Caboose

Caboose

A Casey Cavendish Mystery

Katherine Fast

LEVEL
BEST BOOKS

Cover Photo Credit: David Pierce, President of the Chester Foundation

Authot Photo Credit: Ali Rosa

First edition

ISBN: 978-1-68512-968-2

Cover art by Level Best Designs

*This book was professionally typeset on Reedsy.
Find out more at reedsy.com*

In memoriam: Barbara Harding, Handwriting Mentor and Dear Friend

Praise for Caboose

"With engaging characters, quirky settings (an antique train station!), snappy dialog, and wry humor, readers are again rewarded with *Caboose*, the third installment of the Casey Cavendish series. The mysteries of a missing hobo and the privacy-obsessed tenants of the estate Casey manages are deftly intertwined into a fast-paced tale of betrayal, murder, and redemption. Add ex-con Casey's attraction to the hunky local cop and readers will be glued to this gripping tale to the final satisfying page." —Connie Johnson Hambley, award-winning author of *The Jessica Trilogy*

"Casey Cavendish can't seem to stay out of trouble in the leafy town of Welton despite her best efforts. Even a dull job in estate management for her one surviving aunt leads to betrayal, greed, prostitution, and murder in a swiftly moving tale of a lonely little boy and strangers haunting her home in a converted train station."—Susan Oleksiw, author of the *Anita Ray* series

"For fans of Casey Cavendish, who need to catch up on what's happening with her friends, and her hunt for a welcoming family, this mystery has it all—a compelling whodunnit, fascinating, quirky characters, and of course, a protagonist you can't help but root for."—Barbara Ross, award-winning author of the *Maine Clambake Mystery* series

Chapter One

Welton, Massachusetts

C asey reached high overhead to scrape peeling paint from the side of the caboose. She'd need a taller ladder to get to the corner unless she could inch up just a little more. She leaned against the siding and very carefully raised her left foot toward the top rung.

The shrill of the telephone from the window of the little train station next to the caboose startled her, and she teetered between rungs before regaining her balance. Let the call go to the answering machine. There wasn't a soul in the universe she wanted to speak to.

"Close call." A man's voice behind her surprised her a second time. She steadied herself with both hands on the ladder and turned toward the sound. A lanky, blond man with a red beard stood about ten feet behind her, his thumbs jammed into the pockets of his jeans. She lowered herself down the ladder. At the bottom, she shook paint scrapings out of her hair and off her shirt. When she wiped the perspiration from her forehead, she left a trail of red flecks behind.

She waited for the man to introduce himself, but he stood silently appraising her. Something about his stance seemed familiar, but his cap shadowed his features.

Her gray kitty, Little Mother, emerged from the train station cat door, plumped down the stairs, walked to the man, and rubbed against his boots. Little Tart, more like it.

He leaned over and brushed her away.

"Worthy? Drew?" she exclaimed, staring at his hand.

"Finger's still a giveaway, I'm afraid." The top joint of his forefinger was missing. He offered a lopsided grin. "Name's Chauncey now."

"Chauncey?" she repeated. Casey hadn't seen the man she'd known first as Worthy and then as Drew in two years, ever since he was exposed as an impostor in a disastrous plot to collect Worthy Waddington's inheritance. The real Worthy also had a digit missing from a forefinger, which made the pretense believable.

"Not a normal name, I know." He spoke slowly with a touch of the South. "I was named Chauncey Andrew Cunningham, after my father. I chose Drew for Andrew as a teenager. Who wants to be saddled with Chauncey? Since Worthy's dead and Drew was disgraced, I made a few changes. Friends call me Chance."

As Worthy, he'd been clean-shaven and had dark brown hair. Now he wore his dark blond hair a little longer and sported a well-trimmed beard. She recognized the amused glint in his eyes and the way he moved with graceful elegance.

Facing such a tall, handsome man, Casey was aware that she was dressed in a ratty man's shirt tied in front, cutoff jeans and sneakers.

"Thought I'd drop in to see you and your Aunt Mary." Chance hesitated a second. "Truth be told, I really wanted to see you."

Casey's face fell, and she looked down.

He shifted position, and she was aware that he was studying her.

"I'm sorry, uh…Chance." Her eyes filled, and she felt a lump in her throat. "Mary died last year."

"Aww, no." An expression of surprise, followed by distress and concern, washed over Chance's face. In two long steps, he reached her and engulfed her in his arms. Startled and a little alarmed, she swallowed hard, determined not to break down. She backed away, but he held onto her hand. Casey shook her head and bit her lip, willing herself into control. She barely knew this man, hadn't even recognized him at first.

"Don't be embarrassed. I know how you loved her. She thought of you as her daughter."

He released her hand and followed her toward the little Victorian train station. "I see you still have the Muttmobile," he said as they passed a battered Honda Civic with a Great Dane hood ornament.

They entered the station. Casey sat on a church pew against the wall, and Chance in a rocking chair across from her, the very positions they'd occupied the last time she'd seen him.

He leaned forward, arms on his thighs, and looked into her eyes. When he spoke, his voice was gentle. "I wanted so to kiss you the afternoon I left, but it wouldn't have been right. The police wanted me for questioning, and I had to make myself scarce. Believe me, I had no idea how violent things would become. I read it in the papers and saw footage on the news." He shook his head. "It was hard to see you so battered and..."

Casey just nodded. It seemed like a hundred years ago. Or yesterday. She didn't want to think about it.

They sat for a moment, lost in their own thoughts.

"Where did you go?" Casey asked.

"Maine. I'm licensed to work as a lawyer there. It's taken the better part of the last two years to clear everything up."

"Believe me, I understand." They both knew the long process Casey had gone through before she'd been exonerated from a crime she hadn't committed. Little Mother popped through the cat flap and jumped into Casey's lap. She began kneading her claws into Casey's thigh, offering a rusty purr. Moments later, a small dog pushed through the same cat door. She rushed toward Chance, her plume of a tail wagging in greeting. She had a pointed nose and floppy ears, white wavy hair, and delicate featherings on her legs, and a black spot over one eye.

Chance sat back with a frown and crossed his legs. "Lot of fur here."

"The kitty, Little Mother, came with the station. Isabella," she gestured to the dog, "came with the caboose."

"What's with the caboose anyway?"

Casey gazed out the window up a steep hill at a white mansion a hundred yards away. How to explain. "You knew about Mary's plan to move from the White House to the carriage house and to donate the White House, the A-frame guest house, and the land to a foundation."

Chance gestured for her to continue.

"She considered many causes for the foundation: a battered woman's shelter, a home for troubled teens, a halfway house for recovering mental patients. She bought and installed the caboose as a place for residents to sell goods they made during their stay at the White House. Before she died, she signed the station and caboose over to me."

Little Mother jumped to the floor and stalked toward Chance. She stopped a foot in front of his chair and glared up at him. Seeming unnerved by her unwanted attention, Chance shooed her off. She moved a few feet away and resumed her vigil.

"Welton wouldn't have any of it. No 'undesirable elements' were welcome here. There were petitions, protests. Even a few threats. The turmoil and stress took its toll on Mary's health. That's when Agnes appeared." Casey spat out the woman's name. "Agnes is Mary's adopted sister." She paused, unsure of how much to share.

"Tell me about this woman, Agnes."

Isabella's hackles rose, and she emitted a low growl. Casey glanced out the window again. Wouldn't you know, the minute a handsome man visited, the battle-axe appeared. "See for yourself."

A tall woman with a blade for a nose stormed through the door without knocking. Isabella and the cat scattered. "Why don't you answer the tele—" She stopped short when she spied Chance. "Who are you?"

Chance stood slowly and looked down upon the woman with the superior mien of an aristocrat. "A friend."

"Is that your car in front of the White House?"

He nodded once.

"Move it."

"Let me guess. You must be Agnes." He turned his back on her and walked to Casey. He bent and brushed paint off her cheek. "I'll be back."

CHAPTER ONE

Casey watched him go. Besides being handsome, he was also an untrustworthy devil. But she couldn't help but welcome one of the only people who had known her and her Aunt Mary two years earlier, before everything changed and Agnes took over.

Chapter Two

"If you'd answer your telephone, you'd know that we have an appointment to show the property in a half hour to a potential tenant. You look a fright. Brush off the paint and change into something presentable. Meet me at the carriage house in fifteen minutes. Don't be late." Agnes turned on her heel and slammed out the door. From the front window, Casey watched Agnes march back up Station Road.

The tiny station had an open floor plan consisting of a single long room with a small bathroom and kitchenette at one end under an open sleeping loft above. Casey rose and bolted the door from the inside. Then she assumed a stiff posture, mimicking Agnes' awkward marionette strut as she crossed to the kitchenette, where she relaxed and put on the kettle for tea. In the bathroom, she splashed water on her face and then climbed a spiral staircase to the loft where she dressed in slacks, a blouse, and loafers.

Downstairs, she walked to an antique mahogany desk against the side wall. She drew her fingers across the smooth wood and opened the lid, revealing carrels for documents. She withdrew a folded document from one of the side slots and carried it to a round oak table by the front window.

Two years earlier, Casey's Aunt Mary had paid Casey to help formulate the plans for a non-profit foundation for the White House. After Mary died and the plans were rejected by the town, Casey had to take part time temporary clerical work to make ends meet. She'd even had to sell the little Porsche roadster that an old love had given her to pay quarterly real estate taxes on the station. Recently, she'd launched a fledgling career as a handwriting analyst, teaching an adult education course in graphology. Luckily, there was no mortgage on the station. Even so, Casey was perilously close to broke.

After fifteen minutes, Casey spotted Agnes stomping back down Station Road. The doorknob turned, and Agnes pushed on the door. The knob turned again. Then she pounded. "Casey? Casey!"

Casey sauntered to the door, working hard to suppress a grin. She opened the door with an insincere smile.

"Why'd you lock the door?"

"You just never know who's going to drop in."

Agnes gave her a sharp look. "Who was that man?"

Casey gestured toward the table before returning to the kitchenette. "Care for a spot of tea?"

"I told you, we're expected at the White House. I need you to—"

"You need a lot of things, Agnes. Sit. We need to talk."

Agnes glared at her but didn't budge.

Casey continued, speaking deliberately. "I've helped you with many requests during the transition because I had a vested interest in the foundation project, but now that you've decided to rent the property, you need to realize that I do not work for you. My time is not free." Casey selected two mugs from a cabinet.

"Those are Mary's mugs."

"Not anymore. Sit."

Agnes looked pointedly at her watch but pulled out a chair and sat at the table.

Casey pushed the paper toward Agnes. "If I'm to do skilled work for you, I expect more than minimum wage." She poured water into the mugs and served them with teabags, a small jug of milk, and a plate of cookies.

Agnes ignored the paper but couldn't resist a chocolate chip cookie. As she munched, she cast her eyes about the room, settling on the desk and rocking chair, two old treasures from her family home.

Casey watched her take inventory and waited until she'd snagged a second cookie before continuing. "We need to reach an understanding."

"What don't you understand?"

Agnes wasn't mellow enough yet, but Casey was losing patience. "I've done quite a bit of work for you over the past year, and I'm willing—"

"And I've paid you well. Probably more than you deserve. Looks like you've already received quite a bit of largesse from my family."

"You forget. I'm a member of your family."

"Prove it."

"I don't need to. The desk was my father's, and the chair a special gift from Aunt Mary, who said I was the spitting image of Mother Dempsey—your *step*mother." Casey put a not-so-subtle emphasis on the "step" to goad Agnes.

"So, what is this? You want a raise? You have another source of income?" Agnes challenged. She swiped another cookie and smirked at Casey.

Casey took a deep breath. *Keep cool, Casey girl.* "Actually, I do. I'm working for several temp agencies, and I recently taught a course in Cambridge. A few of my students have expressed interest in another course and in having me analyze handwritings."

"Oh, that woowoo stuff! Who'd pay for that nonsense?"

"A banker, a nurse, and two teachers have asked me to develop personality profiles based on applicants' writings. A detective is particularly interested in spotting forgeries." Casey fixed Agnes with a long look. "Something I'm also interested in pursuing on my own."

As Agnes waved her hand in dismissal, Casey noted that she was wearing Mary's emerald ring, and if she wasn't mistaken, one of her blouses. The woman had been helping herself to Mary's belongings but had never been so blatant before. During Mary's last illness, Agnes had moved into the carriage house that guarded the main gate to President's Lane and the White House ostensibly to care for her sister.

Agnes twisted a stray gray hair and poked it into the severe bun at the nape of her neck. Her beak of a nose detracted from her more positive features, an English peaches and cream complexion and hazel eyes. Her expression of dyspepsia and pursed lips made her look as if she smelled something bad. "Extortion. You wait until the very last minute to demand money."

"Exactly." Casey gestured toward the single sheet which proposed that she be paid an hourly rate on a bi-weekly basis.

"I'm not inclined—"

"But you should be. If you're to become a landlord, you'll need someone to manage the properties. I've been doing that work for the better part of two years. We've had our differences, but I'd rather work here than commute into Boston. I'm available and right next door should there be an emergency."

"Seems like you've got it all figured out." Agnes' resentment at being surprised boiled over. Fuming, she read the short document and pushed it back toward Casey. "Okay. Let's go."

Casey nudged it back across the table. "Date it and then sign it." She offered a pen and a small smile.

"Oh, for heaven's sake!" Agnes took a deep breath and complied. Without another word, she rose and stalked to the door.

Good. The paper was worthless as a contract, but now Casey had a recent sample of Agnes' handwriting, however small. Casey sipped her tea and very briefly examined the quirks and jabs in the writing. She suspected that Agnes had forged Mary's signature on a note that had been used to give Agnes control over the estate. Casey knew her analysis wouldn't hold water legally. She was a graphologist, not a certified document examiner, and graphology couldn't be used in a court of law. But she would know.

She tucked the document into the drawer of the desk before hurrying to catch up with Agnes.

Chapter Three

C asey joined Agnes at the top of Station Road where it met President's Lane before continuing to the main road, Church Street. "Tell me about the people who are interested in renting. How did they hear about it? Did you list the place with a realtor?"

"One question at a time. The man's name is William Kennedy. He's got a wife and a little boy, and two servants. He's in some kind of financial business—venture capital or something—and is looking for a place within commuting distance of Boston."

Casey noticed that Agnes had to pause to catch her breath. Maybe that's why she hasn't bothered to visit the station. No, Casey knew better. She and Agnes were oil and water. In the two years Casey had been living in the station, Agnes had only been inside the building once. When Agnes wanted something done, she called and summoned Casey to the carriage house. They avoided each other whenever possible.

"I got a call a few days ago from a realtor asking if the White House or the A-frame were available. I said yes, and the woman called me back and arranged for Mr. Kennedy to visit today. He's only interested in renting."

"Looks like he's already here." A black Mercedes sedan was parked before the stone gate guarding President's Lane. "You locked the gate?"

"Can't be too careful these days." Agnes marched toward the sedan with Casey pulling up behind. As they approached, two men got out of the car.

The driver was a brick of a man, solid and square, dressed all in black. He stood behind his passenger, a tall, well-dressed man with dark hair and a complexion that suggested time outdoors.

"Hello, I'm Agnes Dempsey." Agnes stepped forward and extended her hand.

"William Kennedy." He didn't take her proffered hand.

Neither Casey nor the brick were included in the introductions. "My name is Casey Cavendish. And you are...?" she asked, looking to the larger man."

"My driver, Vladimir," answered Mr. Kennedy. "We have an hour and a half."

Agnes unlocked the gate and swung it open so Vlad could drive the car through. Kennedy, Agnes, and Casey followed on foot while Vlad parked the car. "What would you like to see first?"

"What you call the White House."

"It's up President's Lane an eighth of a mile. Would you prefer to walk or ride?"

"Walk." Vlad fell in a step behind his boss as they followed Casey and Agnes up the hill.

When Agnes began to struggle, Casey set a slower pace. Couldn't have her stroke out. They needed this rental. They should present a dignified, unified front if possible.

Because Agnes was breathing hard, Casey acted as tour guide. "The house on the left is the carriage house where Ag...where Miss Dempsey lives." Casey gestured to a gingerbread bungalow painted in teal with white trim that guarded the road up to the main house. "The carriage house and surrounding property are not included in the rental." They continued until they encountered a drive off to the right. "The guest house is at the end of the drive. It's a four-bedroom A-frame with full accommodations for company and includes a pool."

They trudged up to the crest of the hill where the lane dead-ended in a circular drive before an imposing mansion. "You can see now why they call it the White House." The grand building had east and west wings and a commanding view of the environs. "From the rear, you can see the Boston skyline."

Agnes withdrew a key from her pocket and unlocked the front door. Vlad brushed her aside and entered first, looking left and right before nodding for Mr. Kennedy to enter.

A bodyguard as well as a driver? Time for Agnes to take over and describe the interior. Casey fell behind and took in the finery of the wide foyer. She hadn't been inside the building since her aunt died. Although familiar, the grandeur and ostentation took her breath away. Vlad pushed forward as they entered a conservatory with a grand piano and priceless antiques. French doors led to a porch and patio. Next, he led them into a dining room with an enormous banquet table and a breakfront full of delicate china. Throughout, Oriental rugs quieted their footsteps.

Behind the dining room, was a fully equipped kitchen. The servant's quarters occupied the east wing. They returned to the foyer and toured the other side of the house. The formal living room featured a fireplace decorated with Delft tiles and surrounding sofas and chairs under protective covers. Pictures worthy of a museum graced the walls throughout. Following Vlad through another doorway, they entered a cherry-paneled library with floor-to-ceiling shelves of books. Nothing had changed since Mary had left years before.

Mr. Kennedy remained silent throughout Agnes' enthusiastic description of all the unique features of the first floor. When she paused, he asked, "What's upstairs?"

"There's the master bedroom suite and other bedrooms. A playroom for children and…"

"Okay." Apparently, Mr. Kennedy wasn't interested in sleeping arrangements. Up close, Kennedy had dark, deep-set eyes under bushy brows that met above a large nose and a wide, thin mouth. His Italian shoes were polished, and he wore a starched shirt with gold cufflinks, a cashmere vest, and pleated wool slacks. Yet another dandy, although he was an older, much darker version compared to the more aristocratic Chance. Kennedy walked to the large oak desk in the study and sat in the swivel chair behind it. Vlad stood next to the door.

Agnes glanced at Casey. Casey shrugged, and they pulled up chairs facing Kennedy.

Kennedy gestured to Vlad, who withdrew a paper from inside his jacket and handed it to Kennedy with a pen. Kennedy shoved both across the desk toward Agnes. "Draw me a picture of the property."

Agnes looked at Casey for help.

The request also surprised Casey. Surely the real estate agent would have shown him a diagram and description of the property. No matter, whatever it takes. Casey drew her chair closer and took the pen. "You drove up the larger road, Church Street, from town, and turned off onto Station Road, here." As she spoke, she drew a map on the paper. "The road leads down to an antique railroad station where I live at the bottom of the hill. The old railroad lines run behind it and under the Church Street arches." She drew in a small building and crosshatches for the railroad tracks.

"President's Lane branches off Station Road and continues to the gate. There it turns left up the hill past the carriage house where Miss Dempsey lives. The lane continues past the A-frame guest house on the right and finally to the White House." She marked where the buildings were as she spoke. "You can see by the map that Station Road parallels President's Lane. Station Road runs downhill while President's Lane ascends. There is no road completing the rectangle from the White House to the station, but there is a small pedestrian gate and stone steps that lead down to it."

"Besides those gates, is there any other access to the property?"

"Yes. At the back of the acreage, there's a fire road and a gate." Casey marked the location of the three gates on the diagram and sat back.

Kennedy took a moment to examine Casey's map. "Before my lawyer signs a lease, we need to reach an understanding about services."

To Casey's surprise, Agnes spoke up. "Would you like to see the guest house? Won't Mrs. Kennedy want to see the property?"

Kennedy waved a hand, cutting her off. "Maybe the real estate agent didn't explain our circumstance. Our home burned to the ground. We're living in a hotel."

"Oh, how dreadful!" Agnes exclaimed. "How did—"

"I'll need either you, Miss Dempsey, or someone you designate, to arrange for the delivery and billing of services listed here." Vlad stepped forward and handed him another paper.

"All financial matters and contact must be made through my legal representative, Mr. Fisher. His contact information is at the bottom of the page. He will not meet you in person. He operates from out of state."

Agnes frowned and accepted the paper Mr. Kennedy pushed across the desk. "If we need additional services such as equipment replacement or repair, or decide we'd want to upgrade utilities—basically any additional work or materials—arrangements shall be made through Fisher, LLC."

He settled back in his chair and waited for Agnes to scan the page. "We accept the rent you're asking, plus $50,000 for managing these affairs, and, of course, the services at cost. Questions?"

"This is highly unusual, Mr. Kennedy." Agnes smiled. "May I call you William...or Bill?"

"'Mr. Kennedy' will suffice. We are not normal tenants. We agree to pay top rates to ensure our privacy." He thought for a moment. "The current security system is inadequate. Install an automated system with pass codes and an intercom linking the gate to the two properties. We'll need at least two telephone lines."

Agnes frowned again. "I'll need time to review these requests. Of course, we require references as well as a month's security deposit."

Kennedy's mouth turned down, and his fingers tapped on the desk. "Mr. Fisher will send you a signed lease and a certified check. We intend to move in at the first of next month. He'll set up an account you can draw from for expenses—keep records for reimbursement or have an accounting firm represent you." He waited a few moments in silence before asking, "Who should Mr. Fisher call to establish the details?"

Agnes chewed her lip. She glanced at Casey and passed her the paper. "Have him contact my assistant, Miss Cavendish."

Mr. Kennedy studied Casey with interest and the first hint of a smile. "Miss Cavendish," he said. "What should I call you?" He wasn't ogling or flirting, but rather signaling dominance that he could take whatever he wanted.

"'Miss Cavendish will suffice.'" She wasn't having it.

The smile faded to a smirk. "Very well. Have you a card?"

"No. Have you a paper and pen?"

"No."

Casey tore off one corner of Kennedy's list and wrote "Miss Cavendish" and her phone number and shoved the scrap of paper his way.

"Questions, Miss Cavendish?"

"I'll ask Mr. Fisher," Casey replied. "Meanwhile, I'd appreciate it if you would add the last few items about security and telephones to the list." She handed back the paper with the list of requirements.

"I don't expect there to be any contact between you and members of the household which includes my wife Loretta and son Peter. Vladimir is my butler and driver and his wife Olga, is our housekeeper and cook." He wrote the additional items on the list, returned it to Casey, and rose to conclude the meeting. Vladimir led the parade silently back to the front door.

Chapter Four

Casey and Agnes walked their new tenant and his butler/bodyguard down the hill to the Mercedes without further conversation. "Can you beat all?" Agnes muttered as they watched the car drive through the open gate and out to the main road.

"Looks like I just got myself a full-time job," Casey replied.

"Can you handle it?" Agnes asked, walking toward the carriage house.

"Sure, but you and I will need to reach a new agreement."

"Don't get greedy," said Agnes.

"I do the work. I get the money. I'll want a monthly salary and benefits if I'm to devote full time to the upkeep of the White House properties. The agreement will state my new responsibilities. I'll be keeping a separate set of books, upgrading security and current facilities, and hiring and supervising new service providers. There's a lot to be done to make the place ready for renters. I also assume I'll be on call for any unexpected problems and new requests as they occur. They're making a lot of demands."

Casey paused before continuing. "But we need to be careful."

"Why?"

"This arrangement is really strange."

Agnes came to an abrupt halt.

"Think about it. He's not signing his name to anything. Everything flows through some mysterious, remote lawyer known only as Mr. Fisher. This paper doesn't even give his physical address."

"Don't you get paranoid and let your little criminal mind sour the deal. I asked a realtor in town what we could expect for a rental, and Mr. Kennedy offered more with cash up front to seal the agreement." Agnes glared at Casey. "We both need the money."

Casey waved the page of tenant demands. "Clearly, Mr. Kennedy already knew he would take the property before he arrived. Vlad acts like a bodyguard, and we don't know why his house burned. We don't even know where they lived."

Casey's criminal mind was in overdrive. Something was definitely off when there would be zero record of Mr. Kennedy, if that was really his name, and his entourage living in the White House. Should she turn it down? Fifty thousand was twice, more like three times what she could earn at an entry-level job, a job she currently didn't have. No commute. Work from her little station.

Deep in thought, Casey left Agnes at the carriage house and walked to the gate. They'd need a totally new system, with an intercom that visitors could ring and speak into to gain access. Casey and Agnes would both have to know the code. She had a lot to do in a very short period of time. As uneasy as she was about the tenant, she welcomed the challenge, and she really welcomed the money.

Casey decided to call her buddy LouAnne for advice. LouAnne had served time with her in the Marysville State prison in Ohio. Although Casey had been exonerated of any crime, she was still very uneasy in any situation that could place her in the crosshairs of the law. LouAnne had a level head, and besides, she was Casey's best friend.

She turned right at Station Road. When she caught sight of the little station at the bottom of the hill, she smiled. She'd fallen in love with it at first sight when she'd come to Massachusetts to find the man she believed to be her father. She shook her head. So much had happened since. She'd found and lost her family, but the station was still hers, and she was determined to do whatever she needed to do to keep it.

As she drew closer, she spied her little dog Isabella down below, sitting on the platform of the caboose stairs. What was so interesting? Casey squinted. Isabella's attention was fixed on something inside the caboose. But surely, Casey would have closed the door. She picked up her pace. She put fingers to her lips and whistled. Isabella whirled about, dashed down the steps, and shot like a bullet up the road toward her.

Casey knelt and welcomed her with open arms. "What you up to, pup?" she asked as she tousled Isabella's ears. When she looked up, a tall figure emerged from the rear door of the caboose and ran down the steps on the far side of the car and out of sight. No automobile in the parking area. No bicycle. And by the time she sprinted down the road and reached the caboose, no person in sight. She circled around the train car. Behind it there was dense shrubbery and overgrowth. She would have seen him if he'd run left behind the station toward the underpass arches below Church Street. He must have run to the right, down the tracks.

This man was real, not her criminal imagination working overtime. She entered the caboose and cast about. It was empty except for cleaning products and painting paraphernalia she was using to refurbish the interior. When they purchased the caboose, she'd found a few belongings that a homeless man who'd been living in the railcar had left behind in a backpack which she'd hung on a peg by the door. Huh. Her visitor had absconded with a pack jammed with old clothing, a pipe and tobacco and a few paperback books. He'd missed the clunky combat boots. No loss, but Casey didn't appreciate an uninvited visitor who helped himself.

Could the intruder be Hobo, Casey's mental tag for the person who had been squatting in the caboose before Mary bought it? They'd purchased it in New Hampshire and had it towed to Massachusetts. How could Hobo track the caboose to its new location? Not hard if Bella was his dog. Casey had found the little dog hanging around the caboose when they had arrived to move it to Welton. She'd taken Isabella to the local veterinary clinic in search of her owner and had also tried to trace him by the number on Bella's dog tag. Both efforts proved unfruitful. The owner was listed as John Smith with a bogus address. He'd paid in cash for Isabella's rabies vaccination and for her tag. She'd left her name and address with the vet and the town.

She opened a large storage closet under the cupola, ducked down, and looked inside. She peered into the dark recess at the back of the closet at an ancient cast-iron safe. Looking closer, she noted the dial of the combination lock on the front plate was still set to 34, her age, so if the man had come for its contents, he'd been careful to leave it as he'd found it. Casey had played around trying to guess the combination, but it was hopeless. Maybe the intruder didn't have time to open the safe after hearing Casey's whistle. He couldn't move it—the thing weighed a ton. Time for padlocks front and back.

She left the caboose for the station with Isabella tagging behind. Now she'd had two unexpected visitors. This one wouldn't be Drew—or rather, Chance—returning. He'd have no reason to skulk away, and he had no need for smelly old clothes. She smiled. He wasn't only handsome with his new beard and blonde hair. He annoyed Agnes. Didn't seem to like cats, though.

"C'mon, Bella. Whoever that was, he didn't take you with him. You're my dog now. I've waited long enough for someone to claim you. I need to fit you with a new collar and ID tag. You're a fancy Welton pooch now and should look the part." Isabella responded with a full-body wag.

Chapter Five

Agnes

Agnes watched Casey walk toward the gate. Who did she think she was, demanding big money for what she'd been doing for Mary for a pittance? Ever since Agnes' sisters Mary and Vera died, and the foundation plan fell through—and thank the good Lord for that!—Casey had been hitting her up for every little thing. Now she assumed she'd get all the funds for managing the White House properties.

There wasn't a whole lot Agnes could do about Casey's demands. Agnes didn't know anything about the suppliers and services at the White House. Mary had taken care of those details until she got too sick and handed the responsibilities over to Casey and her nephew Jackson. Agnes wouldn't know how to manage the properties. Nor would she want to. She shouldn't have to deal with those details. Now with Jackson gone, Casey was the only one she could depend upon to get things done. Much as Agnes resented the scheming little ex-con, she'd need her for a little while.

She turned up the heat and fixed herself a cup of tea. Such a lovely little house! She was so glad that she'd moved back in with Mary when Mary took to her bed during her last illness. Finally, Agnes got what she deserved, the home she wanted. Soon, she'd have a guaranteed income from the rental of the White House.

It hadn't happened without a struggle. First Mary sold their old homestead in West Boylston. As a family member, Agnes should have gotten a portion of that money, but no. And then, her little bungalow had burned to the ground. "Irish lightning," the fireman had called it, and Mary hadn't denied that she'd had hand in the arson. The final blow came when Agnes had to retire from her job with the dear old priests at the Jesuit home because Mary parked her as far away as she could in Chatham on the Cape, knowing how much she hated the heat and couldn't bear the sun with her delicate complexion. Mary knew she couldn't swim. Shunned. Exiled from the family.

Mary had been determined to give away everything—the White House, the A-frame guest house, and the land—with some altruistic notion of a foundation for battered women or recovering mental patients. Thanks to quick thinking on Agnes' part and objections from the town, the plans had been defeated.

Agnes sipped her tea. The shrink was right. She was fixated on events in the past, things she couldn't change. But it was so unfair! With no proof whatsoever, Casey claimed to be the illegitimate daughter of their older brother Jed. What blasphemy! He was a priest! And he, dead and buried, with no recourse to protect his legacy.

By insinuating herself into Mary's affections—Vera's as well—Casey got a lovely, renovated antique train station and a caboose in the bargain. The girl was as immoral as Mary, who had slept her way to a fortune. Two peas in a pod. Rumor had it that Casey had had an affair with a married man in Ohio. She'd even flirted with her cousin Jackson, the crazy spawn of Vera's transgressions. Just this morning, there was another man sniffing around her! All the while, Agnes had lived a quiet life of piety, caring for the retired priests who had devoted their lives to God.

She'd need Casey for now, but the time would come when she could sell the property and be free of her. She already had a sizable nest egg from the sale of the Chatham property. It had felt so good to unload that place! Too big, on the water, hours away from all she knew.

She'd get the last laugh. With both Vera and Mary dead, the cute little carriage house and everything in it was all hers. She'd gotten rid of Vera's illegitimate son Jackson by threatening to put down Mary's enormous Irish wolfhounds. He'd moved to Connecticut with them, or was it Rhode Island, she couldn't remember. And didn't care. Casey said he'd decided to go into the priesthood.

She should be celebrating, although it was difficult with all the pictures around the cottage reminding her of her dysfunctional family. So do something about it. She rose and took down the pictures from the mantle and off the side tables and stuffed them in a bureau drawer. She felt as if a weight had been lifted from her shoulders. Better already!

Time for big changes. She withdrew and unfolded a colorful brochure from her desk. Now with the rental of the White House secured, she could channel her bitterness and anger and make a new life.

But it was too soon to let that little gold digger know her plans. Agnes scolded herself for wearing Mary's ring. Casey had recognized it. Don't get ahead of yourself. One change at a time.

Casey had arrangements to make, but so did she. She was in the catbird seat now. She picked up the phone and dialed.

Chapter Six

Casey

Thursday, 10/20

For the better part of the morning, Casey sat at her desk cataloguing what needed to be accomplished before the property would be ready for the Kennedys to move in. Now, reviewing her list, she realized there was no way she could get it all done. Time for triage and setting priorities.

She'd found listings for security system providers in the Yellow Pages and made a note to ask the realtor who had recommended Kennedy contact Agnes which companies were the most reliable.

Telephones shouldn't be a problem if she could arrange for a multi-line phone system and purchase the physical phones locally. Utilities would just require multiple accounts—one for Agnes' carriage house and a separate one for the rental properties. She'd change the billing address to her address, 1 Station Road. She'd collect the old records from the carriage house and keep them at the station. Or maybe the caboose would make a good office. There was plenty of storage space there. She needn't clutter her home with all those records and files.

Once the foundation proposal had fallen through, there was no reason to fix up the caboose, but Casey found that physical labor helped relieve some of the stress while she waited to hear from prospective employers. Now it could be her office.

What a godsend! A big fat salary for work she knew how to do, right next door. Kennedy and Vlad and the mystery man Fisher were worrisome, but how crazy could it be? Be responsive, keep your nose clean, and relax. Well, relax once all was operational.

She rose and stretched and walked to the kitchenette to refill her coffee.

She stopped short as she passed the window. A sedan drove down Station Road. Instead of parking in the lot across from the station, the car pulled up beside the caboose. Probably another train buff coming to see a vintage train car. When Mary first had the caboose installed on the siding, there had been a steady stream of curious townsfolk visiting, but that traffic had dwindled to a trickle over the past two years.

She poured herself a new cup and returned to the window in time to see the man walk around the caboose and disappear behind it. Moments later, he reappeared at the front after making a full circuit. He looked around and then climbed the three metal stairs up to the platform by the front door. He shielded his eyes to peer inside the window, and then to Casey's surprise, looked around once more and opened the door.

Rats! She should have put the padlocks on the doors yesterday. Now she'd have to shoo the nosy neighbor away. She donned her jacket and went outside to investigate with Isabella at her heels. When the man didn't leave, she climbed up to the door to see what he was doing. The inside was bare except for the painting supplies—rags, brushes, and scrapers—that she was using to refurbish the car.

She and Isabella stood in the open doorway and watched as the man, dressed in jeans, a leather jacket and ball cap, lifted up the mats and opened the tops of the storage benches that lined the sides of the car one at a time as if he were looking for something. He lifted the heavy boots that were under the peg where Hobo's backpack used to hang and examined the soles.

Continuing down the length of the car, he opened the cabinets under and above the galley sink and even lifted the lid of the old cast-iron stove. At the end of the car, he raised the latch on the large storage closet under the cupola, bent low, and entered.

Without a sound, Casey walked through the car. She was tempted to slam the closet door and lock the man in but restrained her impulse. He was probably a harmless curiosity seeker, and the caboose was a real novelty. Admit it, if a caboose had been parked in her neighborhood in Ohio, she'd be the one nosing around inside.

He must have spotted the antique safe at the back of the closet. She stood in the closet doorway, blocking his light. "May I help you?"

Bang!

"Shit! The man grunted and cursed, as he emerged, one hand atop his head.

Serves him right.

He scowled at her as if she were the offender and then approached, crowding her.

She backed away, arms akimbo.

He followed, and she raised her arm and stopped him before he got too close. She refused to be cowed.

He appraised her slowly. "Mary Waddington?" he asked.

"No. I'm Casey Cavendish. Mrs. Waddington died a year ago."

"Who is the current owner of this railcar?"

"I am. Who are you?" He wasn't a friendly explorer. More like an angry intruder. Up close he had hard eyes with no laugh wrinkles, a pocked complexion, and a sharp nose.

"Officer Granger, New Hampshire State Police."

Sure didn't dress like a policeman. But he did have the wide, confident stance of a cop. Or a bully. "Well, Officer, unless you have official business, you're trespassing on private property."

"We're conducting an investigation regarding an individual who was living in the caboose before it was sold to Mrs. Waddington."

Casey crossed her arms. "Have you some identification, Officer?"

He patted his jacket pocket. "I'm not carrying my badge today." He must have registered Casey's skepticism. He reached into his shirt pocket. "But I do have a card." He withdrew a card and handed it to her.

The card read "Detective Sergeant Theodore Granger, New Hampshire

State Police" and gave a phone number and address at the bottom.

Okay, better cooperate. "I understand that the man Mr. Smith—who I refer to as Hobo—was nowhere to be found during the sale and moving process. What do you want with Mr. Smith?"

"You know Mr. Smith?"

"No, but I think Bella here might have been his dog. He left her behind. I got his name tracking her dog tag to the town clerk and through veterinarian records."

"Did you ever meet Mr. Smith?"

"No. Why are you looking for him?"

"Got a light in here?" he gestured toward the closet.

"No." She wasn't about to help this man until he was more forthcoming.

"What's in the safe?"

"I have no idea. It came with the car. It has a combination lock, and, no, I don't know the combination, nor does the previous owner who sold us the caboose."

Officer Granger attempted a smile and backed off. He modified his direct, threatening manner of questioning to a gentler approach. "I'm sorry to seem so abrupt and secretive. I didn't mean to offend you. We're involved in an ongoing investigation. Mr. Smith is a person of interest in the case, and we need to find out as much as we can about him. I can tell you that we have found a body in the woods not far from where the caboose used to sit on the rails. We're trying to identify the individual."

Bad cop. Good cop. All-in-one, cop? Casey didn't cotton to the false face Granger was presenting, but regardless of this man's bad manners, she didn't like the idea that the dead man could be Hobo. That could be the reason no one had claimed Bella. Working around inside the caboose, Casey had developed a feeling of kinship with Hobo and hoped he hadn't come to a foul end. "I should tell you that there was another man snooping about the car. He took a backpack full of Hobo's clothing and ran off when I approached."

"Describe him."

Bad cop was back. She described what little she could remember of the man's appearance from a distance.

"I'll return in a few days with another man to remove the safe. We'll appreciate your full cooperation."

"You'll need a court order to take anything."

"It will be in your interest to cooperate with the law." Officer Granger brushed past her, strode down the length of the caboose, and out to his car.

"Everything seems fishy these days," Casey muttered to Bella. She fingered the card he'd given her. Wouldn't a policeman come to the door of the station, introduce himself, and ask to see the caboose instead of skulking around and entering property without permission? If he was investigating in an official capacity, shouldn't he be carrying a badge?

She returned to the station with a growing sense of malaise. How worried should she be about all the new interest in the caboose? Two sketchy visitors in as many days. What was Hobo's story? She fastened Granger's card to the refrigerator door with a magnet. She didn't know what to make of the man's visit, but she didn't feel good about it.

Chapter Seven

Casey's musings were interrupted by the shrill of her telephone.
"Miss Cavendish, Fisher here."

She held the receiver away from her ear. What a strange, tortured voice! Something between a breathy gargle and a high, unnatural strangled tenor. Before Casey could even say hello, the man continued.

"Place top priority on securing the perimeter of the property. Repair the electronic fence at the rear gate. Immediately install a new intercom system at the main gate. Change the locks on the White House and the A-Frame. Call me immediately when the new systems are operative."

Secure the perimeter? When systems are operative? Was he some kind of military—

"The document Mr. Kennedy left you has the requirements for the installation of two telephone lines. As he explained, nothing need change from the current billing arrangements for utilities. All arrangements and payments are to be made through you."

Casey decided to press the issue that was bothering her. "Just to be clear, the names Kennedy and Fisher are not to appear on any documents related to the rental and operation of the property, correct?"

"Correct. Do you have a problem fulfilling these requirements?"

Casey let the silence hang a moment before committing. The arrangement was highly unusual, bordering on suspicious. Then again, she was highly broke. "No."

"Who was the man walking around the caboose?" the voice demanded.

Huh? She shook her head, momentarily stunned. "If you're in Rhode

28

Island, how do you know someone was walking around the caboose?"

"You don't know him?"

"No. The caboose is a novelty. Folks are curious about it." No way did she want to scare away the new tenant with a suspicious cop searching for a vagrant.

"Call me." Click. The line disconnected.

Casey stared at the receiver for a few seconds before replacing it in its cradle. Was Chuckles watching? Possible, but he'd need binoculars. Casey grinned at her new nickname for Vlad, Kennedy's bodyguard and butler, but she didn't like the idea that someone was watching her home. She walked outside and peered up the hill toward the White House and then turned full circle. Trees shrouded most of the view except for the Church Street bridge that spanned the railroad tracks. No one was on the bridge.

She'd been surprised when Kennedy asked her to draw a map of the properties. Kennedy might have been buying time for someone to install a security camera around the station while she and Agnes were giving them a tour of the White House. A chill ran down her spine. Before the meeting, Kennedy didn't know she would be the one maintaining the property. Keeping an eye on the neighboring station would represent some serious paranoia.

Interesting that Fisher called right after she'd left the caboose. She shuddered, wondering what she had gotten herself into. Walking around the sides of the station, she checked out the most likely places to hide a camera. Nothing.

Was her criminal mind working overtime? Kennedy was probably some kind of gambler, or maybe a high-powered finance mogul who didn't welcome visits from Latter Day Saints, or—

The damn phone was ringing again. Casey caught it before the answering machine clicked in.

"I've decided to take some time off, now that the rental is firm." Agnes never announced herself, just blurted out whatever she wanted to say. "I'll leave on Saturday. You should be able to set things up to Kennedy's satisfaction. The records for the White House and guest house are in Mary's file cabinet."

I know. I've been keeping them for the past year. "Rather sudden, Agnes. Is everything okay? Are you sure you're all right with Mr. Kennedy's demands?"

"You know I have a delicate constitution. This last year has been exhausting with all the worries with the foundation failing and settling Mary's affairs. I deserve some time off."

Time off? You retired two years ago and have been sitting on your hands ever since. Casey assumed her sweetest, most understanding voice. "Good for you. Where are you going?"

"I'll leave contact information. Water my plants when you're here." Click.

Yet another dial tone. Casey chucked the phone into its cradle from a foot away. Was Agnes really taking a vacation, or was she dodging responsibility, or both? Why so sudden and why hadn't she said anything at all to Casey about her plans?

Casey decided to place a call of her own and dialed her old cellmate and best friend, LouAnne, for some much-needed comfort and advice. After multiple rings, the answering machine picked up. She left a message and stared out the window.

Little Mother jumped into her lap and nudged her cheek. Ah, time for dins. Good thing she had the animals. Otherwise, she'd be totally alone.

Chapter Eight

Friday, 10/21

Casey sketched in the fangs of a dragon and began working on scales as she listened to Muzak playing on Hold for the telephone company. She refused to hang up and lose her place in line, although she was worried that she might bite the head off any "Customer Service Representative" who would dare answer the call. She looked up from her hellish sketch when she heard a car in the drive outside the station window.

A big man with dark hair dressed in jeans and a flannel shirt got out of the driver's side of a station wagon and waited for a young boy to join him. The kid ran toward the caboose, but the man called him and, to her surprise, the two approached the station and rang the bell.

Grateful for the long telephone cord, Casey walked to the door with the telephone against her ear.

"What's your name, sweetheart?" The man said in a tender baritone as she opened the door.

Casey was stunned until she realized that the man was kneeling, fingering Isabella's tag. As he rose and she saw him up close, he looked familiar, but she couldn't place him. Although she would definitely like to. Heavy eyebrows shaded his deep-set dark eyes above a straight nose, a generous mouth, and strong jaw. He either had a tan or was of Mediterranean descent. The boy looked like a younger copy. He, too, would undoubtedly grow up to be a

31

lady killer like his father.

"Sorry to bother you, Miss Cavendish. I'm Mike Fortune, and this is Davey. We'd like your permission to look at the caboose."

Miss Cavendish. So, she should know him. She cocked her head and chewed her lip, as she studied him, searching her catalogue of handsome hunks.

"Detective Fortune, Welton Police," he added with a smile to allay her confusion. "I interviewed you a few years ago in the hospital. You may not remember."

Wouldn't you know, a cop. Casey had had one good friend who was the Chief of Police in Ohio, but after ten years of prison guards, she was leery of the law. She'd already been wrongfully incarcerated once.

Okay, now she placed him. At the time she'd met him, she'd been drugged to manage pain, her jaw wired shut, broken arm in a sling, recovering from a concussion after the horrendous series of events when her Aunt Vera was killed, and her Aunt Mary's life threatened. She closed her eyes to dismiss the images that still haunted her.

This was the second time in as many days a man popped in and found her in less than flattering condition with her dark hair scrunched into a rough ponytail, dressed in a sweatshirt, jeans, and flip flops. She scowled at the paperwork on the table. Isabella had already befriended Davey, who was fondling her ears. The boy looked to her with hope in his eyes.

"If you're in the middle of something, we can come back at a better time," Fortune added.

Oh no. "Actually, I've been on hold forever," she said, hanging up the phone. "I could use a break." She grabbed her jacket and led them to the caboose.

Davey clambered up the metal steps and waited impatiently for permission to enter. "Go on. The door's unlocked," Casey said, following father and son into the caboose. "Lots of folks interested in the caboose in the past few days. You're the only one with manners. The first guy took off with a backpack that had been left by a man who'd been squatting in the caboose when my Aunt Mary bought it. The second guy was another detective, but he was from New Hampshire." Casey stopped, realizing she was babbling.

"Really. Local or State Police? What did he want?"

"State. He asked about the man who had lived in the car. He said there was an active investigation to identify him because they had found a dead man in the woods in the area where the caboose used to be. The squatter could either be the dead man or a person of interest in the ongoing investigation."

They spoke as they walked the length of the car. Casey noticed that Fortune's eyes never stopped moving, taking in every detail. "I'm planning to hook up water and electricity soon. So far, I've mostly just cleaned and re-stained the wood and replaced the bench covers. The detective, Granger, opened every storage place as if he were searching for something."

Davey scooted ahead of them and reached the end. He stood next to the tall storage closet door. Again, he looked to Casey for permission, and she nodded. Like a little monkey he grabbed the rungs and climbed up into the cupola and sat on one of the two facing benches. "Wow! Dad, you gotta see this!"

Fortune smiled and waved up at him. "What's in here?" he asked at the latched door.

"It's a large storage area." Casey flipped the latch and reached inside for a flashlight. She turned it on, crouched, and ducked inside. Fortune followed, his shoulders just making it through the door. There was room inside for the two of them, but it was close. She aimed the light at the old safe against the wall. "The officer was particularly interested in the contents of the safe." They could hear Davey above them romping about in the cupola. "I explained that neither I nor the former owner knew the combination. He said he'd return with another person to remove it. It weighs a ton. You can see it's on rollers, but it would take two strong men to get it off the caboose."

Davey climbed down the rungs and crept in between them. He was drawn to the safe like a magnet. "What's inside?" he asked.

"I don't know. It's a mystery. Maybe you can figure out the combination."

Davey toyed with the dial for a few moments in the spooky atmosphere lit by the flashlight. Casey reached under the narrow space between the bottom of the safe and the floor and withdrew an old book with worn edges. She carried it with her as the three exited the closet.

33

"I found this book inside Hobo's backpack. That's my nickname for the guy who lived here, although I never met him. According to these records, the railroad conductor changed the combination monthly for security. There are instructions for resetting the combination, so if I can ever figure out the current one, there's a button inside to push and enter a new combination." She led them back toward the front door.

"I didn't like the detective's attitude. I told him he'd need a court order to remove anything. The safe came with the railcar and should be mine."

Fortune seemed to consider her comment but then made an abrupt change in the topic. "I understand the White House has been rented."

Casey's expression must have registered her surprise.

"The real estate agent keeps me up to date on sales and rentals. Do you know the new tenants?"

"Agnes and I met the husband, Mr. Kennedy, just yesterday with his bodygu...butler. He seemed very security conscious. I'll be managing the property for them. The couple and their little boy and two servants will move in at the beginning of the month."

"That soon? Just a couple of weeks. Do you know where they're from? What does Mr. Kennedy do for a living?"

Why was he so interested? "No. I'll be dealing with their lawyer in Rhode Island for all the arrangements and paperwork. Otherwise, I know precious little. Your agent friend may know more."

"Where's the man, Jackson Dempsey, who used to live over the garage?"

"He moved to Connecticut. He and Agnes Dempsey had a bit of a falling out. The last time I spoke with him, he'd decided to join the Jesuits."

"Ah, yes. I seem to remember Miss Dempsey." His comment was delivered with a straight face. "We should let you get back to work."

They walked back outside to his station wagon. He hesitated. "Did you say the officer's name was Granger? Usually, if an officer is operating in another force's jurisdiction, they stop in to let the locals know of their interest as a courtesy."

"Hold on a sec," Casey trotted to the station and returned with the card Granger used for identification.

Fortune fingered the card. "Mind if I hold onto this for a bit? I'll be sure to return it."

"No problem."

Fortune looked back at the caboose. "You'll need to install padlocks on both ends of the caboose and get a more secure system for the station."

Casey wrinkled her nose and nodded.

"And the town of Welton requires all dogs be registered and wear both an identification tag and proof of rabies tag."

Casey still hadn't gotten around to buying a new collar, and Fortune had noticed that Isabella was wearing a ratty old one without a Welton tag. "She never leaves the property without me," she objected.

"Doesn't matter. It's the law. Both your dog and kitty could also use a flea and tick collar as well. We have Lyme disease here in Massachusetts."

Yes indeed, the law. Casey executed a mock salute.

Fortune grinned. "You don't like to take orders much, do you?"

"Detective Fortune, I have all the bossy I need with Agnes."

Fortune backed off, but the smile didn't leave his face. "Call me Mike. I've been told I can be rather overbearing." He returned her a mock salute as he and Davey piled into the station wagon.

Casey watched them leave. Six visitors in four days: Chance, Agnes, backpack thief, Detective Granger, and now Fortune and his son. Busy little place. Not sure she liked all the attention, although Chance and Fortune would be welcome anytime. As if she were playing her own custom version of Monopoly. Ha! Take a ride on the Welton Railroad. Chance: Go directly to Jail or collect from Community Chest. Fortune: Collect $200 for passing Go on your new job.

She shook her head. Get to work.

Chapter Nine

Agnes

Saturday, 10/22

A gnes looked at her watch—well, Mary's watch—for the fourth time. She had fifteen minutes before the taxi was supposed to arrive. She felt rushed, but energized and excited. She scrunched another pair of shoes into the sides of the suitcase. She really liked the leather shoes. What a bonus. Everything of Mary's fit. Always had. As teenagers in Ireland, she'd snuck out to flirt with fellows wearing Mary's clothes. Jewelry, too. She admired the depth of green in the emerald ring on her finger. For now, she'd turn the stones inward for safety and wait until she got to her destination to sparkle.

Agnes had been surprised when Kennedy's lawyer with the screwy voice had called earlier that morning to say the family would be moving in a week or so earlier than expected. Officious man. She'd successfully wrangled more money out of him and then told him to contact her assistant, Miss Cavendish, when he had a firm date. She would be the one to make expedited arrangements. Let Casey earn her outrageous salary. The abbreviated time frame had made Agnes change her plans and alter her flights and accommodations. She didn't want anything to do with managing the rental and planned to be far away when the Kennedys arrived.

She was probably taking too much, but she didn't know what to expect.

She still had things she'd planned to purchase for her trip, but she'd buy them after she arrived. She'd have a few days extra now, so plenty of time to shop. Relax. Let others worry. Others, ha! Casey.

She latched the suitcases and carried them one at a time to the top of the stairs. Careful now. She bumped one down, stair by stair, and returned for the other. She checked her watch again and made a tour of the house. She'd left a note for Casey telling her when to water her plants and clean, and where to check off on the calendar when she did so.

She'd taken the rental agreement and her own banking materials and placed them in her safe deposit box. Casey needn't discover how much the Kennedys were paying for rent or how much she'd made from the Chatham house sale.

Casey had made a number of insidious comments about Mary's handwritten note that had been used to assign Agnes Power of Attorney over Mary's finances, suggesting that it might not pass legal scrutiny, but what could Casey do? She was a dabbler in graphology, not a court-certified document examiner. That matter, as well as ownership of the White House properties following Mary's death, had been determined a year ago. The court had awarded Mary's estate to her closest living relative, which just happened to be Agnes.

She was ready to come into her own. She'd sacrificed enough. She heard the toot of a car horn and peered out the front window. Her taxi had arrived. She gathered a lovely silk scarf around her neck and donned Mary's camel hair coat and purse. She pushed her bags out the door and beckoned for the cabbie to collect them.

He got out of the taxi and opened the door to the back seat for her but didn't make a move toward her luggage. She pointed to her bags again, but he ignored her. She hauled the bags to the taxi one at a time and lifted them into the trunk.

There goes his tip. Don't worry about it. She smiled to herself. No one would ignore her when she returned.

"Logan Airport."

Chapter Ten

Casey

There was not much more Casey could do on the weekend except make lists and figure out how she planned to keep records. She'd spent the afternoon arranging a notebook with tabs for out-of-pocket expenses and different types of bills: utilities (water, electricity, oil), cleaning, landscaping and lawn care, telephones, security system, pool service for the A-frame. She'd add tabs as new requirements presented themselves.

She'd move the current billing records from the carriage house, where she'd kept the books for the past year, down to the station. Casey had no intention of having Agnes breathing down her neck. She picked up the phone and dialed Agnes' number to let her know she'd be coming up to get the files in a few minutes, but Agnes didn't answer. Unlike her to be out, but no matter.

She and Bella jogged up Station Road and turned down the road to the gate guarding President's Lane. At the carriage house, she rang the bell twice with no answer. No matter, she had a key. Inside, it looked as if Agnes had already left on her vacation. Without so much as a fare-thee-well. Bella curled up next to the door for a nap.

In the study, she opened Mary's filing cabinet next to the big oak desk where Casey kept billing and tax records for the White House properties. She groaned at the number of individual files. She'd need a box to transport them. All the clutter and detritus that Agnes hadn't dealt with following Mary's death had been dumped in the cellar, and that's where Casey found the right-size box. She loaded up what she thought she would need, including supplies, bank records, and checkbooks, and headed for the door.

As she passed a side table, she noticed a handwritten note addressed to her. In the waste basket next to the table, she saw a scrunched-up glossy brochure. She dumped the box on the floor and picked up the brochure. Wow. The Rejuvenation Spa in New Mexico advertised itself as an all-in-one plastic surgery and regenerative spa, with physical fitness, diet, and the best skin care money could buy. A "Fresh New You!"

Blow me away! Who would have guessed? The middle-aged spinster was off for a complete makeover. Casey didn't know the woman at all. She'd taken her at face value, with the beak and attitude leading the way. But why wouldn't the woman dream of a better, fuller—prettier—life? Why wouldn't she want everything that Casey did? Especially since there were no longer any obstacles in Agnes' way. She had money with the new renter, time, and no pesky relatives to burden her. And Casey to do the work.

The bitter, hypochondriac bully was free to break loose and buy a new look. Would it come with a modified, positive demeanor? Would she be less bitter with a lovely face? Sure would be easier to live next to her, if Agnes could tamp down the acid. A month or so at a spa might just raise her pH level.

Casey hadn't been to the carriage house since she'd paid the last month's bills. Now as she looked around the living room, she noticed that most of the signs of Mary had been removed. A cross and a religious scene replaced two paintings. Agnes had worked for years in a home for retired and ailing Jesuit priests.

Curious, Casey began snooping about to see what else had changed. Mary's sick bed had finally been removed and, in the area next to the window, Agnes had set up a table of house plants, orchids, and African violets, and some green things Casey couldn't name. Agnes had a green thumb, something else Casey would never have suspected.

She had guessed what she would find upstairs. Agnes had moved into

Mary's old room and claimed her nicest clothing and jewelry. In the bathroom cabinet, she found unused fingernail polish, rouge, and mascara. Anticipating her new look? Casey pocketed the fingernail polish. She could use it to mark the keys for the front and back padlocks she'd buy for the caboose. In a drawer, she spotted new underwear, not racy but not high-hipped old lady nylon pants either. Casey grimaced. More than she wanted to know.

On the bedside table, she found a photograph of three girls—Mary with her arm around Agnes and Vera, the youngest in front—all three of them fresh and full of youthful energy. Agnes was actually appealing with bright eyes and a wide smile, hair free and flowing. They were hopeful innocents before the tragedies of the Troubles destroyed their family and caused them to flee Ireland for America.

In another picture, the whole family—three girls, two older boys, and a young lad—posed before Rose and Joseph Dempsey. The youngest fellow had to be Casey's father. She looked closer and took in a sharp breath. Casey was the spitting image of Rose with the same wavy dark hair, light eyes, and upturned mouth.

Mary had recognized Casey the instant she met her because she so resembled Mary's mother. Casey remembered seeing a portrait of the matriarch in Mary's room at the White House. It was nowhere to be seen here and may not have made it in the move to the carriage house. Before Mary died, she had planned a large estate sale to empty the White House of its contents, but it had never happened. Now the rental came furnished, reminding Casey that she needed to have a cleaning service do a last sweep of the building and of the A-frame guest house before the Kennedys moved in.

She returned to the desk and found the address of the service Mary had used in the past. While there, she opened Agnes' note to see when she was supposed to water the plants. She frowned at the handwriting with its downward slant, tics of irritation, wide spaces between words, and tight letters within words. The script showed what Casey already knew, that the woman preferred to keep others at bay, was uptight and a pain in the butt.

But it also showed that she was despondent. Could she be depressed or as lonely as Casey? *Now, don't be getting all empathetic.* Much more fun to dislike her than to understand her.

In the note, Agnes instructed Casey to dust and sweep once a week when she came to pay the bills. Fat chance.

Time for a little sport. She opened the top drawer of the desk with its regimented organization of pens, pencils, paper clips, and scissors. She considered shaking the drawer violently, but then decided to be more subtle. She buried a few pencils in the slot reserved solely for pens. In the kitchen, she mixed dessert forks with salad forks and re-ordered a few spices to upset their alphabetical precision. She set the electronic clock five minutes slow. Nothing too obvious, just enough to make Agnes pause and doubt.

Finally, she sat at the desk, picked up the telephone, asked for New York City Information, and got the phone number for *Penthouse* magazine. She ordered a subscription for Agnes Dempsey to be delivered to #1 President's Lane. Enough for now, she had work to do. "C'mon, Bella, let's go." She hefted the box of records to her shoulder and left the house.

Halfway down Station Road, she spotted a man ducking out of the rear door of the caboose. By the time she got to the bottom of the hill, there was no one in sight. Fortune was right. Past time to get those padlocks and a more secure system for the station.

Was she in danger, a single woman living at the end of a road with no close neighbors? She couldn't even call Agnes for help. Until this week, she'd never worried about being alone. Now she wondered how worried she should be.

Chapter Eleven

Fortune

Sunday, 10/23

Fortune sat in his car and sipped his coffee, grateful for a few minutes of blissful silence. Davey had chattered all through breakfast about the caboose and the safe and the little dog. Fortune's mother was full of questions about the single woman who lived in the station. She'd heard all the local gossip about the ex-con who claimed to be the daughter of a priest, a young woman who'd wheedled her way into the good graces of the owner of the White House before she died. Fortune was amazed at the level of information and misinformation that warmed the Welton wires. When he set her straight on a few issues, his mother demanded a detailed description of Casey.

"She's about five feet two, brunette, with an independent streak."

"Pretty?"

"Yeah. But relax, Mom. She's not my type," he'd reassured her.

A rap on the passenger window interrupted his reverie. Blair Forsythe, his type personified, opened the passenger door and scootched in beside him. A local beauty queen, blonde bombshell, and Welton's premier real estate agent, Blair, seemed to pop up more and more often. He'd taken her out a few times and enjoyed her flirtatious…well, seductive…manner, but had let things cool off a bit, not wanting to become entangled in a new relationship.

He needed time to recover from the debacle at the end of his marriage to another blonde bombshell.

"Missed you Friday," she opened after a quick peck on the cheek which made him juggle his coffee. "Oops," she giggled.

He rewarded her with a smile. He'd ducked out of a party early last weekend before she arrived.

"What are you up to today?" she asked, toying with a lock of hair.

"More dog training. And I'd like to find out more about the new family renting the White House off Church Street. You?"

"A few showings. Slow day."

He waited for her to tell him all she knew about the Kennedys and was soon rewarded.

"The Kennedys' lawyer left a message over the weekend asking if the family could move in sooner. I called Mr. Kennedy and got his wife. Did you know they were living in a Boston hotel? I asked her why, and she said their home had burned to the ground! They want to move in ASAP. What's your interest?"

"Nothing official. I took Davey to see the caboose at the old Welton railroad station. The woman who lives there will be managing the White House properties for her aunt. She made some comment about how security-conscious the new tenants were."

"Look out for that woman, hon. I hear she's got quite a lot of baggage."

Before Blair could parrot the litany of gossip swirling about Casey, Fortune drained and crushed his cup. "Much as I enjoy your company, I've got to pick up Captain. Can't be late for school."

"You and that dog!" she teased as she got out of the car.

He watched her, as she knew he would, walk with enough sway and suggestion to turn a celibate's head. Those legs went on forever.

Cool it, man. He checked his cheek in the rearview mirror for lipstick before entering the station. He had a half hour before canine training with his German Shepherd, Captain. He had time to look into one thing that irked him, the out-of-state cop who had ignored normal police protocol, paid a visit to the caboose, and spoken to a resident without informing the

Welton police. At his desk, he toyed with the card Casey had given him and then dialed the number.

"New Hampshire State Police, how may I help you?"

"Detective Fortune, Welton, Massachusetts Police. I'd like to speak with Detective Granger."

With a click, he was connected to Homicide.

"Granger."

Fortune introduced himself. "I understand you paid a visit to my neck of the woods last week."

"Say again?"

The man's stalling. "Why were you visiting a resident in Welton, Massachusetts last week?" he said more forcefully.

"I haven't been out of state in months. You must be misinformed."

"Detective Sergeant Theodore Granger, New Hampshire State Police," repeated Fortune. "I have your card in front of me."

"That's me. Who gave you the card? I leave my card when I'm pursuing leads, as I'm sure you do. One of them evidently made its way to Welton. I'd like to find out more about the person who used my card."

Fortune frowned, now fully engaged. He looked up Casey's number and gave it to Granger, and then related what Casey had told him about the cop's visit to the caboose. "He was very interested in finding out more about a vagrant who was squatting in the caboose when it was located in Conway, New Hampshire."

"Okay. Now I get the connection. We have an ongoing investigation regarding a homicide committed close to where that caboose used to be located. There was a body found in the woods not far from where the car sat on the rails. The vic was shot in the head. We don't know why and have only circumstantial evidence to go on regarding the identification of the man. The body was in bad shape, exposed to the elements, animals, and insects. It was difficult to determine when he'd died because of the deterioration of the body.

"Alex Ferguson from Concord, New Hampshire, identified the body as his brother James Ferguson based on the remains of a leather Army jacket the dead man was wearing and the fact that his brother had been living in the caboose for a while. He claimed the body and buried it in their family plot."

"Interesting. The man Miss Cavendish spoke with seemed to be looking for the squatter. Is there a chance that he's still alive and the brother was wrong?"

Granger was silent for a moment before replying. "I suppose it's possible, but I doubt it. The brother was convinced, and we had no reason to think otherwise."

"Does the situation pose any danger to Miss Cavendish?" asked Fortune.

"I don't see how, although I wouldn't rule anything out at this point, given what you've just told me. I'd suggest the lady take extra precautions, just in case. Someone has gone to some trouble to track down the caboose and pose as me."

Fortune finished the call. Casey didn't need any more trouble, that's for sure. Clearly, townsfolk had her pegged as an outsider with questionable credentials. Living alone in an isolated train station with her animals, she'd be an easy target for someone with malicious intent. He'd stop by and make sure she'd follow his advice about security.

Chapter Twelve

Casey

Monday, 10/24

C asey spent the morning traipsing around the properties with a representative from the security company she'd selected. She ordered a new system with an intercom for the main gate and also keypad locks for the gate at the rear of the acreage and the small gate at the top of the stone stairs that led from the White House down to the station. Four front doors—the White House, the A-frame, Agnes' carriage house, and her station—would get new locks and keypad security. After Casey showed the agent the locations and requirements, the man sat down at her table in the station and wrote up the detailed order.

As a temporary measure, she'd set the code for all the keypads to 1974, the year she'd been released from Marysville Reformatory for Women in Ohio. She'd change the code at the residents' request but would record the new code to maintain control. As the person in charge of maintenance and security, she might need access.

After the representative left, Casey went to the bank to set up an account for Fisher to seed with monies for expenses and bills. For the time being, she was paying everything out of her personal account, and it was making her plenty nervous as the orders and amounts grew. Her next stop was the hardware store, where she bought padlocks for the front and rear doors of the caboose.

Now for the telephone company. She hadn't been able to reach them via telephone, ironic as that might seem, so she decided to make a personal visit to the local office. Although she had to wait a half hour, she eventually placed the order for the new lines for the White House and the A-frame as per instructions on Kennedy's list and purchased the physical phones.

Her answering machine was blinking when she returned to the station. She hit play. "Who was that man? Call me." Fisher's voice demanded. Click. That was all. Huh. He must have seen the security fellow and called right after she left. She tossed the phone into its cradle. She didn't have time for his nonsense.

Now for a few personal errands. She stopped just outside the station door and waved at nothing in particular. "I'm going to be in and out during the week, preparing the White House and guest house for the Kennedys' arrival. I'd appreciate it if you'd let me know if any visitors or shady characters come lurking around the station or caboose in my absence." She wrinkled her nose and threw a kiss for Fisher or whoever was watching.

Feeling pleased with herself for sassing the rude lawyer and ordering him to look out for her property, she drove to the pet shop for supplies. She bought two small flea and tick collars and a handsome black leather collar for Isabella. Next stop was Town Hall, where she paid a fee and registered Isabella and received an official, very legal owner's tag. Finally, she purchased the week's groceries at the super expensive local market.

Time for lunch. As she entered the station, the phone rang. She caught the call on the third ring.

"I spoke with your boss yesterday about a change in plans." Fisher's annoying squawk announced. "She was supposed to call me back, but hasn't done so. Now, she doesn't answer the phone. Have her call me immediately," Fisher demanded.

My boss? Oh, Agnes. "Miss Dempsey is out of town at present," Casey replied in a prim, receptionist voice.

"It's imperative that we speak."

"I'm sorry, but she left on vacation. I can leave a message at the place she's staying—"

"Not very professional," Fisher interrupted.

"Well, we're a work in progress. You're our first renter." Casey paused. Her mind raced with negative possibilities. She'd already committed her own personal funds arranging things for the new tenants and didn't yet have access to any money from Fisher. "What plans? What's changed?" she asked, dreading the possibility of a cancellation of the rental contract that could leave her holding the bag.

"The Kennedys plan to arrive Saturday. Their living arrangements have changed."

"I'm sorry, but we're not ready for them yet. It's too soon. It was already a stretch to have them move in at the first of next month."

"Make it happen."

"Why the rush? Is there something wrong?"

"I'm not at liberty to discuss my client's situation. Money talks. Do what you must." Click.

Casey held the phone at arm's length, glaring at it as if it were a rotten fish before making what was now a practiced shot into its cradle. "Insufferable prick."

She sank into the rocker and began scribbling an emergency to-do list. It would be a long night. She still needed to set up appointments with a landscaper, hire cleaning personnel, do a ton of paperwork, and make phone calls to establish separate billing accounts for utilities for the rental properties. Everything was to be itemized by structure: White House, A-frame, and carriage house.

As she made the list, she vowed to be meticulous about arrangements. She had no desire to be accused of skimming or overbilling. She'd be so law-abiding, she'd frighten herself. She wouldn't be one of the recidivist ex-cons who revisited the penal establishment.

However, part of her mind whirled on a different plane. She wasn't too busy to worry, wonder, and speculate about recent events. Who was the early visitor to the caboose? A hiker? Hobo? Someone looking for Hobo? Or was Hobo the unidentified dead man in the woods? Why would Hobo leave his personal belongings behind crammed into a backpack? Was he planning to run? If he ran, why didn't he take the pack—and Bella—with him? Why were things happening a full year after Mary bought the caboose and brought it to Welton? Thoughts raced through her mind like a runaway train.

The New Hampshire cop was definitely interested in the safe. Would he return? Did she need protection? She had Fisher keeping an electronic eye on the place. Was that enough? The last thought wasn't useful, because it led to the realization, yet again, of how alone and lonely she was. Should she call LouAnne again? It was unlike her not to return a call. Should she be worried?

She had a home if not a family, friends albeit unusual ones, her health and two wonderful furry companions. And a heck of a lot to do before the Kennedys arrived. Little Mother popped through the cat door and marched to her cat dish with a disdainful backward glance. Bella rose from her dog bed and joined her. Time to quit dragging her toenails and feed the animals.

Chapter Thirteen

Tuesday, 10/25

In the morning, Casey called the security company to change the installation date and discovered that, yes, money talked, and enough money wangled an appointment with a technician in a matter of hours. However, her next calls brought no joy. The regular cleaners she'd counted on didn't have available personnel on short notice. She called every listing in the Yellow Pages, but none could come before the next week. She groaned thinking of all the plastic furniture covers and floors and dust and...

She left a message with the landscaper's answering service, but the nice woman said her boss was on vacation and wouldn't return for another week and a half. Let the grass grow! There was only so much she could hope to accomplish. When a different security technician arrived for the appointment, Casey had to explain the contract to him and spend the remainder of the morning overseeing the installation of the new locks and systems.

When she was confident the workmen knew what they were doing, she left them and drove the Muttmobile to town to purchase more cleaning supplies. While she was out, she treated herself to a full breakfast at the local coffee shop. As she was leaving, she noticed the realtor's sign across the street. Maybe she could get a little information and advice on suppliers from the woman who had recommended the White House to the Kennedys.

She crossed the street and checked out the listings and pictures of estates in the window before entering. She knew the town was an exclusive suburb, but the prices were outrageous.

Inside the tastefully appointed office were three desks with facing chairs suitable for discreet conversations with clientele. At the front desk, a blonde woman dressed in a burgundy silk shirt and camel slacks rose and smiled as Casey entered. "How may I help you, Miss Cavendish? I'm Blair Forsythe." The woman's voice was as low and smooth and well-modulated as her blouse. She held out a be-ringed and manicured hand to shake with Casey's calloused and unadorned hand.

Small town indeed. Casey didn't know anyone, but evidently everyone knew her, or of her. "I believe that someone from this office helped rent the White House on President's Lane."

As the woman's eyes took in Casey's jeans and denim work shirt, her expression changed from welcome to lukewarm. "Yes. I called Miss Dempsey for the Kennedys."

"We appreciate the referral. I'll be managing the property. They're planning to move in on Saturday."

Blair's eyebrows rose, but Casey couldn't tell what surprised the woman more, Casey's employment or the tenant's early arrival.

"Have a seat. What brings you in today?"

"Two things. Miss Dempsey and I would like to know more about our new renters. We haven't had time to explore their background or get to know them or check references. And second, I'm having a hard time finding cleaning and landscaping services that can come on such short notice."

Blair sat back with what Casey could only interpret as a smug smile. "Mike, uh, Detective Fortune, asked me the same questions about the Kennedys. He mentioned his visit to the caboose."

"I gave him and his boy Davey a tour of the railcar and station. He seemed like a nice fellow. He asks a lot of questions," replied Casey.

"Yes. Well, he likes to be on top of things." Blair's proprietary, rather suggestive, tone was not lost on Casey. Not hard to imagine what a guy like Fortune, uh, Mike, might like about Blair.

"Unfortunately, I don't know much about the family. Mr. Kennedy said the family of three and two servants were living in a Boston hotel because their home in Rhode Island had burned to the ground.

"As for service companies, I don't think I can be of much help." She flipped through a Rolodex and stopped at a few places to copy names and numbers onto a pad. She wrinkled her perfect forehead into a frown at something that caught her attention out the front window. "Is that your car?" She pointed across the street at the Muttmobile. A little boy was admiring the pupils painted on the headlights and the Great Dane hood ornament.

"My Porsche is in the garage," said Casey.

Blair ripped off the top sheet of the pad and handed it to Casey. "Sounds like you might be a little over your head. It's a lot of responsibility."

Casey accepted the paper. "Thanks for your help. I'm not worried. It's just real estate. How complicated could it be?" She gave Blair her most endearing smile and left. As she crossed the street, she admitted that her comment probably wasn't her smartest move if she wanted to make connections with the community. She hopped in the Muttmobile and twirled the Great Dane's head a full rotation for the boy and for Blair, who undoubtedly was watching. She was tempted to tap the horn and release a howl of hounds but restrained herself. Overkill.

Driving home, she imagined what a handsome couple Mike and Blair would make, their picture in the *Town and Country* society page, the local beauty queen and rugged quarterback. Nah, that's too small-town Ohio. Think Welton. Prep school, lacrosse... Oh, stop!

As she drove down Station Road, she spotted a gleaming, English-racing-green Jaguar parked in front of the caboose.

As she drew closer, she saw Chance sitting on the station stairs, now clean shaven and easily recognizable, looking like an ad for LL Bean, wholesome, casual and confident, as if he belonged there.

He rose and walked toward the Muttmobile in greeting. Isabella jumped out and dashed toward him, tail helicoptering. He knelt and opened his arms wide and was immediately covered with doggie kisses. He looked up at Casey with teasing eyes and spread his arms wide again in invitation. Much as she might like to cover him with kisses, Casey maintained her cool and offered him her hand. Besides, she was probably on camera. "The prodigal returns."

"Things take twice as long as you think they should." He didn't release her hand.

"Unless you work for our new tenant. Then everything is expected to happen instantly or yesterday."

"New tenant?"

"Yes. At the White House. His lawyer may be watching you right now with a camera he's installed somewhere around here." She twirled around and gestured to the universe. "Mr. Fisher, meet my friend Chance."

Chance frowned and looked around the front door of the station for a likely spot to hide a camera. He searched around the caboose and then peered up at the struts supporting the roof overhang by the front door. "Got it." He picked up one of Casey's painting cloths and stuffed it around what looked, at closer inspection, to be the lens of a camera.

Camera shy? "Come inside. It's good to see you."

Chance followed. "What's with the camera?"

"Our new tenant is rather paranoid. I'm putting up with it while we get things set up, but I'll make it disappear soon." She watched Chance, who seemed uneasy. "There have been a number of strange visitors here in the past week, so I don't mind having someone watching the place."

They made small talk while Casey puttered about in the kitchenette fixing tea and a plate of cookies.

"Tell me what's happening," he said when she finally settled down at the table.

Once again, Casey found herself describing events of the past week: her mystery visitor, the New Hampshire cop who was interested in the squatter and the safe, and Fisher with his camera and demands. "Now it's your turn. What's happening in your world?"

"First things first." Chance rose, took her hand, and pulled her into his arms. His kiss was gentle yet demanding. He looked into her eyes, cocked his head and raised his eyebrows as if asking permission for another kiss. She pulled away and sat abruptly, confused, and embarrassed. Chance watched her struggle with a small smile.

Too much, too soon! "Fancy car," blurted Casey.

Chance chuckled and sat down across from her. "It was my father's. We just settled his estate. It was tricky because, as you may remember, I was declared dead—it's difficult to re-emerge amongst the living to claim your inheritance. That's why I've been gone so long. Luckily, Mary never pressed charges against me for posing as her stepson, so there was no legal barrier to my claim. A photograph, blood test, and fingerprints—such as they are—finally proved my identity." He held up his hands with nine fingers and one stub. "Easier to pose as Worthy than to become myself," he finished with a wry smile.

"So, now what will you do?"

"I sold my share of the family business to my uncle. The company makes furniture. I'm not interested in chairs."

Casey watched him as he spoke of recent events. She realized how little she knew about him. Handsome as he was in a southern, rather dashing way, she wondered if she could trust a man who had willingly tried to deceive her and her aunt. Was she falling for the dangerous, exciting bad boy? Slow down, Casey girl. You don't have a very good track record with men, and you have everything to lose. *But he's so delicious.*

"I seem to have lost you. Maybe you're also bored with chairs?"

"Sorry. I have nothing against chairs." She rolled her eyes at her lame response. Try again. "What would you like to do?"

Chance's gaze left no question.

Casey's hormones battled mightily with common-sense warning bells. She squirmed and turned a few shades of pink.

Chance rose and leaned forward with a teasing expression, and then shook his head. "Unfortunately, I have an interview in Maine in an hour or so with one of the fellows I went to college with. He's considering a number of options that require legal counsel. But I hope to pass through again soon."

Too close. She backed away. Passing through sounded awfully casual, and he was acting as if he expected more than a kiss on a later pass. Maybe a little nookie with the ex-con on his way to and fro? She couldn't do much to ruin her reputation in town, but she could lower her self-esteem another notch if she acted like a doormat.

Sounds of a car in front of the station distracted Chance. "You have company."

Chapter Fourteen

Casey looked out the front window. "Oh my," she muttered, watching Fortune get out of an unmarked car. He walked around the Jaguar and checked the plate before approaching the station. Casey opened the door. Beside her, Isabella stood on her hind legs in greeting. "Hey, Bella." He ruffled her ears before greeting Casey. Glancing about, his eyes settled on Chance. "You have company."

Was there an echo? What was the likelihood two hunks would appear on her doorstep on the same day? "Yes, an old friend." She smiled and stepped aside, ushering him in, relieved for the interruption and embarrassed at the same time.

Chance watched the detective with hooded eyes as Fortune took in the scene. The room seemed to shrink with two dominant males facing one another.

"Chauncey Cunningham, meet Detective Fortune of the Welton Police." Chance nodded but didn't step forward to shake hands.

What a contrast. Neither man looked pleased. Fortune, a buff five ten with his Mediterranean complexion and firm jaw, looked like a Roman legionnaire compared to the lanky, sandy-haired Confederate gentleman across from him. Chance could probably outrun and outjump Fortune, but he was toast the second Fortune caught him.

Fortune smiled down at Casey. "Call me Mike." He gestured to the door. "I see you changed the locks."

He doesn't miss anything. "Uh-huh. The new security systems and locks were installed this morning. The tenant has a camera fixed on the station,

56

so there's also surveillance."

"Camera?" Fortune frowned.

Casey shrugged. "Yes. Mr. Kennedy's lawyer uses it to keep tabs on the comings and goings here. I told you the tenant was paranoid. Chance found it attached to one of the struts under the roof." She turned and pointed to two packages on the table. "You'll be happy to know that I bought padlocks for the front and back doors of the caboose and got a town tag and collars for Bella and Little Mother."

"Good girl."

Was he going to pat her on the head? Casey was about to give him another mock salute when he smiled down at her. Better.

"We have information about your Hobo and about the New Hampshire State police officer who visited. He's an impostor. Call me if he shows up again. You have my number. I'll return at a better time." Fortune's expression hardened as he glanced at Chance, turned, and left.

Damn! Casey was burning with questions, but Fortune was already at his cruiser.

"Buddies with the law these days?" Chance asked, watching Fortune drive away. The charming Chance was replaced by an aloof inquisitor.

Casey smiled and crossed her arms. "Yes." Let him stew on that.

"What's going on?"

"It's a long story."

Chance surprised her. "Some other time. Much as I'd like to hear it and continue our earlier... discussion, I must be on my way." He rose and made a production about brushing off cat hair. Apparently, dogs were okay, not so cats. Casey pointed to a sign attached to her refrigerator with a magnet: "Cat hair, both a fashion statement and a condiment."

He shook his head. As he approached, his expression changed back to the familiar, intimate Chance. "Keep me in mind." He stroked her cheek and was out the door.

From the window, Casey watched him saunter to the Jag and drive off without a backward glance. Wow. You have my number, but I don't have yours. I don't even know where you live. Seemed like every day ended with a good reason for a glass of red wine.

The phone shrilled.

Had to be Fisher.

"Who were your visitors?" Fisher demanded.

Plural? Chance had covered the camera. How had Fisher seen Fortune?

"I heard the second car and voices."

Now he could read my mind? "Enough of your spying. Why are you watching, anyway?"

"You can't be too careful, especially when our main contact is an ex-con with former inmates for friends."

How would he know that? He wouldn't dare tap her phone, would he? No, much easier. Kennedy had spoken with Blair, and she probably gave him an earful of local gossip about the properties and their residents. Folks in town had noticed LouAnne and Rosie, the tall black couple who came to visit Casey. One of the local cops had given them special attention as they drove through town.

"Believe it or not, I have zero interest in you or your clients as long as you're happy with the rental, and you pay. Speaking of which, listen carefully and write down this bank account number. Fund the account soon so that I can make your money talk." Casey retrieved a slip of paper, read off a series of digits, and hung up.

Enough. She was exhausted by all the arrangements, paralyzed by her reactions to the two men, and pissed off at Fisher.

Chapter Fifteen

Wednesday, 10/26

Early the next morning, Casey hung up after pleading, to no avail, with another cleaning service. The instant she replaced the receiver, the phone rang. She almost blew off the call but answered at the last minute, hoping for a reprieve from Fisher on the imminent arrival of the Kennedys, or a return call from a landscaper.

"What's up, girlfriend? You okay? Your message sounded crazy," LouAnne said.

"Over my head, Lou. The tenant moves in Saturday, not next week. Agnes took off. A fake cop wants to locate Hobo, and I can't find anyone to—

"Whoa! Slow down, sugar. Back up. Take a deep breath. Talk to Lou."

Casey obeyed her old friend and cellmate. She started with the rental and filled her in on the bizarre events of the last week. After her recital, the line went quiet for a few moments before LouAnne responded. "Let's figure what we can do. Rosie and I can take a day off, no problem. The security—you say they fixed up the gates and the house locks, so that's set. You did the phones. How about cleaning?"

"I can't get our regular service to come until next week at the earliest. I've called every other service in the book. No dice. Same with the landscaper and pool company."

"Okay. You and I can clean. Nobody's been living there to mess it up, right? Freshen up a few bedrooms, bathrooms, and kitchen. Run a vacuum.

Dust. Make it pretty. We can do that."

"Sorry, I was losing it."

"You got a mower there that fellow Jackson used to ride around on. Rosie can cut the grass and trim about the house and garage. Leave the rest for later. Forget about the A-frame house till next week. They'll just have to understand. You go buy some supplies for the bathrooms and kitchen. Meet me in an hour at the White House. Leave the gate open."

"Y'asm." Lou was one take-charge lady. Casey hopped in the Muttmobile and drove to the store. She bought cleaning products, and she also purchased steaks and salad fixings and potatoes for Lou and Rosie for later. When she got to the White House, Lou was waiting, arms akimbo, all business. Over six feet and muscular, with a long neck and high cheekbones and a two-inch Afro, she was a force of nature. "How many folks we talkin' about?"

"Two adults and a child and a married couple, their servants."

"So, we fix up four rooms upstairs: the master bedroom for the parents, a room for the kid, and an extra for good measure, and then the servants' rooms downstairs in the wing. Three bathrooms. Seems a whole lot of house for a small family." LouAnne knew the layout of the White House from a tour she had given her and Rosie a year ago.

Casey and Lou worked all day, uncovering furniture, airing out stuffy rooms, dusting and mopping the floors. They made the beds with fresh linens and scoured the bathroom surfaces and stocked each one with towels, toothpaste, soap and shampoo. The sound of the mower through open windows serenaded them as Rosie rode circles around the immediate grounds.

They tackled the kitchen next, cleaning the counters and refrigerator and washing and waxing the floor. After they finished, Casey disappeared into the cellar and emerged moments later, juggling four bottles of wine.

"They drinkers?" asked Lou.

"Don't know. A white and red for them. Two reds for us. Party at the A-frame in fifteen minutes. Get that handsome husband of yours and bring him down for our last laps in the pool, a soak in the hot tub, and a steak before the tenants take over."

Casey took the back path from the White House to the A-frame carrying the bags of food and wine. Outside by the pool, she fired up the grill and then went inside to put potatoes in the oven and cut up veggies for a salad.

When LouAnne and Rosie arrived, they stripped to their underwear, ran outside to the pool, and dove in.

"I'm hungry," LouAnne announced fifteen minutes later, stepping out of the pool.

Casey and Rosie swam a little longer and then followed. Rosie stood a half foot taller than Lou and was at least fifty pounds heavier. Casey felt like a shrimp. She stared at the bottom of the pool. "I don't have time or energy to vacuum it."

"Simple, girl. We just roll out that tarp over there and cover it until the pool service can get here. You grab one end; I'll get the other."

Casey tried to move her end of the tarp into position, but it was too heavy. When Rosie noticed, he called out for Lou to help, but she was fussing with the sound system by the door to the house. Moments later, music blared from their favorite oldies station, and LouAnne joined them.

"Don't turn around," she warned. "There's a camera by the audio equipment. Has a giveaway little red light. I turned up the music, so whoever is spying can see us, but not hear us. Talk mush mouth in case he can lip read."

"Good grief!" said Casey. "Someone's wired this place, too. I told you about the camera on the front of the station. Think they had one in the White House?"

LouAnne frowned. "Maybe the front and back doors. Not inside. Too many rooms. But this here camera is seriously weird."

Casey thought a moment. "They could have installed the cameras during our rental meeting with Kennedy. I think they'd already decided to rent the place before the meeting, and just met us to set out their demands. No problem getting in. Agnes left the gate open all the time."

They finished covering the pool and then uncorked the wine and sank into the hot tub on the far side of the pool away from the camera. Casey noticed that Lou wasn't drinking. "You the driver tonight?" she asked.

LouAnne shot a look to Rosie. He nodded as if agreeing to something.

"There's a reason I didn't answer your calls right away. We've got news." LouAnne grinned and rubbed her tummy. "For the first few months, I was sick every morning."

It took Casey a second before she erupted. "No! True? Wonderful!" She raised her arms for a congratulatory hug that encompassed both her friends. With two giants and a shrimp in the tub, the water splashed over the top. When they finally released her, Casey asked, "When are you due?"

"June, best we can tell," said LouAnne.

"Boy or girl?"

"Don't know. Not asking," Rosie answered. He leaned forward and kissed LouAnne on the cheek. They talked for a few moments about plans for the baby before Rosie changed the subject. "Where's the battle-axe?" he asked, referring to Agnes.

"Off at some spa. I'm actually glad she's not here. She'd just get in the way," said Casey.

"Afraid that woman doesn't approve of us," Rosie said as he bounced up and down, making waves.

LouAnne interrupted. "I don't care where she is, or who's looking. I'm starved." After they dried off, Rosie uncorked the second bottle of wine, and Casey threw the steaks on the grill. They retrieved the baked potatoes from the oven and dressed the salad, and then settled down to eat by the glow of pool lights.

"Be nice, 'cepting for the uninvited guest," said Rosie.

"Watch me chew," said Lou, carving up her steak.

They made quick work of the meal. Casey and Rosie managed to polish off the last of the wine. After cleaning up, they walked back up President's Lane to their cars they had left parked in front of the White House.

"I can't thank you enough. You two are the best," declared Casey.

"Keep close, girl," said LouAnne as she and Rosie gave Casey another hug. "Write everything down, maybe even buy a little recorder and tape that lawyer guy, Fisher. Call us if there's trouble."

Chapter Sixteen

C asey slumped into the driver's seat of the Muttmobile, exhausted and tipsy, wondering if she had the energy to drive down the hill to the station. She was thankful for her dear friends, but worried about what she'd gotten herself into. The tenant Kennedy had to be seriously paranoid for his lawyer, Fisher to watch both the station and the A-Frame for him. Why? What, or whom, was Kennedy afraid of? Although only a week had passed, it was too late to extricate herself from the situation.

She'd call Lieutenant Fortune, except she didn't want to admit to holding a party in the A-Frame with her old cellmate and her husband. She wasn't exactly trespassing, but she was taking advantage. What could he do, anyway? She sank lower in the seat. She sure was alone, living in the station. She didn't want anything to do with a firearm, but she could get some Mace spray for protection.

Too tired to worry more, she fired up the beast and drove slowly down President's Lane, past the carriage house and through the gate. She turned down the Station Road, thinking about how nice it would be to sink into her bed in the loft and pull up the comforter. She blinked. Huh? Was she seeing things in an alcohol-induced stupor? She squinted. Sure did look like a light inside the caboose. But the electricity wasn't hooked up yet. Casey hit the gas, and the trusty Muttmobile leapt forward.

Halfway down the hill, Casey rocked back and slammed on the brakes. The wheels locked and the car slewed sideways, shuddering to a stop and stalling. *What was she thinking!* If someone was inside the caboose, he broke in. Any self-respecting intruder could pick a lock. What did she think she was going to do? Scold him? Unarmed, a five-foot-two-inch, hundred-pound female. She'd learned some valuable defensive moves in prison, but this was beyond stupid.

She waited until her breathing returned to normal, her hands quit shaking, and her heart stopped thumping before turning the key. The Muttmobile responded on her second try. She righted the car and pointed the Great Dane hood ornament straight down the hill before killing the engine and lights.

The car rolled silently down the hill. She braked in front of the station. There was no light inside the caboose. As quietly as possible, she got out and ran to the door of the station, opened it, and punched in 1974. She locked and bolted the door and then raced to look out the side window. Huh. No light in the caboose.

Bella and Little Mother weren't spooked by a vagrant or intruder or strange noise, just hungry. Was she crazy? Was the light a reflection off the caboose window from a passing car's headlights on the Church Street overpass? Or from the Muttmobile headlights as she turned down Station Road? Was she becoming as paranoid as her tenants?

While feeding the animals, she forced herself to concentrate on more positive thoughts. When was Chance coming back? Could he help somehow? But how could he protect her—or how could Fortune, for that matter—without staying on the premises full time? Interesting and rather appealing as either option might be, it wasn't happening. She wasn't ready for a male roommate, at least not yet. Not that she'd had any offers.

Tomorrow she'd buy some Mace for protection. She wouldn't trust herself with a gun. She could imagine the headline: "Ex-con shoots intruder." At age thirty-four, she'd had enough violence for a lifetime. Where there were guns, there were dead people. She'd check her locks and watch her back. While she was at it, she'd also get a little tape recorder for Fisher's rude calls.

Her friends, LouAnne and Rosie, could only do so much. They had their own lives and work to do, lived two towns away, and were expecting a baby. What a bombshell their announcement was—the last thing she'd expected to hear! She was truly delighted for them, but at the same time, she felt saddened and somehow left out. The days of the carefree trio were over. They'd be a family unit. Maybe the kid would call her Aunt Casey. They must really want this baby. LouAnne was in her forties and was pushing it. She and Rosie looked so happy.

Although LouAnne rarely spoke of it, she'd had a child earlier. When she caught her first husband molesting her little girl, she'd killed him. Both were severely traumatized, and LouAnne served hard time for manslaughter while her mother raised the girl. LouAnne and her daughter had missed much of the developmental years and were still somewhat estranged after the long years of separation.

Casey sat at her desk and opened her notebook, dated the page, and thought about entering the events of the day. No, not tonight. Tired and stiff from a full day of cleaning and woozy from the wine, she took a couple aspirin, called her fur family up to the loft, and fell into bed.

Chapter Seventeen

Thursday, 10/27

Casey awoke in the morning with a cat paw in her face. She rolled over only to meet a wet dog nose. Okay. Okay. She'd overslept. She dragged herself downstairs and fed the animals. After her second cup of coffee, she began to feel human. She peeked outside. All was calm and bright. Other than feeding a couple of demanding pets, she was free to do whatever she wanted to do today. A day off from Fisher and his demands and away from the annoying telephone.

She'd like to buy a few things to spiff up the inside of the caboose and some fire engine red paint for the outside of the caboose, but that would have to wait for the first installment of her new salary. Until then, she was sorely strapped for cash. She could raid the White House wine cellar for a few more bottles. They'd never miss it, and renting a place furnished didn't include food and drink, did it? Or maybe not. Don't do anything that could even be frowned upon.

She attached the new keys to her key ring. How official, holding all the keys to the kingdom dangling from the belt loop of her jeans. Six keys in all: White House, A-frame, carriage house, station, and two for the caboose. She was either the person in charge or the janitor. She found Agnes' red nail polish and marked F and R on the keys to distinguish between the front and rear doors of the caboose.

Casey unwrapped the new collar she'd purchased at the pet store and affixed Isabella's official new Welton tag to it. "Come here, girl." Bella obeyed and waited patiently as Casey removed her ratty old collar and replaced it with her handsome new one.

As she was removing the previous owner's tag from the old collar, she noticed markings on the inside material in faded ink. Looking closer, she could make out a series of numbers and letters. She squinted to read them. 11R-17L-35R. Not a name, but numbers and letters separated by dashes. This was the collar Hobo, or Mr. Smith, had put on Isabella. It was probably his writing.

R then L then R.

Could it be? She dashed out the door and unlocked the caboose. Inside in the storage closet she grabbed the flashlight and focused it on the safe. It took her a number of tries to twirl the numbers around correctly, but finally the heavy door opened.

She pointed the light inside, illuminating three items: a handgun, a stack of what looked like hundred-dollar bills, and a tattered black and white photo of a lovely young woman. Wow, was this hers? She could sure use the money, and for that matter, with strangers snooping about the premises and Mr. Fisher seeming so, well, fishy, she might need a gun. No, she reminded herself. Guns...dead people. She'd leave it.

She reached in to retrieve the money and then sat back abruptly. For the second time in as many days *what was she thinking!* You know nothing about this money. It could be related to a crime. Don't ask for trouble.

She slammed the door of the safe closed and returned to the station. She took a deep breath and called the Welton Police and asked for Detective Fortune.

"Officer O'Malley," a gruff voice answered.

"This is Casey Cavendish.

"I know who you are. You're the girl in the train station."

"I'd like to speak with Detective Fortune."

"He's not here."

"Please take a message for—"

"I'm the officer on duty. Tell me what this is about, miss."

"Just tell him that there's a gun in the safe."

"I need more details."

She was getting nowhere, so she sighed and explained as quickly as she could that there was an old safe that came with the caboose and that neither the former owner of the caboose nor she knew the combination to the safe until today.

"Where did you find it?"

"On the inside of a dog collar."

"Really?" O'Malley sounded incredulous.

Casey couldn't blame him. She quickly explained about the stray dog she'd found around the caboose when they were loading it up for the move to Welton. "The former owner believed the dog belonged to a squatter who had been living in the railcar. The owner fed the dog for a week or so, but couldn't keep her, so I brought her with me to Welton. When I replaced her collar a few minutes ago, I saw faded numbers and letters inside the old collar."

"Quite a story," he commented.

"I'm holding the old collar in my hand. I can show it to you."

"What is in the safe?"

"A gun, a stack of bills wrapped in twine, and an old photograph."

"How much money?"

"I have no idea."

"I'll give Fortune the message." Click.

Was that the way people in New England ended phone conversations, or was she just lucky to speak with three rude individuals—Agnes, Fisher, and now O'Malley? With a practiced hand, she tossed the phone into its cradle.

She took out her paints and stared at an empty blank piece of watercolor paper for a while, unable to concentrate. Okay, so prepare for the handwriting class she was scheduled to teach at the beginning of January. Figure out how to hook the class during the first lesson. Easy. Start with the most common objections people parroted when they found out she was a graphologist: "My handwriting changes all the time." "My writing is a mess. You can't tell a thing about me." "I only print." She'd answer a few objections and then have class members write, "The quick red fox jumps over the lazy brown dog," on a plain sheet of paper. She'd post them on the wall and have the class appreciate how different the writings were and—

The phone rang just as a Welton police cruiser drove down Station Road. When she answered, Fisher's voice demanded, "Why are the police there?"

Chapter Eighteen

"Where are you?" Casey was fed up with Fisher's attitude and intrusion.

"Why are the police there?" Fisher repeated.

"Join us and find out." She tossed the phone into its cradle and went outside to speak with Fortune and Officer O'Malley, whom she now recognized from interviews conducted after her Aunt Vera was killed. He had the build and personality of a fireplug.

She showed them the old collar with its numbers and letters written inside and then walked with them to the caboose. Fortune smiled at the newly installed locks, but otherwise was all business. Before unlocking the caboose, she asked them to hold on for a moment, rushed back inside the station and returned with a small camera. The phone began ringing again as she entered the caboose.

"Do you want to get that?" asked Fortune.

"Nope." She'd had enough of Fisher for a while. Inside, she led the officers to the storage closet. Fortune and Casey ducked inside. She asked him to hold the flashlight while she manipulated the dial.

When the heavy door opened, Fortune whistled. He handed back the light and put on plastic gloves. He took an evidence bag from his belt and placed the handgun inside it. Casey stopped him as he started to bag the stack of money. "Count it," she said. As he untied and counted the bills, Casey took photos of the gun, bills and the picture of the woman.

"Don't you trust me?" asked Fortune with a slow smile.

He was close enough that she could see how his black hair was turning white at the sideburns. "You can never be too careful." *You best be careful, girl.* But she couldn't resist sneaking a look at the ring finger of his left hand. Bare. He caught her glance and raised his eyebrows.

O'Malley interrupted her embarrassment with a comment from outside the storage closet. "She's the ex-con who flew down the hill taped to a wheelchair—"

"That'll do," interrupted Fortune with a grimace. "Police will keep possession of the contents of the safe. A year from today, if there's no evidence that the contents were involved in any criminal activity, they'll be considered abandoned property that will revert to you. We'll give you a formal receipt for the money and the gun." He continued counting the bills and placed them in a separate bag. "That's a tidy little $2,510." He studied the picture for a moment, turned it over, said, "No identification," and left it in the safe.

Fortune backed out of the closet, and Casey followed. "Will the gun be mine?" she asked.

"You'll need to be registered to claim it. In the meantime, we'll need to take fingerprints on the surfaces of the caboose. If I remember correctly, we won't need your prints." He tempered his remark with another smile that made her blush. "I'll be right back. I need to call Detective Granger—the real one in New Hampshire—and a fingerprint team." He left the caboose for the cruiser.

Casey and O'Malley waited for Fortune to make the call. O'Malley continued to badger her. He was like a dog with a bone. "I seem to remember there are a lot of dead bodies wherever you are, in Ohio and here, both."

Casey turned on him. "Have you noticed one other thing? I've never been responsible for any felonies or homicides."

"Smoke, there's fire, young lady, and I have you well within my sights. I happen to know that one of your close associates *was* convicted of murder— a nasty one at that, and you spent the better part of ten years bunking with her. My sources suggest you are still in close contact with Mrs. Washington."

Huh? It took Casey a minute to remember that LouAnne was now Rosie's wife, Mrs. Roosevelt Washington, although she continued to use LouAnne

Jones, her incarcerated name at work. Good thing Casey'd been distracted for a moment. No reason to poke the bear. There were altogether too many people interested in the happenings around the station and the caboose.

When Fortune returned, she invited both officers into the station for coffee while they awaited the arrival of State Trooper Granger. Casey retired to her desk and retrieved her sketch book. While the men talked and arranged for fingerprinting in the caboose, she drew a picture of the man who had claimed to be Detective Granger. An hour later, she examined her sketch and had to admit it was a good likeness. Maybe it would help.

When Granger arrived, Casey showed him the caboose and the safe. Fortune gave him the bagged gun to test against the bullet that had been lodged in the head of the dead man found in the woods.

They returned to the station where Granger wrote out a receipt describing the gun with the date and time, and his name and badge number. "The body of the man in the woods was identified as James Ferguson by his brother Alex Ferguson. He claims his brother was the vet who was living in the caboose, the man you call Hobo. The gun may be from his service in the Army. We can check it against Army ordinance records." While they spoke, the fingerprinting team arrived and carried their equipment into the caboose.

Casey handed Granger the sketch she'd been working on. "I drew a picture of the man who gave me your card. He didn't look anything like you."

Granger examined the picture. "You're really good," he commented. "I don't know this man," he said, handing the picture to Fortune.

"I'll make a copy and send it to New Hampshire," said Fortune as he walked Granger to his car. "We'll be in touch about the results of the fingerprint analysis."

Casey waved goodbye and then affixed the new card from the real officer Granger to her fridge. He'd arrived in a cop cruiser and flashed a genuine badge. He was quite handsome but not as personable as Fortune. *Good grief, girl. Anything in pants? Well, not O'Malley.* Chance's appearance must have re-awakened her dormant hormones. Damn him. Before she was working on being depressed. Now she was actively lonely.

Before Fortune left, Casey showed him the camera.

He reached up to remove it, but Casey stopped him. "The man who watches is Jeremy Fisher, Kennedy's lawyer in Rhode Island. He bosses me around, makes demands and looks out for me from a distance. The camera saves me long-distance phone calls."

"Okay," he said, but he didn't sound pleased. "Take care. Call if you have any unwanted visitors."

Casey saluted with a smile and watched him drive away. Inside, she cleared coffee cups from the table and noticed that Fortune had forgotten the picture she'd drawn of the phony Granger. Good. Now she had an excuse to see him again when she delivered it.

As she placed the dishes in the sink, she noticed the blinking red light of the answering machine. Probably the earlier call she'd blown off. Possibly Agnes. Could Agnes be fighting some dreaded disease? Possible, but experience would suggest not. Agnes whined about every stubbed toe and hangnail. No, she was off on vacation. Maybe LouAnne. She punched the Play button. To her dismay, it was Chance.

"I'm so sorry to have missed you. I had to rush home. My father has been threatening to die for a year now and is finally succeeding. Much as I despise the old man, I'm a good southern boy, and I must do my filial duty. I would dearly love to see you upon my return."

Wouldn't you know, she'd missed the one call she was waiting for. But wait. Didn't Chance say he'd been wrapped up in settling his father's estate? You didn't settle a man's estate before he died. He must have misspoken. He did have a lot to do just proving that he was Chauncey Cunningham. He must have been getting affairs in order prior to the expected death of his father.

Her mind returned to the conundrum of the day. Who had owned the goodies left in the safe? If Hobo, why would he live off the grid when he had a pile of money? The gun was worrisome. Especially since the dead person in the woods had met a violent end.

Was Hobo killed before he could run? Or did he kill someone and disappear? Either scenario could explain the backpack of clothing and boots that had been left in the caboose. The phony cop was definitely interested in the safe. Maybe he was chasing after the money. In that case, he'd probably return. Her thoughts ran in circles, and all ended up with the conclusion that she just didn't have a clue what had happened.

Officer O'Malley was right about death and destruction stalking her. Casey counted up the number of people she'd known who had died in her presence by violent means and stopped when she reached eight. Two fires rounded up her resume. She drove a car that barked. Okay, okay, but what was the point?

She was vulnerable.

Chapter Nineteen

I n the morning, Casey carried her second cup of coffee and her ring of keys to the caboose. Inside, she surveyed the mess of graphite fingerprint dust left on all the surfaces by the forensic team. She unlatched the storage closet and shined the flashlight on the safe.

She leaned forward for a better look. Damn! How could that be? She'd left the dial on 34 on purpose. It was now on 8. She hadn't heard anything during the night, but someone had been in here and moved the dial. Someone who knew how to pick the outside locks. She examined the dial. No fingerprint residue. Wiped clean—even the dirty prints she'd left when she set the dial after the police left were gone. She backed up. Same with the latch on the outside of the closet. A very careful intruder.

She reached for the dial to the combination lock and realized her hand was shaking. Quickly, she twirled the dial back and forth to the correct combination numbers and opened the heavy door. Only the picture of the young woman remained. Had the intruder opened the safe and seen that the money and gun were gone? If so, would he assume she'd taken them and come for her? She thought for a moment before returning to the station where she wrote a note. "You can claim your money at the Welton Police station. The New Hampshire State Police have your gun. After a year, if no claim is filed, both will belong to me." She signed the note and taped it on the outside of the safe and reset the dial to 34.

To keep from completely freaking out, she hooked up a series of extension cords between the station and the caboose and spent the rest of the morning vacuuming fingerprint dust. She used household cleaners to remove the smudge residue from harder surfaces. Would have been so much easier just to have accepted the money as manna from heaven. But no, someone had messed with the combination lock. If he knew the combination, why would he have left the money and gun? $2,510 was an odd amount of money to store in a safe. Maybe he had been using the safe like a bank, sneaking in during the night, thinking no one else had access to it. Well, now he'd be plenty upset! Good idea to leave a note.

Curious though, the caboose had been on the property for over a year. Why the recent interest? Could be that she just hadn't seen anyone before. After the initial curiosity from townsfolk, there had been very little attention paid to the railcar.

She was tired and hungry, but the only prospects in the fridge—a half-brown apple, an onion, and a butternut squash—weren't appealing. Time to go grocery shopping. Too bad she couldn't afford the little restaurant next to the store. She made a list and was about to leave when the phone rang. Hopefully, Agnes was returning one of her many messages.

"Don't hang up."

No such luck. It was Fisher. "You weren't kidding when you said you were a work in progress. The account numbers you gave me are for your *personal* account. That's not how things work. Miss Dempsey is the Kennedy's landlord. Rent and remuneration for utilities and services will be handled directly with her and her only. We have no formal arrangement or agreement with you. You need to work out financial matters with her." Click.

Double damn! For over a year, Casey had prepared checks for payment which Agnes reviewed and signed. No problem when the woman was available, but Agnes had taken a hike and hadn't bothered to answer Casey's increasingly desperate phone messages.

Casey dialed the only number she had for Agnes and instructed the answering service to deliver a message. "Unless you come home and sign checks, the rental will fall through. I'm out of money and cannot cover the bills from my personal account, and Kennedy's lawyer won't deposit money in my account. The new gate code is 1974. I have new door keys for you. Casey." That ought to get her attention.

Before she left, she folded the picture she'd drawn of the phony cop and tucked it into her purse. On the way home from shopping, she'd drop it off at the police station for Fortune. She grabbed her keys and drove to town. No more steak dinners with friends—just tuna and macaroni and cheese, plus pet food and a few replacement cleaning supplies. At the grocery checkout, she realized she was perilously close to broke. She juggled the heavy grocery bag through the automatic door and walked past the restaurant toward the Muttmobile.

"Hello, Casey."

Startled, Casey almost dropped the bag. Blair and Fortune and another blonde woman stood at the door of the restaurant. Casey took in the three of them, momentarily speechless. She recognized Blair and Fortune. While Blair was flashy and curvaceous, the other woman looked like a model for *Vogue,* tall and elegant and rather austere in muted colors.

"Anita, this is the girl I was talking about who lives in the little train station. Casey, meet Anita Fortune," said Blair. She watched Casey's reaction with interest.

Casey glanced at Fortune with raised eyebrows. "Sister?" she asked.

Fortune shook his head. "Ex."

Blair continued. "Casey's managing the White House rental properties. You remember the Waddingtons' place. You know, where Worthy lived before his parents split."

"Oh yes, I remember Worthy for sure." Anita's voice was sultry and suggestive. "If I recall, he and his mother moved to California. There was quite a scandal at the time."

"Yes, a rather sordid affair between Worthy's father and his secretary," said Blair.

Casey clenched her jaw to maintain composure. The secretary was Casey's Aunt Mary.

"Last year the town defeated that woman's scheme to gut the main house and convert—"

"Davey says you live in France?" Casey interrupted Blair and addressed Anita with a polite but forced smile.

"I'm just over from Provence," said Anita, pronouncing the last word in perfect nasal French. She cocked her head to the side and studied Casey's clothing, head to toe. "You've met my son, David?"

"Positively lovely boy." Casey turned to Fortune. "I have something for you. I was going to bring it to the station, but since you're here..." She handed the bag of groceries to a surprised Blair and took her drawing of the fake Granger out of her purse and gave it to Fortune. "He sure didn't look like the real Theodore Granger we met yesterday."

Fortune accepted the picture with a smile. "I realized too late that I'd left it. I'm impressed with your drawing."

"Thanks. You'll send a copy to New Hampshire?" Casey ignored Blair's attempt to give back the groceries by edging closer to Fortune.

Fortune grinned, seeming to enjoy the interaction. "No problem. Any more prowlers around the caboose?"

"Someone got in overnight and turned the dial on the safe, but as you know, it's empty except for the photo."

Fortune's expression darkened to a frown. "I thought you installed new locks."

"It's not hard to pick a lock." Casey turned her head and wrinkled her nose at Blair and then returned her attention to Fortune. "I set the dial on the safe to 34 after you left. It was on 8 this morning. I left a note saying where the intruder could claim the contents."

With mischief in her eyes, she took the groceries and thanked Blair. "*Au revoir, madame,*" she said to Anita as she walked with her head held high, well, relatively high, toward the Muttmobile.

Back at the station, she fixed herself a sandwich before reluctantly pressing Play on the answering machine.

"Leave checks for me to sign on my desk. Yours should be $833.33. Write separate checks for other bills I need to pay. Create an invoice for the

Kennedys' portion of utilities and expenses. Attach all appropriate receipts. I'll need a separate accounting for any expenses you've incurred that need to be reimbursed. Leave the new key in the pot of ivy next to the front door." Click.

Not "Hello. How are you? How have you been? Have the arrangements for the new tenants gone smoothly? Is there anything I can help you with? Thank you."

Still, she sure could use the money.

Her thoughts returned to Fortune and his bevy of blondes at the restaurant. She was a little surprised that a local cop would keep such high society company. But what did she know? The two women appeared to be friends, but how long would that last with the prize hunk in between? She'd sensed competition for Fortune's attention. All yours, ladies. Great eye candy, but in a league she didn't aspire to or appreciate. Blair was easy to read, and if Casey's impression of Anita was correct, she was both aloof and mercurial, tightly wound and used to control. Poor Davey.

For the next hour, she prepared the paperwork and checks for Agnes to sign. Agnes hadn't bothered to tell her when she planned to return, but there was nothing more Casey could do. She arranged the bills and checks in a folder, and then she and Isabella hiked up the hill to the carriage house where she left the folder on Agnes' desk. As she was leaving, she poked Agnes' new door key as far down as she could into the pot of ivy. A little spiteful, but Agnes wasn't exactly being helpful.

Chapter Twenty

Fortune

Fortune suppressed a smile as he watched Casey walk toward the Muttmobile.

"Is *that* her car?" Anita asked Fortune.

"Yes, she says it runs like a top. Can't beat it for a hundred bucks." Fortune ushered the ladies into the restaurant.

"Now you're befriending the local pariah?" asked Blair.

"Protect and serve. She hasn't had an easy time of it." Fortune didn't bother to keep an edge out of his voice. Blair could be such a snob. Well, so could Anita. They'd grown up best friends. He'd dated both off and on until they went off to Wellesley, and then he'd linked up with Anita after college. Big mistake.

"She should go back to Ohio," Blair continued.

Fortune was about to ask how Blair knew Casey was from Ohio when he reminded himself that the woman was the repository of all information regarding Welton residents. The women interrupted their badmouthing while the hostess led them to a booth. Anita sat on one side, Blair the other. Fortune refused to make a choice and remained standing.

Anita picked up the thread when they were seated. "How does David happen to know that woman?" She smiled but her words weren't kind.

"He wanted to see the caboose that's on the track behind the station. Casey owns it," responded Fortune.

Blair turned to Anita. "Mary Waddington née *Dempsey* bought it for her. Remember, she claimed Casey was the illegitimate son of Mary's brother, the priest."

To cut the recital short, Fortune jumped in. "Davey's been after me to stop at the station for months. Perhaps I should refresh your memory, Anita. He loves everything to do with trains." Fortune's sarcasm wasn't lost on either woman.

"Sounds like you have other interests in the caboose and its owner," prompted Blair. "Very exciting. A safe, money, a gun, a cute little ex-con— very intriguing. Want to clue us in?"

"No. There should be enough other local dirt to keep you two busy for a while. Sorry, I can't stay. I've got to go to work."

"Sit a minute, Mike." Anita's voice lowered to invitation. She stroked the leather seat next to her.

Personal now, so she had a request. Fortune slid into the booth reluctantly, wondering what Anita had in store for him, and instantly regretted his decision as she lit a cigarette. The warmth of her and the mixture of her perfume and tobacco blindsided him. He struggled for composure. Something must be off with her lover, or she wouldn't be running home to Mommy. Or Daddy more likely if she needed money. She was a high-maintenance woman.

"We need to talk about David's schooling."

She knew his Achilles' heel was the boy, and he was quick to respond. "The schools in Welton are rated the highest in the state. He's doing well, making friends, and he likes his teacher."

"My parents and I think he would benefit from the valuable social contacts and opportunities offered by a private school."

"Where? In France?"

"Maybe. Although I may decide to relocate to be closer to David during his formative years."

"Huh. Missed a couple already. Why now? How about Phillipe? Your French lover willing to 'relocate' with you?" Fortune was aware that Blair had leaned in and was listening attentively to every word.

Anita lowered her head and gave a small shake, and then slowly raised her eyes to his. "We were good once, Mike," she whispered. When they locked eyes, he felt the old chemistry sucking him in. Oh God, she'd been better than good. Leave it, man. He broke eye contact to escape her magnetic field and eased out of the booth.

"Will I see you later?" Anita asked.

"Mom serves dinner at six."

"No, just us." She placed a possessive hand on his arm.

She wasn't giving up. Sure. A romantic dinner with candles and wine, where she could wear down his defenses. He wasn't sure he'd be strong enough to resist. "You've been here a week and only seen Davey twice. Mother's an important player in our little drama, and she's doing an excellent job of raising your son. You need to show up and give her the time of day. If you come, you'll have to smoke outside."

"Have it your way." Anita withdrew her hand and sat back, her expression turning cool and controlled.

He gave her an obligatory peck on the cheek. As he passed by Blair, she whispered loud enough for Anita to hear, "We still on for Saturday?" He winked in response, and she gave him a thumbs up. Hey, second fiddle still played a valuable part, and Blair was quite practiced.

He was sure their exchange didn't go unnoticed by Anita.

Fortune knew he was stirring the pot and didn't care. It was like tying two cats' tails together and throwing them over a clothesline.

The farther he moved away from the two women, the more his brain took over. Anita had always been the best, the queen, the prize: every man's dream lover. And the mother of his boy. Maybe two years of Phillipe was enough. She'd left Fortune when Davey was five, and it had torn the boy apart. Inconsolable. Even though she didn't take to mothering like some women, she was still his mom.

She'd nearly broken Fortune when she admitted to an affair with the rich Frenchman she'd met at some gala fundraising event that her parents supported. Now she was back and playing with fire with him. Did she really think they could still make it together, or was this a ploy to get Davey into a private school? He didn't doubt that her parents wanted to give their grandson all the advantages of an elite upbringing, something Fortune couldn't afford to do. He wondered if Anita and Phillipe were having a rough patch. He didn't have the full story yet.

What he did know and was committed to was giving Davey a stable home with his father and grandmother, not some damn private school.

When he reached his car, he realized he still had Casey's portrait in his hand. What a contrast she was to the two he'd just left! Had to hand it to her, she was feisty. Didn't back an inch, confronted by the blonde duo. Frankly, he'd been embarrassed by their snobbishness. He loved it when Casey handed Blair her groceries. She was a little powerhouse. But a vulnerable one.

Life certainly hadn't been kind to her. She'd lost so many years. Didn't help in town that her best friends were black and that the woman—according to Blair gossip—was Casey's cellmate who'd done hard time for stabbing her husband to death. There had also been years of gossip about her aunt, the "shanty Irish interloper Mary Waddington," and her plan to establish a non-profit that would have invited undesirable elements into Welton's pristine white suburb. Although Fortune admired the altruism, the dream was a non-starter with the conservative elements in the community.

He'd send a copy of Casey's picture to Granger and ask him for more details about the body found in the woods, and anything he knew about the squatter who had stayed in the caboose when it was in New Hampshire. They might confirm his identity from the fingerprints. He was glad Casey let the police hold the money and gun, but in truth, she probably didn't realize she could have refused. Safer for the police to have custody.

He'd also see what he could find out about the Kennedys. Why would they need to keep tabs on Casey with a hidden camera? According to Blair, the rental agreement was rather sketchy with all arrangements signed by some lawyer from Rhode Island.

Fortune was surprised at how protective he felt. Protect and serve, but still. On another note, she didn't have the best sense for men. He'd done a little extracurricular checking on the license plate on the Jag driven by

Chauncey Cunningham. The car was registered in North Carolina to an older gentleman, evidently the father, Cunningham Senior. Fortune knew that the younger man had been a person of interest in the investigation of a boating accident in Maine in which two people had died. He'd also been impersonating Mary Waddington's stepson in an attempt to claim the dead man's inheritance. Deceitful at best, and very close to a series of events that left four people dead and one imprisoned. He'd charmed Mary. She refused to press charges. The man wasn't good company for Casey.

Nothing he could do but offer advice, and he was pretty sure she wouldn't appreciate his interference. Who was he to counsel with his own failed marriage? And admit it, one who, just five minutes ago, was sorely tempted to repeat his earlier mistake.

Chapter Twenty-One

Agnes

Agnes pretended to struggle lifting her travel bag.

"Let me help." The man behind her took the bag and hefted it easily into the overhead compartment.

"Ah, a gentleman. A rarity these days. Thank you." And evidently a scholar wearing a Princeton University class ring. He settled into the first class aisle seat next to her. The moment they were seated, the stewardess appeared dressed in a pair of red hotpants. Agnes was reminded of the ad for the airline, "Hi. I'm Cheryl. Fly me." So much sex everywhere. She ordered a glass of white wine, and he ordered a double scotch. His eyes followed every step of the stewardess as she retreated to get their drinks.

Agnes hadn't wanted to make a sudden return trip to Welton, but there was no way around it if she wanted to maintain control. Evidently, that sneaky little ex-con had set up a separate personal bank account and had the nerve to ask Kennedy's lawyer for money. It wasn't going to work that way! That strange-sounding man had left Agnes a message that he wouldn't deal with anyone but her for financial matters. Good for him.

She'd planned her trip and left explicit instructions for Casey on her answering machine. She hoped Casey remembered to leave a house key in the ivy and had prepared the checks for her signature as instructed. She hadn't advised Casey of her travel plans. She had no desire to see the girl.

She was aware that her seatmate had checked her out when he helped her stow her travel bag. After the stewardess returned with their drinks, he turned to Agnes and surveyed her face. "Ouch," he said, with an empathetic frown and a grimace.

"Nasty fall. This helps." She raised her glass with a smile. She had two black eyes, and her nose was covered in bandages. The man couldn't help but notice the emerald sparklers wrapped around the stem of her glass.

"Good plan," he agreed, sipping his drink.

Agnes hadn't expected to enjoy her "vacation" anywhere near as much as she had—so much so in fact, that she'd signed on for a second round. After the first few days of awkwardness, she'd relaxed a bit and enjoyed the company of other rich ladies at the spa. She'd even tried a cigarette because one of the women she admired looked sophisticated and dramatic smoking with a long filter. So far, Agnes hadn't gotten the knack of it without a coughing fit. Early days. She liked the red lipstick on the filters.

She had to admit, she was developing a taste for wine, although she much preferred white because it wouldn't stain her new teeth. The front caps had cost a bundle, but now she could flash a smile with the best of them. At first it had felt unnatural—she wasn't used to smiling—but after practicing in the mirror, she gained confidence. It felt good.

Damn! Mary's little purse slid from her lap to the floor. She stopped her hand before automatically crossing herself for the blasphemy. Pain in the ass having to be so careful, she giggled, feeling the wine. Recently, she'd been lax going to Mass, but she had an excuse. She was short on cash, and going would require a hefty taxi fare, money she'd rather spend on her newfound habits.

When her seatmate reached down and retrieved the little bag, he handed it to her and introduced himself. "Bob Brooks."

"Casey Waddington," she answered without hesitation. She'd discovered it was fun to try out different names and personalities when the other person had no way to know who she really was. Today, she could be whoever she wanted to be, free of the burden of her past. At least until she landed.

"Business? Pleasure?"

"Business." She was relieved when the stewardess interrupted with a second glass of wine and her dinner. She turned aside to focus on her meal. She'd learned a lot already from the ladies that frequented the spa. Never appear too eager or interested. Make them work for information and smiles and offer only an occasional encouraging glance or nod. After the tray was cleared, she retrieved a book from her carry-on tote and pretended to read. Bob busied himself with papers from his briefcase.

She planned to make a quick turnaround at the carriage house. Although she was pleased to have Casey manage the property and accounts, she liked the idea of a surprise visit. In and out. Keep Casey guessing and on her toes. Agnes was determined to keep control over the purse. She enjoyed hands free ownership, but she couldn't be too careful, operating from a remote location.

Even though she appreciated the charm of the carriage house, Agnes had decided that she didn't want to live in Welton. There was too much baggage associated with the White House. Mary had certainly done them no favors in the community with her harebrained foundation scheme. No matter. It had been soundly rejected. But as Mary's sister, Agnes wouldn't be welcomed into the community.

At the spa, it was just the opposite. The ladies were charmed by her lapses into an Irish lilt when she'd had a few glasses. They were friendly and included her in their plans. She felt, for the first time in years, that she was making friends.

She'd see how the rental arrangement went, but she had other options. She didn't have to stay in Welton. She could split the property three ways and sell off the White House, A-frame, and carriage houses separately. There was enough land to give each parcel at least two acres to qualify for the Welton zoning laws. There were many more acres around the White House, but she'd never paid attention and would have to ask Casey how many total acres there were. No. Bad idea. Don't let Casey in on her plans. That real estate lady from town, Blair Somebody, would be all too willing to help her.

When they announced the final approach into Boston, Bob stowed his briefcase. "What kind of business are you in?" he asked, as if their earlier conversation hadn't been interrupted.

"Real estate."

He wrote his number on a business card. "I'm always interested in real estate," he said, handing it to her with a wink. "Feel free to call for a coffee or a drink if you're in town again."

By God, he was flirting. Agnes actually blushed, something she hadn't done since she was a teenager, and accepted his card. They exited the aircraft and said their goodbyes when he turned off to Baggage Claim. She headed directly for the taxi stand.

She gave the driver directions to President's Lane in Welton. Much to her relief, the gate opened when she input 1974 into the security box. At the carriage house, she asked the cabbie to wait for fifteen minutes while she gathered a few things.

"Meter's running," he said, waiting for her reaction.

"No problem." How empowering it was to have money!

At the door, she had to dig into the pot of ivy with her newly manicured nails to find the key. Why did Casey have to bury it so deep in the dirt? Inside, she washed and cleaned her hands and checked her plants before sitting at her desk and quickly reviewing and signing the checks Casey had left for her. Agnes had to admit, Casey did a thorough job. Receipts and bills were attached where appropriate.

After she'd attended to business, she rushed upstairs and selected a few dresses and blouses, plus two pairs of shoes from Mary's closet, and silk scarves from a drawer. Much as she had resented her sister, she was enjoying Mary's elegant taste now. Downstairs, she selected a suede jacket from the hall closet. She packed her new wardrobe into a small case. That should do it. She'd call Casey while waiting for her return flight. Expensive trip, but it was worth it for the control and the clothing.

She locked the door, pocketed the key, and returned to the taxi.

"Logan airport."

Chapter Twenty-Two

Casey

Saturday, 10/29

Showtime! Casey woke early, excited about the arrival of the new tenants. After breakfast, she drove into town and purchased an orchid for the White House foyer, a bouquet of yellow and orange mums for the kitchen, a fresh pastry assortment, and orange juice. She couldn't think of anything else. She'd given Fisher the code to enter the gate to President's Lane and left the front door of the White House unlocked. She placed a set of house keys on the table in the foyer. She'd deliver extra house keys in person and introduce herself after they'd had a little time to settle in.

She made a last tour of the house to check preparations following the whirlwind clean-up with LouAnne and Rosie. She'd ask Mrs. Kennedy if she'd want to employ the cleaning service, although there were servants. One thing at a time. Relax. Oh, one more thing. She ducked down the stairs to the cellar and snagged two bottles of cabernet.

As she drove back down President's Lane, she was surprised to see the taillights of a car pulling out of the carriage house driveway. A yellow light on the roof of the car identified it as a taxi. Could it be Agnes? No other reason for a taxi at the carriage house. Casey's message sure got her attention! Casey pulled into the drive and walked to the door. Yup. Agnes had dug in the ivy for the keys.

She found the correct key on her key ring and entered. Inside, she caught a whiff of Mary's favorite perfume, Chanel No. 5, and was immediately overcome by an acute wave of déjà vu, as if Mary were right in the room with her. But she knew better, and the pleasurable sensation turned to irritation. Agnes didn't spray it on in remembrance of Mary. Chalk up another treasured part of Mary's memory that Agnes was besmirching. Nothing she could do about it. Well, actually, there was. She mounted the stairs and entered Mary's room. She located the bottle of perfume on her dresser and pocketed it.

Downstairs, she found the signed checks and a scribbled note which looked a bit looser than Agnes' normal tight writing next to two piles labeled "Mail" and "File" and a separate check made out to Casey. "We'll invoice Mr. Fisher for expenses when I return."

Who is "we," thought Casey, knowing she would be keeping the books. And when will you return? Her rather sarcastic thoughts were interrupted by movement outside a side window. She rushed out the front door as an unmarked van, followed by two large, black Mercedes sedans, pulled up to the gate. Kennedy's servant rolled down the window in the van and punched a number into the keypad. A large woman sat next to him in the front. The gate swung open, and the entourage drove by.

Casey waved but got no reaction from drivers or passengers. The windows were tinted for privacy, so Casey couldn't tell who was driving or riding in the cars behind the van. She knew the Kennedys were renting the White House furnished, but still, she expected them to arrive with a moving van. None of her business, but she was curious.

She returned to the station a bit untethered. Until she received another request or demand from the Kennedys, Fisher, or Agnes, she was free of responsibilities. But after the frenetic activity of the past week, she was still full of nervous energy. Time to make her own plans. She walked over to the caboose and examined the exterior. She needed to finish scraping and prepping the back side of the car, and then paint it fire engine red.

Inside, she'd install a mini-fridge and purchase a propane tank for the two-burner stove. Mentally, she added pellets for the large potbellied stove to her growing list. She liked the idea of drawing and painting in the caboose as a change of scenery from the station. She'd bring over an afghan and a few blankets to ward off the evening chill.

Most all of the furnishings for the caboose were dump picks. The Welton "transfer station" had proved to be a treasure trove of eclectic items: an old picture frame, a caned chair, a mirror, all manner of kitchen gadgets and wares, and books galore.

She returned to the station and made a few calls to arrange for workmen to come and hook up the caboose's electric and water systems. Her new salary sure was coming in handy. This afternoon she'd cash her first salary check, buy some pepper spray and a little tape recorder to capture Fisher's demands, and maybe get some pellets. On her way home, she could stop by the dump and see what treasures had been left today. Maybe celebrate in the evening with a pork chop and a glass of purloined wine. She was free.

Chapter Twenty-Three

Casey waited until Saturday afternoon before hiking up the stone stairs to the White House to meet the new residents. The same huge fellow she'd met when she and Agnes first interviewed Mr. Kennedy answered the door.

"Hello. I'm Casey Cavendish from the station," she said, but she knew that the man she'd mentally nick-named Chuckles recognized her.

"No visitors." The man blocked the door.

"I've come to meet the new tenants and also to bring copies of extra keys Mr. Kennedy requested."

He held out his hand for the keys.

"I'd like to deliver them in person." Casey wasn't going to be put off by this aging and rude Mr. Clean.

He didn't move or retract his hand. Behind him in the hallway, Casey spotted a tall blonde woman in a caftan. An adorable little boy peeked out at her from behind the blonde.

"Who is it, Vlad?"

"No one." He extended his hand in demand.

Casey turned and left. If they wanted extra keys, they could send Chuckles to get them.

At the station, with no more excuses and time on her hands, Casey set about chipping away more peeling paint on the outside clapboards of the caboose. It was a mindless task, but required concentration. After a few hours, she was happy to be distracted when the little boy she'd seen at the White House appeared beside the ladder.

"Hi. I'm seven." He held up seven fingers.

"Hi, Seven. I'm Casey."

The boy cocked his head to the side and frowned. "No. I'm Petey." Isabella joined them, wagging, but safely just out of reach.

Casey shook her head. "I thought you said you were Seven. Are you Seven?"

Another frown. "Yes."

"Seven, meet my dog, Isabella. Isabella, this is Seven."

The boy stamped his foot, and Isabella shied away. "Petey. I'm Petey."

Figuring she'd tortured him long enough, Casey asked, "Petey, does your mama know where you are?"

Petey looked down and shook his head.

"How'd you get here?"

"Climbed the fence."

The secure perimeter. Breached by a seven-year-old.

Their conversation was interrupted by a high-pitched, frantic call. "Petey? Petey?!"

Casey followed the woman's voice to the top of the stone stairs leading to the White House. "Down here," Casey responded. "That your mother?" she asked Petey.

"No. Olga." Petey made a naughty face as if he tasted something bad.

"We'd better go see her. She sounds worried. C'mon, Bella." Casey led a parade of dog and boy up the steps to the gate where a large, red-faced woman stood, arms akimbo. "Hello. Petey came down to meet my little dog. I'm Casey." She smiled and extended her hand over the gate.

The woman backed away and uttered a command Casey didn't understand. The boy scrambled over the fence and dashed toward the big house. Without another word, the woman turned and stomped after him.

Casey looked at her extended hand as if it were coated in dog doo and shrugged. Poor kid. That had to be Olga, Chuckles' wife. Casey had hoped that the family would be friendly, even if Kennedy was a dud. She missed her Aunt Mary so much, and now her cousin Jackson had moved, and LouAnne and Rosie were busy with their own lives. Heck, she almost missed Agnes.

Time for a different kind of painting. She returned to the station and took out her watercolors and paper and decided to try to capture the image of Little Mother curled on a cushion on the antique rocking chair. She was surprised when it grew dark. Amazing how she lost track of time with a paintbrush in her hand.

When the phone rang, Casey grabbed the little tape recorder she'd purchased earlier and pushed Record before she picked up the receiver.

"Mrs. Kennedy says to thank you for the flowers. She has a few matters to discuss with you. Expect her call." Click.

Casey pushed Stop and then Rewind and Play. Fisher's strangled voice was just as insufferable the second time.

Chapter Twenty-Four

Sunday, 10/30

Electricians showed up bright and early in the morning to connect the wiring between the station and the caboose. After they left, Casey put down paint tarps and set about staining the inside walls of the caboose, leaving the front and rear doors ajar for ventilation. Isabella trotted in for a drink out of her water bowl next to the rear door. Moments later, Casey was surprised when Petey followed her into the caboose. He was quiet but curious.

Casey ignored him at first. She worked up high on a stool, humming softly to herself. When she looked down, he'd taken up a small brush and was applying stain to lower boards. They worked in companionable silence for a while. She climbed down and examined his work. "Maybe a bit more here? What do you think?" He nodded and filled in a small gap he'd missed.

"I'm thirsty. I'll be right back." She walked to the station and returned a few minutes later with two glasses of lemonade. She crossed the drive and sat with her back against a tree. She gestured to the boy to join her and handed him a glass. "Thanks for your help."

Isabella trotted over. "Say hi to Isabella. I call her Bella." Casey raised her hand, palm upward. "Sit." Bella sank to her haunches. "Shake," ordered Casey. Bella offered a paw. They shook. Casey reached into her pocket and gave her a dog treat. "Good girl." She handed Petey a treat.

Petey hesitated. Bella, no fool, had followed the treat transfer and shifted her undivided attention to the boy. He glanced up at Casey. Casey just looked at the little dog and waited. Seconds passed, and Bella inched closer to Petey. "Sit," he said, raising his hand. Bella sat. "Shake." Bella gave an instant paw, and they shook. He gave her the treat. "Good girl!"

Quick study. He must be in first grade if he's seven. "Do you like school?" she asked.

Petey bit his lip and shook his head.

"You don't like school," prompted Casey.

"Don't go to school," he said.

"I thought all kids went to school," said Casey.

"Aunt Loretta teaches me."

"She's the pretty lady I saw yesterday?" asked Casey.

Petey nodded.

"How about your father? Does he teach you, too?" asked Casey.

Petey chewed on his lip and looked away.

"Mr. Kennedy?" prompted Casey.

"Uncle William."

Oh. Not his father. Casey figured she'd quizzed him enough for the moment. "Bella, where's your ball?" Bella had curled into a little ball next to Casey. She jumped up, instantly alert. "Ball," repeated Casey. Bella dashed to the side of the station and returned seconds later with a mouth full of tennis ball.

"Give it."

Bella wagged.

"Bella. Give it."

Bella dropped the ball just out of reach. Casey leaned forward, snatched it, and tossed it down the drive. Bella scrambled and reached it on the second bounce. "Bring it." Bella trotted back to her. "Give it." Casey threw it in the opposite direction.

"Have fun. I'm going to finish up inside." Casey handed the ball to Petey. She carried the glasses to the station and returned to the caboose. As she picked up the brush and climbed onto the stool, she heard a small boy's voice, "Bring it." What a neat little kid.

Boy and dog played outside while Casey finished staining the wall. Enough for one day. She cleaned up the brushes and was leaving the caboose when she heard a bell ringing. Sounded like a cowbell. Petey tossed the ball one last time. "Gotta go!" He waved and ran toward the steps to the White House.

Casey entered the station and fixed herself a sandwich. No fun cooking anything just for one. She poured some iced tea and took it and the sandwich out the back door to the loading platform where passengers had once waited to get on the train. She'd found a couple of old lawn chairs and made herself a low table with bricks and a piece of plywood she found at the dump. Just as she was settling in, the phone rang. She let it go to the answering machine and was surprised to hear a woman's voice. Agnes? She dashed inside and listened.

"Miss Cavendish, this is Mrs. Kennedy. Mr. Fisher suggested that I contact you for help locating a number of services. Please join me tomorrow morning at ten for coffee. Bring the little dog." Click.

Not a request, but not as demanding or rude as Fisher. What more could the Kennedys need? She hoped that requests wouldn't become a regular thing, but she was also curious to meet the woman of the house, presumably the beautiful lady she'd seen behind Chuckles yesterday.

Chapter Twenty-Five

Monday, 10/31

Casey awoke early and decided to go for a run. Although she'd worked hard fixing up the White House and A-frame and now the caboose, she wanted more aerobic exercise. She donned sneakers, shorts, and a t-shirt and warmed up by walking briskly up Station Road to Church Street. From there, she jogged toward town on the narrow road, enjoying the fresh air and morning light and what she could see of the beautiful, but very private, homes she passed on the way. The color of the leaves had peaked, but there were still a few breathtaking displays of orange and gold. One of the things she treasured most after her time Inside was the freedom to walk or run or ride anywhere she pleased whenever she wanted. The joy of—

Honk!

Casey jumped off to the side as a Porsche flew past her so close that she felt the air in its wake. Maybe not her brightest idea. She continued on, but the mood was shattered. Fleeting thoughts of freedom yielded to her more normal attitude of wariness and reminders of all the things she was trying not to worry about. Was she safe? How much free time would she have? What did Mrs. K want? With no experience in property management, Casey had no idea what to expect, no job definition. What the heck was Agnes up to? Was there any reason to hope she wouldn't return?

With her mind spinning in circles, she turned around and ran back to the station. After a shower and coffee, she worried about what to wear. She sure could use some new clothes. Time for another visit to the Salvation Army store? Quit fussing!

She ironed a shirt, donned a pair of slacks, and threw a few treats and a ball into a tote bag. She and Isabella hiked up the stone stairs through the gate to the White House, where she found a note tacked to the front door: "Sorry, I forgot to tell you to join me at the pool."

Casey examined the writing. She enjoyed creating a mental personality profile, imagining what the person would be like based on their handwritten strokes. She rubbed the note between her fingers to feel the indentations in the paper and gauge the pressure of the strokes. Mrs. Kennedy's script was vertical with moderate pressure and regular rhythm. So, she'd be outwardly friendly but controlled.

Other traits indicated that she'd be energetic, probably stylish, definitely concerned about appearances, and appreciative of the finer things. Loops of imagination and flourishes would suggest an artistic flair, although her lower loops were inflated. Her graphologist mentor in Ohio had called such enlarged lower loops "money bags." Well, she'd need a pile of money to live at the White House.

Over-the-top arcade strokes reinforced the need for control and privacy. Her left margin was indented starting close to the center of the page, suggesting an avoidance of issues in the past. Of more concern were the incursions into a few communication letters—a's and o's—and retracings of strokes which could signify manipulation. These last traits were among a group that could cause concern for honesty, although they were also common traits in many writings.

Casey thought for a moment and brought up a mental picture of William Kennedy's domineering writing, with its heavy pressure and sharp angles. He wouldn't be an easy person to be married to, but maybe his riches attracted her. He was handsome in a dark, brooding kind of way and was wealthy enough to rent a whole compound. For that's what the property was with its acres of gated privacy, mansion, and party house.

By the time she reached the A-frame, she'd married the writings and was ready to test her mental image of Mrs. K with the genuine article. Voices and splashing sounds came from the pool behind the building.

"Yoo-hoo," Casey called as she skirted the house and opened the gate leading to the pool.

"Come on in!"

Casey and Isabella entered and found Mrs. Kennedy in a colorful cover-up draped on a lounge chair by the pool. Petey waved and swam to the side of the pool and called Bella.

Mrs. Kennedy patted the lounge chair next to her. "Good to meet you. I'm Loretta, and you already know Petey." She waited until Casey was seated before signaling to a woman sitting in a chair beside the door to the house and raising her hand to her lips. Casey recognized Olga, the grouchy woman who had called Petey home and ignored her greeting yesterday.

"Thank you so much for being so flexible with our arrival!"

"I hope you've found the place to your liking."

"I don't know if the real estate agent told you, but we were staying in a downtown hotel these last few weeks. We had a fire in our home in Rhode Island. Needless to say, it wasn't an ideal situation for us."

"Let me know if you want us to move any furniture or household goods to storage to make way for things you might prefer."

Olga brought Casey a mug of coffee on a tray with cream and sugar and a plate of scones. She didn't speak, and Loretta didn't introduce her. Loretta continued the conversation as if there hadn't been an interruption. "That won't be necessary. Our house burned to the ground, which is why a fully furnished house is perfect for us. I expect that William and the servants will spend most of their time at the main house."

Casey poured herself a cup of coffee and helped herself to a scone.

"Petey and I enjoy this smaller house, and he loves the pool. We had to leave Petey's nanny behind and had hoped to have hired a new one by now, but so far none of the women we've interviewed have pleased my husband." Loretta studied Casey as she spoke, her eyes resting briefly on the scar on Casey's arm. "Olga can't keep up with him. He can be rather high-spirited and adventurous."

Casey watched Petey who was shaking Bella's paw. He'd seemed adventurous and curious, but otherwise polite and helpful.

Loretta followed Casey's eyes. "We can't have animals. William is allergic."

"Maybe I shouldn't have brought her," said Casey.

"No. No. William will probably only come here for parties. It's fine."

Interesting how she referred to her husband as William. Not Bill or Will, but the more formal and respectful given name. Casey glanced at the wedding band on Loretta's left hand. "Petey called you Aunt Loretta," Casey ventured, hoping to learn more about the family.

"Yes. Petey is my sister's boy. She and her husband died in a horrible automobile accident three years ago. William and I have assumed legal guardianship. I have to say, we hadn't planned to have children, but I'm Petey's only remaining living relative."

Casey chose her next words carefully. "I met your husband briefly with Miss Dempsey prior to the rental. He seemed to be a person who knew what he wanted."

"I'm making William sound awful—no pets, no children—but he can be kind and considerate. He calls Petey his Little Goose because he comes with a trust fund."

Little Goose? Okay, for golden goose. "Kind and considerate" sure didn't show up in his writing. "Really tough for a young boy to lose his parents, but lucky you're there for him."

"I called you because I need someone to help me on weekends. In Rhode Island, we often had guests for the afternoon and sometimes in the evening. Socializing with contacts is an essential requirement in William's business. This house is perfectly suited for entertaining and informal gatherings."

"If you don't mind me asking, what does your husband do?"

"He's involved in land management, procuring properties, and arranging development opportunities for interested parties." She frowned and changed the subject. "As you know from Fisher, we place an absolute premium on privacy. We vet our company carefully. Ideally, the person we're looking for would help me serve guests and keep an eye on Petey. We'll pay top dollar for this service. Fisher recommended I speak to you."

No first name for Fisher, making him sound like more of a lackey than a friend. "May I assume you vetted me and Agnes Dempsey as well?" Might as well be direct.

"Of course." Loretta sat back in the lounger and watched Casey's reaction.

That's why she hadn't been surprised at the scar. She knew I'd been in prison and may even have heard about the knife fight. Casey met Loretta's eyes. "Why do you need a camera over there?" She nodded toward the table by the door to the A-frame, where she remembered seeing it.

Casey saw a momentary flicker of surprise in Loretta's eyes before she spoke. "You're very observant."

Casey didn't respond to her evasion.

"You can't be too careful these days. The fire was declared arson. We're in a state of heightened alert."

Casey wondered if Agnes knew anything about the fire. "Have you spoken with the Welton Police or Fire Department about your safety concerns?"

"No. We have no interest in attracting special attention in town."

Loretta's response was firm and definitive. Casey didn't feel she could push the topic any further. "Do you want me to help find someone for you, or are you asking me if I'm interested?"

Loretta smiled and relaxed. "I'm asking you."

"I have no experience with children or serving."

"Petey likes you and adores your dog. If you smile, your service will be a one hundred percent improvement upon Olga." Loretta made the same naughty smile Casey had seen on Petey's face. "Olga and her husband, Vlad, will prefer to stay in the White House. Olga doesn't approve of our parties."

Casey sat back, dumbfounded by the unexpected flood of information and the request.

"Mr. Fisher specifically recommended that I approach you," Loretta repeated.

Not wishing to be rude, Casey decided a few more questions were in order. "What's involved in serving?"

"Drinks and snacks, fetching towels, changing the music. Maybe a little grilling. Petey reads and swims and likes any kind of game. Olga will take him back up to the White House around eight o'clock."

Casey had to admit, she had nothing better to do on the weekend. Loretta hadn't mentioned a specific amount of money, so Casey let the silence hang.

"Would you consider helping us out on a trial basis? We'd pay $300 for an afternoon and evening."

Casey looked down and swallowed hard to keep from jumping at the prospect. She had received zero response to her attempts to find employment. Although she had a very generous new salary, and the prospect of having discretionary income was tempting, she needed to warn Loretta about her lack of experience. "I'm a novice cook, and I don't know the first thing about mixing drinks."

"I have no doubt that you're a quick study. With no background in property maintenance, you managed to arrange for our move in record time."

"When would you need me?"

"This weekend, if possible. I'm hoping my lady friends will arrive around two on Saturday. There will be four of us in the afternoon, and then William and some fellows will join us for drinks and dinner by the pool."

"Let me give a tentative yes. I need to check one thing before I can confirm."

Loretta rose. "Call me when you decide. Nice to meet you." She walked into the house.

Well, that was abrupt. Casey was dismissed. Loretta was clearly in control and intended to remain so. Lots of information and questions, but no warm, fuzzy friendship opportunity here. Casey snagged a second scone and called Bella.

Petey's face fell as the dog trotted to Casey. She reached into the tote for a tennis ball and tossed it to Petey. "Come play with us," she suggested with a smile and pointed toward the station. He caught the ball and grinned.

Her thoughts swirled as she walked back to the station. That was the last thing she had expected. For a couple so private, they invited guests in on the weekends.

At the station, she dialed Fisher's number, and he answered on the third ring, and she pressed Record. "Casey here. I want to check something with you. Mrs. Kennedy just asked me to watch Petey and serve company at a party at the A-frame. Would that be okay with Mr. Kennedy?" Even though Fisher had a camera at the pool, Casey wanted to cover her ass with explicit permission. She had no desire to cross Mr. Kennedy.

"Do whatever she asks." Click.

Prick.

Time to write in her journal. So much had happened lately, she had a lot to record. Much of it was exciting, but also unsettling and downright scary. She wasn't the only one with serious security worries.

Chapter Twenty-Six

C asey wrote down her thoughts in the random order in which they occurred. The Kennedys felt threatened because their home had been torched in Rhode Island and were willing to pay handsomely to maintain security and privacy. However, Loretta had very clearly indicated they were not interested in contacting Welton police or fire departments because they didn't want to attract attention. That didn't make sense. Anyone moving into the White House would be under a microscope in this nosy little town.

Could the close timing of visitors to the caboose and the arrival of the new tenants be a coincidence? Or were they related? Maybe her Spidey sense was justified. The Kennedys weren't just worried about trespassers or curiosity seekers. Arson was a big-time threat to life, limb, and livelihood. When she'd first met Vlad, he seemed like a bodyguard. Now that made sense.

Casey had been surprised by Loretta's nonchalant admission that she'd vetted her, but given the circumstances, she probably shouldn't have been. When she'd worked in the Children's Room of the public library in Ohio, the administration had been very concerned about exposing the vulnerable psyches of the town's babes to a person who had rubbed shoulders with criminals. But even though Loretta knew she'd spent years in prison, she wasn't at all bothered about her potential effect on Petey.

Everything about this rental was strange. Although Casey had been exposed to some of the most seedy and dangerous elements of society, she'd had only a few years' experience with normal adults. Then again, even she could sense that these highflyers were far from normal. More like downright weird. What would the relationship with the Kennedys be like if she refused? They were definitely used to having things their way.

The money. Wasn't $300 for an afternoon and evening of unskilled work a spectacular amount of money? Especially for someone completely lacking in qualifications? She'd ask LouAnne about it. Sure was a tidy sum. She could try it out once and see how things went. She was trainable. She could grill a steak and play Monopoly.

So why did it make her so nervous?

She put down her pen and checked the clock. Still time to get supplies for Halloween. She jumped in the Muttmobile and drove to the garden center where she purchased a large pumpkin and a couple of decorative gourds, and then drove to the grocery store for a bag of wrapped chocolate candies.

She knew it was wishful thinking to expect any goblins to come trick or treating at the station, but she would hate to disappoint anyone who had the gumption to venture down Station Road. At home in Ohio—and yes, she had to admit, Ohio was still home when she felt lonely—hundreds of children would come to the door of the old inn where she lived, and the town was half the size of Welton. For the last two years, not one little trick or treater had come to her door, but hope springs eternal.

Back at the station, she set about cutting off the top of the pumpkin and cleaning out the seeds which she'd bake later. Carefully she sculpted cat eyes, nose, and a mouth with sharp teeth. She formed ears from the carved-out pieces and attached them to the sides of the head with toothpicks. Finally, she gathered straight sticks and poked them into the sides for whiskers.

At dusk, she went outside and shouldered the ladder to the side of the caboose. Very carefully, she climbed up the rungs carrying the pumpkin in one hand, wishing she hadn't been quite so ambitious. She hefted the pumpkin atop the roof and then removed the top piece. She withdrew a lighter from her pocket, tilted the pumpkin to one side, and lit the candle she'd affixed inside, and then replaced the top. Glorious! She turned the pumpkin so that it faced the overpass on Church Street for drivers of cars to see as they traveled to and fro to Welton.

She placed a witch hat and a broom inside the front door with the candy in case a little goblin ventured into her lair.

Chapter Twenty-Seven

Fortune

Fortune trudged along a trail into the woods, grousing to himself about Blair because she hadn't brought suitable shoes for hiking, even though he'd told her he wanted to show her the woods above the Eagle Mountain House in the White Mountains. Open-toe wedges displayed her pedicure perfectly but were more suited for shopping in the town of Jackson, New Hampshire, which is where he'd dropped her off. They agreed to meet later for lunch after his hike.

The farther up the mountain he got, the more relaxed he felt, and he was actually relieved to be free of her constant chatter. He preferred the sound of the breeze rustling through the leaves and his footfalls on the soft earth. As he hiked upward his mind and muscles gradually unwound and relaxed in a natural meditation, momentarily untethered to responsibility.

He wished Captain were with him. The dog would bound ahead, exploring the environs and then return to check on him. Davey would love it, but he was in school, and afterwards he'd be with Anita. Fortune reached an outcropping of large boulders and sat atop the highest, giving him a panoramic view of the valley below, bedecked in what remained of fall's glorious red, orange, and yellow hues. The air was brisk and clear. He stretched out on the stone, basking in the sun, delighted to be free and warm and healthy. He nodded off in a relaxed catnap.

Fifteen minutes or so later, he awoke and sipped from his canteen. His mind returned to the morning's conversation in the car with Blair. He'd been surprised when she had tossed an overnight bag into the back seat. He told her that he appreciated her gifts, but that he wasn't looking for a long-term commitment. He hoped she got the message. He knew she heard and understood his words, but he wasn't sure she accepted them. She was like Anita that way, confident that her charms and wiles could harness him and change him.

Blair struck back by telling him Anita had taken her aside for a little friendly advice: don't waste your time. You can do better. He's a cop, nothing more. Fortune was surprised that Blair would confide that piece of hurtful information, but then she had witnessed Anita coming on to him at lunch. The two of them had always been competitive when men were involved, best friends when they weren't. Blair's intent was probably to discourage him if he had intentions of reconnecting with his ex.

Blair would probably make an eager partner in bed, but he didn't need to complicate his life. He also didn't want to take advantage of her, which is why he'd been so blunt this morning. Her idea was to have a leisurely breakfast and then spend the morning in the little shops that lined the streets in Jackson that carried "the most amazing, clever things." The latter was his idea of one of Dante's levels of hell.

He took another drag of refreshing but metallic-tasting water from his canteen. Everything seemed better outdoors after a week in the station and in his cruiser. The highlights of the week were his training sessions with Captain. The dog had the best nose for scent work and tracking in the class. He'd graduate soon, and then the nature of Fortune's police assignments would change, working with his new canine partner. Captain kept his distance from both Blair and Anita because they often smelled of some combination of nail polish remover, perfume, and alcohol.

As he hiked back down the mountain, he admitted that Blair was the least of his problems. Anita was pressing him at the behest of her moneybag parents to send Davey to a boarding school. The issue came up because the grandparents had secured promises of acceptance at two prestigious American prep schools and one international school. Fortune suspected that Daddy had been supporting his golden girl for the past few years, given the posh address of her home abroad. Of course, Fortune had checked it out. He suspected she liked receiving a check from him every month, knowing the dent it would make in a police officer's paycheck.

Anita had been back in the States for the better part of a week, and he knew the time was fast approaching when he would have to meet with her and hash things out. They hadn't had many custody issues since the divorce due to her living in Nice with Philippe, but evidently, the grandparents, who had never approved of Fortune, were pressuring her to take more control of their grandchild's life.

He'd been surprised at her come-hither behavior at the restaurant and wondered if it was for the benefit of him or for Blair. He still had feelings for Anita, a mixed-up combination of anger, distrust, and face it, desire. Yes, he was susceptible to her. She was a beauty, smart, and sexy as all hell, what he always dreamt of in a woman. He looked forward to seeing her tonight and at the same time dreaded it.

Davey had become the focus of his life and the apple of Fortune's mother's eye. When his father died, she was so depressed that he'd feared for her, but Davey had brightened her days and given her a new purpose. What a loss to both of them if he left.

He couldn't get embroiled in another round with Anita. What would it do to Davey if they reconnected, and she left again? Davey had asked for a whole year when she was coming back. Interesting now to see the two of them forging a new relationship. They hadn't been together for six months, or was it longer? Davey had stopped asking for her or about her. Now he was tense, wondering how to respond to a person he no longer knew very well.

Could Fortune ever really trust her again? The pain of betrayal still blindsided him when he least expected it. When she had thought she might be pregnant again, he had been overjoyed until she admitted that he might not be the father. And then, the abortion, without ever consulting him. Because dear Philippe didn't want a baby. Fortune picked up a large stick in the path and hurled it into the forest. Thank God for Davey and Fortune's mother. Otherwise, he would have been destroyed.

And then Anita had expected him to understand, even forgive her, because she wasn't suited to the life of a cop's wife. Which highlighted the painful reason she'd married him in the first place. Her highfalutin fiancé had dumped her, and Fortune caught her on the rebound. That time when she got pregnant, she hadn't known where to get an abortion.

Enough navel-gazing. He hoped she'd return to France. He and Davey had learned how to get along just fine without her. Besides, she didn't appreciate Captain. Fortune was convinced that Davey would be better off living with at least one parent, not isolated for months on end at a boarding school. Besides, the school system in Welton was one of the best in the state, and for that matter, the nation.

He hiked back down the trail, making plans. When he got to the hotel where they were to meet for lunch, Blair was lounging on the porch in one of the rocking chairs nursing a Bloody Mary. Fortune ordered a drink at the bar and joined her.

"How was the hike?" she asked

"Wonderful. You would have enjoyed it."

"No, I just had my hair done."

"What's that have to do with the price of milk?" he asked.

"Silly. I don't pay big bucks and then go play in the dirt. I'd have to fix myself up all over again."

Fortune looked at his watch. "I'd like to leave in an hour or so. Take in more of the scenery and then make a quick stop in Concord on the way home."

"Oh. I'd hoped we could have a few drinks here and…" she batted her eyes. "…leave in the morning.

"Sorry. I have to be back at a reasonable hour to take Davey to a Halloween party."

"Come on, Mike. Can't your mother take him?" she pouted.

"She could, but I want to take him. He's going as Rocky Balboa in a hooded black robe, with shorts and a belt Mom fixed up for him."

"You wearing a costume?"

"I'm going as Joe Friday from the old Dragnet show. 'Just the facts, ma'am.' Did you know that his badge number 714 was the number of home runs Babe Ruth hit?" He noticed that she wasn't smiling.

The ride through the mountains was glorious and silent. "I hoped we'd be able to spend more time together," Blair sulked.

"We are spending time together. It's a three-hour ride."

In Concord, he parked Blair at a coffee shop and stopped at State Police Headquarters. Detective Granger greeted him warmly, but only had a few moments to spare. After exchanging pleasantries, Fortune got down to the reason for his visit. "Have you learned anything more about the body found in the woods close to the caboose?"

"We contacted the V.A., and they confirmed that James Ferguson was a patient there in the psych ward. They had diagnosed him with a severe anxiety disorder stemming from his military service."

"Huh. Someone has been visiting the caboose in Welton. We don't know why, but have advised Casey, who you met, to install padlocks to discourage intruders. Someone may be looking for the gun and money we took from the safe. Thanks for your help. Keep me posted." They shook hands, and Fortune returned to the coffee shop to collect Blair.

"I've decided to go as Cleopatra," she said as he ordered a cup of coffee to go. He frowned, confused.

"To the Halloween party."

Fortune almost spilled his coffee. "Don't think so, Blair, unless you want to accompany Wonder Woman."

"Anita?"

"Afraid so. She wants to be part of Davey's activities and is butting in on the party."

"So, the day with me; the evening with her."

"Tonight won't be anywhere near as much fun, trust me."

"Drop me at the office."

He obliged. When he pulled into the parking space in front of the realty office, she grabbed her purse and overnight bag. "When you speak with that woman in the caboose, find out how to contact Mr. Kennedy. I need his new phone number."

"Yes, ma'am."

She slammed the car door behind her.

Why did he subject himself to these women with their moods and demands? When would he learn? So far, he'd successfully avoided the clutches of bored Welton housewives desperate for attention while their husbands were off busily amassing fortunes. Slim pickings locally for a single cop his age and little time to explore farther afield. Maybe he should have been a monk. Except for the things that grounded him. Davey. His mom. Captain. His job.

For now, that would have to be enough. As he crossed the Church Street bridge, he was surprised to see a glowing cat pumpkin atop the caboose. Clever. What fun. Davey will love it.

Chapter Twenty-Eight

Casey

Tuesday, 11/1

A sharp report awakened Casey in the middle of the night. Sounded like a rifle. Little Mother shot from the futon and disappeared under a small dresser in the corner of the loft. "Isabella?" Casey called. She turned on a lamp by the futon and peered over the rail downstairs at a nervous pooch pacing the floor. Was it just her paranoia to think it would be a firearm? Heck, it was Halloween, probably some fireworks to scare folks. Or the loud backfire of a truck on the Church Street bridge over the railroad tracks. She went down the spiral stairs to settle Bella.

She peered out the window, but the candle in the pumpkin had either burned down or blown out. All was dark outside. Let it be. She grabbed one of the mini-Hershey bars that not even one little goblin had claimed and went back up to bed.

She awoke before dawn, determined to make progress fixing up the property before winter came. She'd plant daffodils and tulips in front of the station. She had a hoe, a three-claw rake and hand trowel, and two large bags of bulbs. "C'mon, Bella. Let's play in the dirt." She carted her equipment outside and stopped short, dropping everything on the ground.

Shattered pieces of her cat pumpkin were splattered over the ground in front of the caboose. She approached the destruction slowly, shocked at the vandalism. No little BB gun. She'd heard a shot after all.

She imagined the trajectory of the bullet, probably from the road behind and above the caboose, through the pumpkin down to…oh, no. She walked over to where the Muttmobile was parked and found a hole in the driver's door. When she opened the door, she saw where the bullet had pierced through the door and entered the seat. Had to be a powerful rifle. She poked her finger in and hit something metallic. When she retracted her finger, her hand was trembling.

Welton. Such a quiet little suburb with great schools. Six or seven different churches. And snipers to send ugly hate messages. She got a knife and dug into the seat to extract the bullet. Big sucker, no wonder the pumpkin was all over the place. Couldn't wreck the Muttmobile, but sure cast a pall over her earlier optimistic mood. She got a broom and a bag and swept up the remains of her Halloween.

She hadn't felt welcomed, but this was downright threatening. After she cleaned up the mess, she attacked the packed earth next to the station with a vengeance. Well, with the three-claw rake. She had wanted to be part of something. To have neighbors and friends, townsfolk who would smile and greet her. The kind of life she'd had growing up, when she knew where she belonged. Just wasn't going to happen here. She chucked stones to the side and kept digging. Why bother planting bulbs and painting the caboose when there was no hope of living happily ever after in her little station? Irony of ironies: she had a home, pets, a job, and a couple of friends—and was totally rejected by everything and everyone else. Not just rejected. Threatened.

She didn't want to give up, sell, and move to another place. Why would it be different anywhere new? She didn't want to cower under a rock pretending to be someone she wasn't, to have to lie about her history.

The sound of an automobile coming down Station Road interrupted her negative spiral. Great. Covered in dirt with tears of frustration she hadn't expected streaming down her face. All she needed to complete the picture was company. Well, maybe if it was LouAnne or Chance or even Fortune—

No, a black Ford pickup barreled down the road, skidding to a stop before the station. The driver turned the truck around and backed up to the caboose.

The fake detective Granger jumped down from the high seat. She recognized him instantly with his arrogant swagger and ball cap. He'd come back for the safe.

Funny, if he'd knocked on the door earlier like Fortune did and asked, she would have happily given him a tour of the caboose and answered his questions. But he was a rude bully and an impostor. After years of forced obedience and prison guards, she'd honed a sharp sense of authority resistance. One of her reinstated freedoms following release from prison was the ability to say no. She rose and wiped her face on her tee shirt smearing dirt and tears across her cheeks like a warrior painted for battle. She watched his approach in silence.

"You know what I want. I brought a dolly this time to take it away. As I told you before, it's part of an investigation in New Hampshire." His thin mouth formed a grimace of a smile.

"Then let a New Hampshire policeman show up with a warrant, and I'll gladly comply. Someone, say, like Detective Theodore Granger. You don't look a bit like him."

He stopped and adjusted his cap. "Yeah, well, Granger's card was the only one I had on me." He walked between her and the station where she'd been digging in the dirt. He eyed her and smirked. "Wilson, Private Investigator. People are generally more responsive to cops. Has anyone come by to claim the contents of the safe?"

Damned if she'd answer the man's rude questions. His slash of a mouth turned down to one side. Casey glanced at the back of the cab where a long rifle with a scope rested on a rifle rack. "Did you shoot my pumpkin?"

"Yeah. I hate cats."

It took Casey a second to realize he was referring to the cat pumpkin, not Little Mother.

"I don't want to hurt you, but I'm leaving with the safe." He edged closer.

"What for?" she asked.

"To confirm the identity of the man who was living in the caboose when it was in New Hampshire. Move aside."

"No."

He strode back toward his truck.

"By the time you reach that rifle, I'll be inside calling the police."

He turned around. "I don't need a rifle to handle you."

He was right. He was over six feet and had her by at least a hundred pounds. "I can save you some trouble," she offered. "The safe's empty. I found the combination and called the police. They came and took away the contents."

"What was in the safe?"

"Not telling. You could go to the police and claim the items if you knew what they were."

He seemed to consider her words for a moment. "I still need to see inside the caboose."

"Why?" she asked.

"My client's looking for the man who used to live in the caboose. Something left behind might help locate him."

"Who is your client?"

"I'm not at liberty to say."

"The police say that man was killed."

"You believe them?"

"More than I believe you."

The man ignored her comment and focused on Isabella. He knelt and made smooching noises and held out his hand. Isabella cocked her head to the side and gave a tentative wag.

"Isabella, NO!"

"Why so defensive?" He moved closer. "Show me inside the caboose."

"Nope." She skirted around him with a quick move, grabbed the claw rake, climbed to the top stair of the caboose, and sat blocking the way. "Time for you to leave."

"A lone woman and her fearsome guard dog ordering me around? I'm terrified."

As he approached, Casey rolled back the sleeve of her work shirt exposing the long knife scar on her forearm that she'd received in a bloody attack in prison. She held the three-pronged claw in her right hand and ran the forefinger of her left hand down a metal prong, tapping the end and wincing at its sharp metal tip.

He stopped mid-stride, eyeing the scar and the claw. "You threatening me?"

"With this?" Casey shrugged. "Huh." She pricked her finger and drew blood. "Messy but could be effective." She squinted at the New Hampshire license plate.

"Go ahead. Write it down. Ain't my truck. Plate's stolen." He laughed and got into the pickup. "If you meet the fellow who lived in the caboose, tell him Wilson's looking for him. I'll check back another time. See if he shows up."

Casey didn't budge until the truck disappeared. When she rose, her knees were rubbery, and she had to hold onto the railing to descend the steps to the ground. She waited until the truck reached the top of the hill and turned onto Church Street before she entered the station with Isabella close on her heels. Inside, she locked and bolted the door and sank into a chair, trembling. Might not have been her smartest move. Should she call Fortune?

The phone rang. Maybe he was calling her.

"Who was that?" Fisher demanded.

For a moment, she had forgotten about the annoying lawyer. "Said his name was Wilson," she replied.

"What does he want?"

"You must've heard him. He wanted to get into the caboose. I need to hang up and call the police."

"What good will that do? He's long gone."

"I don't like people shooting up my property."

"Can you prove he shot the pumpkin?"

"No."

"Then, no harm, no foul. Let it go."

This time, Casey was the one who hung up. But Fisher was right. There was probably nothing the police could do, but she didn't like being bossed around. Should she report it? Loss of a pumpkin on Halloween. Big deal. Trick or treat. Pretty mean trick. It had to be against the law to fire a rifle in town. She fingered the shell in her jeans pocket. Fisher didn't want police at the station, which, in her mood, was a good reason to call. She looked up the number and dialed.

Chapter Twenty-Nine

Once again, Casey was transferred to Officer O'Malley. "This is Casey Cavendish. Please ask Detective Fortune to call me. My number is—"

"What's it about this time, Miss Cavendish?"

"Just leave him a message, please."

"Do you have a complaint or something to report?" he insisted.

"What I have is a two-inch rifle shell that blasted through the front door of my car and was embedded in the seat. Tell him that." She hung up, frustrated at the pigheadedness of the obnoxious plug who clearly had taken a dislike to her. The feeling was mutual, and miserable as he was, he wasn't stupid and undoubtedly sensed her disdain.

Time to clean up. In the tiny bathroom, she laughed at the smeared clown face that greeted her in the mirror. Fierce indeed. After a quick shower, she set about making a sandwich for lunch. As she was carrying the tray out to the platform, the doorbell chimed. Couldn't be Fortune so fast. She put down the tray and peeked through the peephole. Loretta? With Petey.

Casey unlocked and opened the door. "What a nice surprise. Come on in." Isabella rushed past her to greet her favorite little person. Petey knelt and was covered in doggy kisses. When Loretta saw the lunch tray, she hesitated. "We're interrupting your lunch. We'll come back another time."

"No, no, I'm pleased to have company. Have you eaten? I have plenty. Let me fix sandwiches." Loretta demurred and settled on lemonade, but Casey saw Petey eying her sandwich. Casey led them through the sliding door to the platform and handed it over. He gobbled it in record time and then looked expectantly at Isabella.

"Her ball is in the little bed inside the door." He didn't need more permission and was gone in a second, racing through the station to the front door with Bella close on his heels.

"Your little station is charming. Like an apartment with privacy and land all around. I know I should have called, but Petey was impatient. He saw the pumpkin from his window last night and wanted to come down and see it in person."

Casey's face fell. "Good thing he's distracted. We had a bit of vandalism last night. No more pumpkin. I found it splattered on the driveway this morning. I was hoping to attract little goblins for treats, but got a mean trick instead." As she spoke, she wondered how much, if anything, Fisher would tell Loretta about this morning's visit from Wilson. Might as well fill her in. "Someone shot it."

"That's horrible!"

"I called the police, but there's really nothing they can do about a smashed pumpkin on Halloween." Casey downplayed the event, unwilling to provide more information or alarm her tenant unless she asked questions.

"I'm so sorry. You certainly haven't had an easy time of it."

What did that mean? "You've only been here a week. What have you heard?"

Loretta chuckled. "The real estate agent, Blair, has been up to see William twice already. He wasn't home either time, but she stayed for coffee and talked a blue streak about the history of the White House, the tumultuous and violent saga of the two Waddington wives, and your Aunt Mary's last few years—and you. How you, as she said, 'weaseled your way into Mary's affections' and ended up with a station, a caboose, and now a job. Fisher also researched you a bit, so we know about your prison years and education."

"Wow. You have the advantage over me for sure. Tell me a little about your story."

Loretta chewed her lip for a moment. "I grew up in Queens." She smiled at Casey's raised eyebrows. "Took me years to lose the accent. After high school, I joined a modeling agency, made a number of commercials for television, and played in summer stock. I hoped for an acting career. A few of us in the agency worked for an escort service to pay the rent, and that's how I met William. He was already well established in his business and ready to settle down. He wanted a wife who would help entertain his customers at home and look good on his arm and quickly nixed the idea of an acting or modeling career. Although we've moved around a bit, that's basically my story."

She thought a moment before continuing. "The girls you'll meet Saturday worked with me in New York. William doesn't like me to leave the property right now, so they've agreed to come and play with me here. It's okay if I have my friends in, because he knows them. He's a bit paranoid these days. With good reason. As I mentioned, the Fire Marshall declared the fire at our home to be arson. So, William's protective, but I have to admit I'm feeling rather confined."

"Why would anyone set fire to your house?" Casey asked. Her underlying question was how worried should she be that the arsonist would follow the Kennedys to Welton? She'd sure hate to see the White House and A-frame go up in flames. She made a mental note to check on the home insurance policy.

"He's received threats related to his work. I really can't talk about it."

"Sorry. I didn't mean to pry. I hope you're not in any danger."

"Thank you." Loretta shifted in her seat. "I'm curious about the caboose."

"Let me show you what I'm up to." Casey took the keys from a hook by the door, and they walked outside to the caboose. "I've been working on the outside in good weather, stripping the peeling and loose paint, and staining the wood inside when it rains...or when I get sick of being on a ladder." She unlocked the padlock and showed Loretta the features of the old car. "I just had the electricity and water hooked up. After the next paycheck, I'll get a mini-fridge and propane gas for the cook stove. The potbellied stove takes pellets and coal."

"What will you do with it when you're finished?"

"Not sure. It's a nice change of pace from the station. I may paint or sketch here." She walked toward the rear. Petey raced past them to the back of the car and climbed up into the cupola. Casey laughed and saluted, "Conductor Pete." She unlatched the door to the storage closet. "You might find this interesting." She turned on a flashlight and ducked inside. For the second time that day, she stopped short. The note she'd left taped to the safe was gone.

"What's wrong?" asked Loretta, bumping into Casey as she entered behind her.

Petey saved Casey from answering by pushing past them to the safe. "Can I open it?" He looked to Loretta and then added, "Please?" Casey hesitated and then gave him the numbers of her mother's birthdate along with directions on how to turn the dial. "Make one circle all the way around to the right and stop at 2; now back around left to 2 again; and right to 19." It took three tries before he mastered it and opened the heavy door with a tug. "Cool!" he exclaimed.

"Interesting," said Loretta. "But empty."

Casey didn't tell her about discovering the combination, the contents of the safe, or the fact that the police had hauled away a handgun and a pile of money. No reason to worry her about Hobo, who was probably dead and buried, or that someone had broken in and removed her note.

"Can I do it again?" begged Petey.

"Once more, and then we must go," said Loretta.

Petey's mouth moved with the direction and numbers of the combination. He got it on the first try. Clearly, he didn't want to leave, but Loretta took him firmly by the hand just as a car drove down Station Road.

"Busy little station this morning," said Casey, watching Fortune get out of the car and walk toward them. She backed up a step or two, self-conscious in cut-offs and sandals next to Loretta, who looked like the million dollars she probably had, nicely coifed, tall and elegant in slacks and an ironed blouse.

"Got your message," he said as he approached. He gave her a smile and nodded to Loretta. Casey introduced Detective Mike Fortune to Loretta and Petey. Loretta shook his hand, but then surprised Casey by leading Petey toward the steps to the White House. "We must be off. Thanks, Casey."

Petey stopped, withdrew his hand from Loretta, and turned back, his eyes big. "You really a policeman?"

Fortune grinned, amused. "Yup."

"Do you have a badge?"

"Petey!" exclaimed Loretta.

Fortune withdrew a wallet from his rear pocket and flipped it open to his badge, holding it out for Petey to see.

"Do you have a gun?"

"Petey, come!" Loretta had had enough.

Fortune opened his jacket, revealing a shoulder holster.

Loretta yanked Petey the last few feet to the stairs. "We good for Saturday around two?" she called back to Casey. Casey gave her a thumbs up.

Fortune followed their progress up the stairs. Casey suspected he was actually following Loretta and was annoyed with her twinge of jealousy.

"She wasn't too pleased that I'd called you about the pumpkin," Casey explained. "They're super private and don't want anything to draw attention to them or the surrounding area."

Fortune turned his full attention to her. "Tell me what happened."

Chapter Thirty

"Come on in. I have fresh coffee and something to show you." Casey led Fortune into the station. Moments later, they sat at the table with steaming mugs, and Casey told him all about the second visit from the phony cop earlier that morning. "He said he was a private eye." She reached into her pocket, withdrew the rifle shell, and handed it to him. She quickly withdrew her hand, aware of dirt still lodged under her nails from digging. "He said he'd shot the pumpkin last night because he hated cats."

Fortune's eyes widened as he examined the shell.

"It splattered my pumpkin and then pierced the driver's door of my car and lodged in the seat. The truck was a Ford pickup, but the man, who said his name was Wilson, claimed it didn't belong to him and that the license plate was stolen." She wrote the New Hampshire plate number on a napkin and pushed it to him. "He seems to think the man I call Hobo is still alive and possibly around here. He didn't say what he wanted with him or who his client was." She watched him frown and examine the bullet and the napkin.

"Oh, there's one other thing that makes me think he may be right." She explained the note she'd written and taped to the safe and that she'd just discovered that the note had been removed moments before he arrived.

"Whoever your visitor is, he's not bothered by a few padlocks," said Fortune. "I can assign a patrol to come around and make sure everything's okay. Sometimes the presence of police scares away trespassers."

"I'm sure patrols would be the last thing Fisher and Kennedy would want."

"Fisher?"

"Yeah, the lawyer who keeps tabs on me and visitors via the camera I showed you over the door."

"Do you think Fisher is recording or just watching? He may have captured an image of Wilson we can use."

"I doubt either the lawyer or the tenant will welcome any queries."

"If Wilson shows up again, give him the safe. It isn't worth a rifle shot or worse. We'll get it back. I can tell you don't like giving in to bullies, but this guy is armed."

"He probably won't bother with the safe now that I've told him the police took the contents."

"The other thing Granger said that was worrisome was that James Ferguson had a history of mental problems and had spent years in a Veteran's hospital in the psych ward. He'd been diagnosed with a severe anxiety disorder."

"Super. A violent P.I., a mentally unstable trespasser, a paranoid tenant, a nosy lawyer, an absent boss…at least Loretta seems friendly and little Petey is a delight."

"You seem to have made friends with them."

"Hope so."

Fortune tucked the napkin and shell into his pocket.

Casey didn't want him to leave just yet. "Have you ever been involved in a forgery case?"

Fortune cocked his head to the side at the change in topic. "Yes. Why?"

"I have a reason to question the authorship of a note, and I'd like a referral to a court-certified document examiner. Although I'm a graphologist, my opinion isn't accepted as legally binding in court."

"A graphologist? I know about document examiners. How does that differ from a graphologist?"

"Examiners measure and compare writing to prove or disprove forgery. Graphologists evaluate handwritings in order to create personality profiles."

"Mmmmmm." Fortune pushed back and looked at her with an expression she could only regard as skeptical.

His reaction wasn't uncommon. She walked to her desk and selected three handwriting samples she planned to use in her next class. She spread them out on the table before Fortune. "Do you think these three notes were written by the same person?"

Fortune glanced at the writings. "No."

"Okay. Which is the most forceful?"

He pointed to the first one.

"Who is most controlled?"

"Number two."

"Who is repressed?"

He pointed to the third.

"You get an A. This is way too simplified because people are complex mixtures of traits. But you could easily tell something just from the writing. The first is forceful, showing both power and a lack of empathy, a domineering personality, strength, and intelligence. It's William Kennedy, our tenant. The second is harder to read because of its controlled nature, a person who can be both cold and warm depending upon the situation, one who likes the finer things and is flexible and quick on her feet—it's Loretta's writing. And the third is Agnes, wound tight as a spring; repressed. Not a happy-go-lucky soul."

Fortune had to nod in acknowledgment.

Casey wasn't done. "Handwriting is brain writing." She held up her hand. "The brain is a dumb instrument. The brain directs the hand and fingers how to move." She wiggled her fingers. "As you develop and grow, so does your writing. And each writing is as unique as a snowflake. Well, in your case, as unique as a fingerprint." She handed him a blank sheet and a ballpoint pen. "Write something and sign it."

Fortune stared at the page. "What should I write?"

"The quick red fox jumps over the lazy brown dog."

He hesitated a moment and then wrote the sentence and signed it.

Casey picked up the paper and ran her fingers across and under the sheet to feel the pressure. "Print-script shows a compromise between cursive and block printing, written with control and strong pressure. You feel things deeply and can be emotional…yet logic rules and constrains. You show good attention to detail, strong energy and sex drive, and are stubborn as hell. You have the gift of intuition, but you don't trust it, preferring to rely on a factual approach." She wrinkled her nose. "A bit vain. Strong drive toward goals. Persistent, but can get derailed if you push too far in one direction—"

"Good God, woman! Enough!" Fortune laughed, raising his arms in surrender.

"And, there's what we call signature incongruity, showing that you'd like to be quite a bit freer than you are."

"I'll be damned. Unfair advantage. Show me yours."

"Nah."

"C'mon," he egged her on.

Casey picked up a blank sheet of paper and held it aloft. "Lovely garland strokes demonstrate a calm and peaceful nature, artistic with a fanciful sense of humor, great loops of imagination, quick intelligence, makes great cookies, loves dogs and cats—

He grabbed the paper and pulled it to the table, laughing. "I'll ask around for a document examiner."

"I need all the help I can get."

He covered her hand with his. Her hand didn't feel dumb at all and was sending clear electrical impulses to her brain. She didn't dare move or look at him.

"I'll help you in any way I can. You are not alone." He gripped her hand tighter. "Listen to me. You need to be careful. You're dealing with some very sketchy and dangerous people. Wilson is armed and violent. The man, Hobo, may be alive and probably none too pleased to have his money and gun confiscated. He may be a mental case. And your new tenant has had his home burned to the ground."

Reluctantly, she withdrew her hand and stood, gathering cups and carrying them to the sink.

He followed and apologized. "I'm overstepping, but I hope you're hearing me."

"What can I do?" Her voice cracked as she threw her arms into the air and looked to the heavens.

"Anywhere you can go for a bit until things quiet down?"

She shook her head. "This is all I have now." She turned her head to the side, fighting back tears, determined not to cry.

In two strides he enveloped her in a hug and held her head against his chest, rocking her back and forth. After a moment, he held her at arm's length, his eyes seeking hers. "Locks, Mace, telephone…and me." He pointed his thumb to his chest. He released her and, with one long backward look, walked out the door.

Casey closed her eyes and sank into a chair, overwhelmed with longing. "Oh, God, if only." She wanted so much more than safety and comfort.

Chapter Thirty-One

Agnes

Late in the morning, Agnes returned from her exercise class at the pool feeling energized. She loved the air and the wide vistas of the spa. As she passed a mirror, she tucked a few strands of newly coiffed hair behind one ear and smiled at her reflection in the mirror. The swelling had mostly subsided from her operation, but she still needed a bandage to cover the remnants of the bruising. Good thing she'd had the operation the minute she'd arrived. She tapped the end of her new nose. They did a beautiful job! Another month or two, and no one will notice the minute scar tissue.

She practiced her smile and had to admit it felt good. She winked at herself and then leaned in closer. Did she need a lid job? Her eyes were her best feature. She had a few more pounds to lose before Mary's clothes would fit perfectly, but she could already wear them. She wasn't used to material clinging to her figure.

She wished she'd had the operation years earlier. Instead, she'd considered herself hopelessly homely because of her beak and sequestered herself working at the old priests' home. She smiled again. Her capped front teeth made a big difference.

She hadn't planned to return to Welton until the end of November, but the call from Mr. Kennedy— "call me William"—suggested that he was interested in speaking with her regarding her long-term plans for the White

House properties. She had agreed to contact him when she returned. She remembered him as a darkly handsome, rather rude and gruff man from the meeting earlier with Casey, but he was very polite and even friendly during their recent telephone conversation. Could she hope that he might be interested in buying?

Time to call that real estate agent in Welton and see if she knew anything. No reason to involve Casey. Just keep her happy with her outrageous salary. If Agnes decided to sell, it would be best to close the deal before the girl had an opportunity to challenge her. She probably was bluffing with her hints about forgery, but Agnes didn't want to take any chances.

She dialed the number on the real estate agency card and was surprised when Blair Forsythe answered on the second ring. Don't be too direct in your questions, she mouthed to her reflection in the mirror. "I got a strange call from our new tenant at—"

"To whom am I speaking?"

The woman knew full well who was calling. "Agnes Dempsey." Stop frowning, she chided herself. Remember, you can hear a smile.

"Oh yes, Miss Dempsey. How may I help you?"

"I got an interesting call from Mr. Kennedy. Have you spoken to him lately?"

"Not recently, no."

"I believe you told me he worked in finance." She raised her eyebrows and let the statement hang. She could learn to be much more expressive with her new look.

"Well, actually, he's a real estate developer."

"Really." Another silence.

"He buys properties and arranges for builders and contractors to develop them. I'm interested in speaking with him now that he's relocated to the Boston area. Why do you ask?"

"Mr. Kennedy asked if I'd made any long-term plans regarding the White House and A-frame properties. I haven't yet. I'd need more information before doing so. Since you handled the rental, I thought maybe I could ask you to investigate a number of things for me." She nodded to her image.

"Certainly. I'd be happy to work with you. Would you consider selling the property?"

"No, no." She shook her head. "I'm not ready to make that decision quite yet. I'd have to have someone research recent comparable property sales for me."

"I can look around and prepare a list of recent land and estate sales and current offerings and get back to you. It would give you an idea of what's selling in the market and a range of prices, although your properties are in a rarified category." The agent hesitated before continuing. "By the way, you should know that the last project he sealed in Rhode Island was a large, low-rent housing project set in an exclusive suburb. Would such a prospect bother you?"

Agnes shrugged and then actually laughed. "Well, if it comes to that, you can throw in the carriage house. That would make the lot a rather exclusive compound."

"Definitely. All three buildings and the acreage would make sense for either type of project, a family compound or a large-scale development. With the railroad property and Church Street on one side, conservation land abutting the back two sides, and the frontal, gated access to the property—yes, that would make an exclusive and desirable combination for the right buyer."

"I plan to return to Welton in a week or so. I'll call to see what you can dig up."

"That's rather soon—"

"I have confidence in you." She puckered her lips in a pretend kiss. "I need the information before I meet with William." That should impress her. "I'll let you know when my travel plans are confirmed. In the meantime, use the utmost discretion in your research, especially around Miss Cavendish and the Kennedys."

"Of course."

Agnes hung up and then practiced a wink. She'd love to unload that property. She hated Welton.

Chapter Thirty-Two

Casey

Wednesday, 11/2

Casey cursed under her breath as she wrestled with the ironing board. All morning, she'd been worrying about what to wear to serve at Loretta's party. She finally settled on black slacks and a linen shirt. Innocuous. Inconspicuous.

Around one thirty she and Isabella walked to the A-frame. She punched in the new security code and entered. "Yoo-hoo! Anybody home?" she called to announce her presence. Silence.

She walked through the small foyer past the wooden door to the sauna and followed the hallway into the open floor plan. Through the huge windows at the back of the building that spanned the entire A-frame, one could see all the way to the Boston skyline. In the kitchen area she joined Olga who was stocking the refrigerator and bar. Olga scowled at the dog and ignored Casey.

"Good morning," Loretta called from an upstairs balcony. Casey remembered that the upstairs had four bedrooms and two baths. "I'll be down in a minute. Make yourself at home. There's coffee on the counter. Petey's at the pool."

Casey walked across the plush carpeting to the sunken fire pit, continued past the entertainment center, and stood by the window. Below was the familiar pool surrounded by the deck and pool chairs, lounges, tables, and umbrellas. She smiled to herself, remembering how she and LouAnne and Rosie had cavorted in the pool less than a week ago, grilled steaks, and soaked in the hot tub. She found the door between the kitchen and the dining area and went outside to the pool. It was unseasonably warm for a fall afternoon. If anyone chose to swim, the pool was heated.

Petey sat hunched over a project at a table under an umbrella at the back next to the fence engaged in drawing a picture. She joined him and set down her tote which she'd packed with a with tennis ball and dog treats for Isabella and sunscreen for her. "Hi there. What are you drawing?"

"A caboose."

Casey squinted but realized she'd need more imagination to conjure a railcar. "Hmmmmm." Non-committal was good at this stage of design. They sat in companionable silence for a few moments before Olga uttered a command from the door.

"Peter. Lunch." Reluctantly he abandoned the table and entered the house. Casey sat waiting for some kind of instruction, wishing she'd brought a book. She didn't think the help were supposed to dive in. Petey returned with a sandwich and a soda.

Around two-fifteen, Casey heard a car pull into the drive, followed by female voices. Moments later, Loretta and two other women came through the door and settled in chairs beside the pool. Loretta raised her hand to Casey, signaling her to join them. "What would you ladies like to drink?" she asked them. "We have most everything."

The perky redhead asked for a gin and tonic, and the brunette and Loretta both ordered white wine. "And bring chips and nuts," said Loretta.

No introductions. No please. Casey smiled and withdrew with the orders.

The ladies chatted and giggled. Casey sat by Petey at the back, waiting for the next signal from Loretta. The redhead produced nail polish and began painting her toes. Clearly, they knew one another and were at ease. Another blonde woman showed up a few minutes later, and Casey took her order before retreating to the table where Petey was feeding Isabella the remains of his sandwich.

The brunette rose and sauntered over to their table and tousled Petey's hair. He drew back, embarrassed, but she didn't seem to notice. "Your little dog?" He shook his head and looked to Casey. "Remember me?" the woman asked.

He nodded. "Jenny." He looked to the group of women beside his aunt.

She pointed to the redhead and the blonde. "And Ellen and Laura." Jenny glanced at Casey for a second, but apparently didn't see anything that interested her. She turned and rejoined her friends.

They were four strikingly beautiful women. Loretta was tall and willowy and elegant with flowing blonde hair. Next to her was Jenny, the shapely brunette with hazel eyes. The petite redhead who was painting her toes had freckles and green eyes, and Laura the other blonde bombshell who'd just arrived, could be a double for Marilyn Monroe. Casey faded into the woodwork and watched the rich women cavort in their privileged world. Like a movie set. Unreal.

From time to time, the women summoned Casey with requests. According to their sparkling ring fingers, all had married blindingly well. Thin, rich, and pampered. Around four-thirty Casey provided towels when they decided to go for a dip.

Then they disappeared into the house. All was quiet, and Casey was curious. Trying not to be too obvious in her exploration, she wandered over to the area next to the door where LouAnne had spotted the camera. There! A small red light was the giveaway. She would never have noticed the little camera if LouAnne hadn't identified it. Casey didn't like the surreptitious spying, but she had to assume it was okay with Loretta. She carried glasses and plates into the kitchen, and once again found herself contemplating her navel.

An hour later, Loretta appeared in a long, silky light blue dress, hair piled atop her head. "After drinks and hors d'oeuvres, we'll be eating inside. Steaks are in the fridge, and there are baked potatoes, salads, and whatever vegetables Olga left. The potatoes are already baked and just need heating up."

So, I'm to prepare dinner?

Casey was surprised when Loretta actually poured herself a glass of wine. She reached into a drawer and produced an apron. "Wear this. I wouldn't want any of the gentlemen to be confused."

Confused? What gentlemen? What would confuse them?

"Olga set the table, but it looks like she forgot candles. They're in the pantry." Eight place settings were on a long oak table with a centerpiece of anemones. Real silver and china, crystal wine glasses and water goblets, all largesse brought down from the White House.

Loretta nodded toward the window. Outside, Olga was collecting Petey and his belongings, and it looked like he was giving her a hard time. "Go tell him he can play with the dog tomorrow."

Casey was startled by the order but decided this wasn't the time to object. She joined Petey and Olga by the pool gate. She didn't like Loretta's assumption, but she did enjoy the boy. "You can come down to the caboose in the morning if you'd like," she offered as he petted Isabella. He pouted but obeyed Olga, and Casey returned to her serving duties.

Inside, female voices preceded the young women who descended the stairs, dressed for dinner. Casey tried not to gawk.

A sleek green shift emphasized Ellen's elfin figure and gimlet eyes. Marilyn—no, her name was Laura—swirled down in white chiffon, and Jenny dazzled in classic silk mauve. Casey was grateful for the apron.

"Another G and T, but not so much ice," said Ellen.

"Same for me," ordered Jenny.

"Loretta and I'll stick with wine," said Marilyn.

Casey bustled about preparing drinks for the ladies. As she served them, she noticed that their jewelry had migrated from their ring fingers, now bare, to necks and earlobes.

The monitor by the door beeped, and Loretta responded. "The fellows are here." A moment later, a deep baritone voice announced the entry of four middle-aged men dressed in slacks and dinner jackets. They sported varying amounts of hair, some of it natural. She recognized the tall, darkly handsome man as William Kennedy. Loretta took his arm and handed him a drink. Personal service for the husband.

Because there were no introductions, Casey provided her own identifiers for the other men as she prepared a drink for each: the bald eagle she labeled "Beak;" the one with red cheeks and a small round paunch, "Santa," and the austere fellow with military posture and yellow hair, "Colonel Mustard."

Interesting. No intros meant they already knew one another.

"What a pleasant surprise, MISS Cavendish. You look positively fetching in that little apron." Kennedy stood beside her and spoke to her without turning his head. Casey froze, not knowing what to expect. His eyes wandered up and down each of the beauties in turn before landing on Loretta. Finally, he turned to Casey and handed her his glass. "A double Macallan, no ice. It's under the sink. Don't leave it out." In any other setting, Casey would drop the glass on his foot, but instead, she gritted her teeth and walked into the kitchen.

When she served him his drink, he accepted it with both hands, one covering hers for a split second too long, enough that Casey caught Loretta scowling at him. Although the other men held their own, she noted that they deferred to Kennedy. It was as if a magnetic field circled him. His posture was confident, but he wasn't any bigger, or better dressed, nor was he the best looking. His manner exuded ownership of the room. Casey found herself resenting his assumed dominance and wondering what Fortune would think of the man's bearing. Then again, people also deferred to Fortune. She busied herself with hors d'oeuvres and advised herself to stick to her knitting.

She'd heard of people "working a room," but Kennedy managed it without ever budging from the center. One by one, each man approached him, shared a few words, laughed at something at least once, and then faded away. After the parade ended, Kennedy beckoned to Loretta. She joined him, and he leaned over and spoke to her in a confidential manner. Then he waved to his entourage, gave his wife a proprietary peck on the cheek, and, to Casey's surprise, made his exit.

Casey felt an instant change in the atmosphere, a collective sigh of relief, as if the commander had said, "At ease." Either that, or the cumulative effect of alcohol was releasing inhibitions. The men milled about for a few moments and then paired off with what appeared to be predetermined partners.

Loretta caught her eye and signaled time for dinner by raising her hand to her mouth. Casey took orders for how to grill individual steaks while Loretta played hostess, directing Casey to pick up a stray plate or refill a nut dish. Loretta didn't lift a pinky.

After a moment of panic while she tried to remember how to fire up the grill, Casey managed to cook the steaks to order and serve the dinner without a hitch.

As evening descended, the party migrated back to the pool area. Loretta turned on the pool lights and music for a more intimate ambiance. Santa smoked a cigar. Casey served after-dinner drinks and retired to the kitchen.

Exhausted, she cleared the table and nibbled on a few tidbits that were left over. As she loaded the dishwasher, she couldn't help but notice when Beak and Jenny entered, climbed the stairs, and disappeared. Not long after, Colonel Mustard and Marilyn followed suit. Where was Loretta? Casey had lost track of her. How much longer would she be needed? She wasn't comfortable with the goings-on and decided to ask.

She walked outside to the pool area looking for Loretta, but jumped to the side when she felt a warm hand on her hip. She shrank away, thinking she'd bumped into a guest. But no. Santa closed in and reached for her again. "I haven't seen you before, sweetheart. Wha's your name?" he slurred. She backed into a chair, and it clattered to the deck.

"Hank, leave the help alone," ordered Loretta from the doorway to the house.

"Just my size and cute as a button."

Loretta marched over to run interference and redirect his attention to the redhead. "Your favorite's right over here." She pointed to Ellen, who was glaring at Casey.

"Sorry about that," said Loretta. "Nice job tonight. Clean up the glasses out here, and then you can go." The somewhat warmer, friendlier Loretta was back.

Casey circled the pool gathering up glasses, giving Santa and Ellen a wide berth as she passed them smooching on one of the lounge chairs. She made one last trip to the pool area to grab her tote and whistle softly for Isabella, who was waiting patiently under Petey's table. As she entered the house, she was surprised to see Loretta slow dancing cheek to cheek with her arms around a man's neck in the middle of the room. Casey tried not to stare, but this new man looked like Paul Newman. She made it to the kitchen area before Loretta noticed her, stopped dancing, and joined her.

"Forget you saw that," she said. "He came a little too early." Loretta quickly escorted her to the door and tucked an envelope into Casey's bag.

On the way back to the station, Casey shook her head. Not too hard to figure out what was going on. One by one—or rather, two by two—they disappeared to the upper rooms. Bet the women were making more than $300. Loretta had told her Kennedy was a jealous man. She was playing with fire with Paul Newman. But why the camera? That was the most disturbing part.

Thinking about it, she realized that Kennedy was never in the pool area. Never on camera. Neither was Paul Newman, but that was easy to understand if Loretta was fooling around.

Casey hadn't done anything wrong, but she felt sullied if a little richer.

Chapter Thirty-Three

Walking down Station Road with just the streetlights from nearby Church Street to guide her, Casey's mind worked overtime, replaying details of the evening. Had she just been working for a madam in a suburban brothel, or was it a swinging singles party? The men and women seemed paired up by a previous arrangement. The men knew each other, and the women were friends and had met Petey before. The chubby fellow she'd dubbed Santa didn't seem to remember that the elfin woman was for him until Loretta redirected him. Clearly, they'd all come for sex, although Casey hadn't seen Loretta and Paul climb the stairs to the bedrooms. Maybe that was yet to come, so to speak.

Kennedy—or at least Fisher—had to know what was going on because of the hidden camera. Was Kennedy checking up on Loretta? Or was it for protection in case there was trouble with any of the guests? Not likely. If they needed protection, Loretta could just call down Chuckles or Mr. Clean or whatever the refrigerator-sized man was called. Vlad, his name was Vlad. More likely, the recording would or could be used as blackmail. She'd overheard some banter between the men about cutting class, yet they were middle-aged men, and seemingly affluent by their manner and dress. Could be they were attending an executive ed class or a conference and having a bit of sport on the side.

Was it just entertainment for bored suburban housewives? Or entrapment? Along with money, the other probable lures were power and influence.

Earlier, when she dressed for the day, she'd wondered how low she would go to prostitute herself for the Kennedys. Ha! She hated being treated like a servant, pushed and ordered about like a pawn. But her basic authority resistance had warred with her curiosity, and yes, if she were honest, the extra money. She'd been scraping by ever since she came to New England.

The sooner she could distance herself from the scene, the better. She was on the recording serving those involved in possibly illegal activity. She'd bumped into trouble, and she sure didn't need any. She'd have to figure out how to extricate herself from any future dealings.

Another thought. Petey knew the names of the women, or at least the names they used in their evenings out, so this had to have been going on before the Kennedys moved to Welton. Maybe the operation was shut down elsewhere and needed a new place of operations fast, given the demands of their clientele.

Loretta hadn't been straight with her. She knew the men were coming for the evening, yet she'd lured Casey for the afternoon with a three-hundred-dollar babysitting/serving arrangement. Casey hadn't figured out the scene when she agreed to serve dinner—the action began afterwards.

She unlocked the caboose, turned on the light, and went to the storage closet to put her ill-gotten gains into the safe. She twirled the dial back and forth to the combination numbers and opened the door. What better place to store the money than in the safe the police had already emptied?

She reached into her tote and retrieved the envelope Loretta had tucked into it and opened it. Not three one-hundred-dollar bills. Five. Either a lapse of memory, or an outrageous tip. Or hush money. Loretta may have realized how uncomfortable Casey had become and paid five hundred to buy her silence and keep her quiet and happy, especially after Casey had seen her with Paul Newman. She felt dirty.

She shuddered as the walls of the storage closet seemed to close in around her. She shouldn't be here late at night alone without Mace, but she needed to do one more thing. Both Petey and Loretta knew the current combination to the safe. She placed the money inside, punched the reset button, and changed the combination to the last three digits of her Social Security number.

As she walked through the caboose to the front door, the overhead lights illuminated her, vulnerable for all to see. "Let's go, Bella." With shaky fingers, she shut the lights and relocked the door. She and Bella ran to the station.

Inside, she settled into her rocker wrapped in an afghan. Should she call Fortune? What could he do? She could ask him about the fingerprints and the gun, but maybe it was too early to expect results. Well…she should be able to dream up a good excuse and call him first thing.

She was too wired to sleep. Think about it, girl. You are the one who made all the arrangements for the new tenants—set up the accounts, withdrew money, paid bills. If there's something crooked going on, which certainly seemed to be the case, what was her liability? She'd arranged it all. She'd even involved her old buddy, another ex-con, in the cleaning. Not good. Agnes hadn't done anything other than rent the place, and Casey couldn't even find a rental agreement. Maybe she should reconsider contacting the police.

Little Mother nudged her leg for attention, and Casey coaxed her into her lap. As she petted the kitty, random thoughts swirled like dust motes. Her tenuous security could be in serious jeopardy. If they had a camera at poolside, why not upstairs as well? Exhausted, she finally succumbed, and the rocker stopped.

Chapter Thirty-Four

Thursday, 11/3

She awoke the next morning with the unsettling sense that someone was watching her. She opened her eyes slowly and laughed. Little Mother and Isabella sat side by side in front of the rocker staring up at her. When the rocker moved, both fur friends turned and marched toward their dishes in the kitchenette.

Casey checked the time. It was late for her. She must have been really tired to sleep sitting up in a chair until seven o'clock. After feeding the beasts and brewing herself a pot of coffee, she collected her newspaper and led the parade outside to the platform. She'd distract herself with a puzzle. Looking around, she could use some plants, a few inside and a planter or two outside. Maybe a pot at the front door. She closed her eyes and basked in the sun, enjoying the morning quiet, broken only by the sound of an occasional car passing over the Church Street bridge.

The telephone shrilled inside. Casey ignored it and let the call go to her answering machine. She didn't want to speak with either Fisher or Loretta, who would expect her to jump at their every command. Enough. She'd maintain the property. Period. No more special requests. No more parties. She wasn't a babysitter, a cook, or a…enough. Too much negativity. Today, she'd buy a few flowers, paint, take a drive to the ocean, or—

Isabella launched herself off the platform and dashed around the side of the station towards the front.

Casey put her coffee down and listened. Nothing. She entered the station and walked through to the front window and peered out. No one at the door or by the caboose.

A movement inside the Muttmobile gave Petey away. He sat behind the wheel talking to Isabella who rode shotgun.

Casey grabbed her keys and purse and opened the door. Petey jumped out of the car and ran toward the steps up the hill.

"Wait," Casey called. "It's okay."

He stopped and looked over his shoulder, eyes big as if he expected a reprimand.

"Get in. Let's go for a ride."

Petey turned and cocked his head.

Casey slid into the driver's side, reached over, and opened the passenger door. "I'm off to the dump. Don't worry. It's just down the street. You'll have to share the front seat with Bella."

Petey approached slowly and then obediently got in, buckled up, and sat holding Isabella in his lap.

As she drove, Casey showed off the Muttmobile's unique features, pressing the left turn signal to make the Great Dane dog head hood ornament twirl left, pressing the right signal for the opposite direction. When she held either signal down, the head rotated a full three hundred and sixty degrees. Petey laughed and relaxed. Next, she hit the horn, startling both Bella and Petey with the howl of barking dogs. She'd purchased the Muttmobile from an MIT geek who had a dog walking business and a sense of humor. Enough. She decided to keep the siren and portable flashing light device for a later ride.

At the dump, she gathered books from the back seat and led Petey to the swap shop. She took her time exchanging books, giving Petey time to dawdle and poke around. "See anything you like?" she asked.

After Petey chose a book about a train, he circled around a child's bicycle a few times. Clearly, he wanted it, but was afraid to ask.

What would Loretta think if Casey chucked the bike into the Muttmobile and let him ride around the station parking lot? What did she care what

Loretta thought? She wouldn't serve guests, but if Loretta asked if Petey could come down to play, Casey would agree. Maybe not a sleepover, though. She didn't know about the strange vagrant that must have visited the caboose. He was probably safe, but he hadn't come during the day or made himself known to her.

Petey's jaw dropped as she wheeled the bike to the rear of the Muttmobile, opened the hatch and hoisted it inside. She gave him a thumbs up, he hopped into the front seat with Bella, and they were off with new treasures.

At the station, Casey and Petey jumped out of the Muttmobile, eager to unload their dump picks. Just as Casey opened the hatch of the car to get the child's bike, Chance's green Jag drove down the Station Road. She waved to him as he pulled over and rolled down the window.

Chance looked at Petey and frowned. "Whenever I come, you have company."

Casey shrugged and introduced Chance and Petey, and then turned her attention to the bike. As she pulled on the handlebars, one of the pedals caught on the upholstery. She'd have to climb in to extricate it. Unloading the bike would be harder than chucking it in.

Chance watched from inside his car while she crawled into the back of the hatch and freed the pedal.

She backed out and, with a decisive yank, both bicycle and Casey tumbled backward to the ground.

"Nice move, Grace."

Casey ignored Chance's sarcastic remark, got up, and righted the bike. Rolling it to Petey, it occurred to her that she didn't know if he could ride. Good grief! She didn't have a helmet for him. What if he fell and broke his head? She should have thought of that before snagging the bike. "Ever ride before?" she asked.

"Yup." Petey gave a wide smile. Like an old pro, he jumped on and pedaled around the drive.

"Phew," Casey exhaled. She dusted herself off and turned back to Chance. "Petey's the new tenant's boy. We just raided the swap shop at the dump."

"Time for him to go home?" suggested Chance with a suggestive smile.

"No, he's here for the morning. Join me for a cup of coffee?"

"Not what I had in mind. I'm just passing through on my way down to see my father. Some other time." He put the Jag into reverse, turned around, and drove off.

Huh? *Not what you had in mind?* Casey's ebullient mood morphed from delighted to confused to disappointed and pissed in seconds. No time for a little conversation? Couldn't get out of your fancy car to help me with the bike? Just dropped by for a roll in the hay. She should have sent him over to Loretta for a little afternoon delight. She slammed the hatch shut and grabbed her new book from the front seat. Then she slammed the front door for good measure.

Oh boy. Petey had stopped riding and was watching her with worry written on his face. Not his fault. Time for an attitude adjustment. "Sorry, champ. Looks like you know what you're doing."

"The man didn't like me. You're mad at me."

"The man doesn't know you. He's a spoiled brat. So am I. You didn't do anything wrong."

"What did he want?"

More than he got. "Doesn't matter, he's gone now. Let me see you make another spin around the drive."

Casey took her book and sat under the tree at the side of the parking lot with Isabella, pretending to read while Petey pedaled about. A few days ago, she hadn't objected when Chance had kissed her, so could she blame him for his behavior? Damn straight, she could! He was just plain arrogant and rude.

Wait a minute. "On my way down to see my father"? Had he just lied about his father a second time? Had she heard him correctly? Yes. Another lie. No question. She sure didn't like what she'd seen of him today. She didn't need more drama in her life. He was delicious and she was hungry, but no need to be a fool.

"Vroom! Vroom!" Petey twisted the hand grips on the bike as if he were riding a motorcycle. He popped a wheelie and rode over to her with a big grin. "Thank you."

CHAPTER THIRTY-FOUR

Casey laughed. "You're welcome. How about a sandwich?"

Inside the station, Casey let Petey explore while she prepared grilled cheese sandwiches. When she called him to the table, he sat obediently, put his napkin in his lap, and lowered his head.

Oh no, he's expecting me to say grace. Casey took Petey's hand. He looked up, startled by her touch. "In my family, we just hold hands and say, 'Glad to be together.' Will you say it with me?" He nodded, and they spoke the words in unison. Casey noted the boy's excellent manners, chewing with his mouth closed, "please" and "thank you."

Petey finished his sandwich and drink, and then looked up at Casey as if asking permission to speak.

"What?" Casey prompted with a smile.

"May I leave the bike down here?"

Why wouldn't he want to take it with him? "Sure. We can store it in the caboose when you're not here, but don't you want to ride it at home?"

Petey shook his head and looked down.

"Doesn't your Aunt Loretta like you to ride?" Casey worried. Maybe she shouldn't have encouraged him. "Would she be unhappy to know you have a bike down here?"

Petey frowned at her question and chewed the inside of his mouth.

Casey waited.

He practically whispered his next words. "She threw away the bike my mother gave me."

Casey squeezed his hand. "Okay. No problem. It stays down here."

Just then, a bell clanged from the top of the hill.

"Miss Olga." Petey's mouth turned down. He rose and took his plate to the sink. At the door, he turned with a small smile. "Thank you."

Casey followed his slow progress up the stone steps to the White House. She wouldn't become more involved with the adults in the Kennedy compound, but she'd do whatever she could to help that lonely little boy.

With a heavy heart, she called LouAnne and left a message on her answering machine. "Friend, I could use some good company and advice. Any chance I could lure you two to dinner tomorrow?" She ignored her own messages.

Chapter Thirty-Five

Friday, 11/4

The next morning, Casey braved a downpour while shopping for food and flowers for dinner and then puttered about inside the station, alternately delighting in her new domesticity, worrying about the crazy tenants in the White House, and daydreaming about her diminishing romantic prospects. A cop, for heaven's sake, a rude liar and swindler, a mad artist cousin who'd moved to Rhode Island, and a former lover in Ohio who did her dirt. It was more rewarding to slice and dice vegetables and bake a pie.

Around six, LouAnne and Rosie arrived with wine and hugs. Casey served a pork roast with fixings and then surprised them with apple pie *à la mode* for dessert. During dinner, the conversation centered around the couple's work at the women's center and LouAnne's pregnancy. Afterwards, they settled in around the woodstove to offset the chill from the storm, which had picked up again outside. Rosie stretched his long form out on the old church pew, LouAnne draped herself in the lounge chair, and Casey rocked next to the stove with Isabella curled in her basket at her side. Little Mother presided from above in the loft.

"Now tell Lou what's going on. You sounded worried in your message," prompted LouAnne.

"I think the Kennedys are running a high-end brothel and taking pictures, maybe for blackmail. I stupidly agreed to watch Petey for Loretta while she had—"

"Back up," interrupted Rosie. "Remind me about Petey and Loretta."

"Sorry. Petey's this great little boy, seven, who visited the caboose and fell in love with Isabella. He's come to play a few times. Loretta is Mrs. Kennedy. I thought she and her husband were Petey's parents, but he calls them aunt and uncle."

"Uh-huh. Always a sucker for animals and little kids," said Rosie.

LouAnne shushed Rosie with a wave of her hand. "Go on."

"Loretta asked me to serve snacks and watch Petey while she had friends at the A-frame for the afternoon. For $300. Not bad at all, so I agreed. At first, it was only three lovely young women and Loretta, but then William Kennedy and three gentlemen arrived. Loretta surprised me by expecting me to cook and serve dinner. Okay. Kennedy left after a round of drinks. Dinner went without a hitch, mainly because of our earlier experience with the grill.

"But after dinner, they split into couples and began to repair two by two to the bedrooms upstairs. I bailed after one of the drunken men came for me. When I got back to the caboose, I found that Loretta had stuffed $500 into my tote."

"Damn good money!" chuckled Rosie.

"Uncomfortable for sure, but why the worry?" asked LouAnne.

"If the law comes for them, I'm implicated in a crime. I'm on camera as a participant in the evening. And I arranged everything for them at the White House. Remember I told you their names don't appear on anything. I can't even find a rental agreement. And now I've accepted $500 for serving the ladies and their johns."

"Were you on camera when Loretta paid you?" asked Rosie.

"No, but one of the men did make a pass at me in plain view."

"Let's think on it a bit. You worry too much, sugar. You didn't do anything wrong." LouAnne rose and began clearing dishes.

"Don't do that! You're my company." Casey objected and followed.

"Remember our old rule. 'He who cooks, don't clean.' You sit and worry. This will take but a minute."

Isabella jumped up, ears forward. Seconds later, she dashed to the door, jumped through the cat flap, and disappeared.

Rosie put his fingers to his lips and whispered, "Keep talking." He unlatched the rear sliding door and stepped outside into the dark and rain.

LouAnne watched Rosie disappear, arms akimbo. "You've had visitors to the caboose before, haven't you?"

"Yes, but never while I was home with the lights on," Casey replied. "The first guy took some old clothes and ran. Then there was a phony cop. And a few nights ago, I thought I saw a light in the caboose window as I drove down the road to the station. The phony cop showed again on Halloween. Really spooked me." She told LouAnne about the P.I. who was looking for Hobo and who shot her pumpkin.

"Now that's a worry," said LouAnne. They continued talking softly, but their attention was focused outside. Casey couldn't hear anything above the wind and rain. Moments later, the front doorbell rang.

Casey peered through the peephole before opening the door.

Rosie pushed a tall, bedraggled man into the room. "Sit," he commanded, pulling out a dining chair.

Isabella popped through the cat flap and trotted to the man. He ruffled her ears. She shook, giving them all a shower.

Hobo, thought Casey. "You're the man who lived in the caboose before we bought it."

The man glanced up but didn't speak. He wore a filthy Red Sox baseball cap over dark, stringy hair that reached his shoulders. Most of his face was covered by a dense black beard. His sopping wet clothing clung to his emaciated frame. Casey felt a wave of déjà vu remembering another bearded, dark-haired man who had camped out under the Church Street bridge a few years back. The man before her now wore the red flannel shirt that had been taken from the caboose.

Rosie nudged the man to answer. He nodded assent but remained silent.

"I found the combination to the safe inside Isabella's collar. The police have your gun and money." Casey rose and went to the desk and retrieved an envelope. She carried it to Hobo. "I made a copy of the picture."

He opened it slowly and gazed at the photo of the young woman. He hung his head and stifled a sob.

Casey waited a moment before continuing. "They found the body of an unidentified man in the woods close to where the caboose was. They're calling it a homicide. I'm sure they would be interested in speaking with you."

"No!" blurted the man, fixing his dark eyes on Casey. "I'm dead!" He shifted in the chair. "I'm better off dead." His whole body began to shiver uncontrollably.

"Come close to the fire and dry off," said Rosie. He draped his leather jacket around the man's shoulders. Casey and LouAnne walked to the kitchenette and put the kettle on for coffee to give the man time to regain his composure.

When they returned, Rosie pulled up a chair next to the man. "Talk to us. What's your name?"

Hobo gazed about the room, avoiding eye contact, gripping the mug of coffee with white knuckles to keep it from shaking. When he spoke, his voice was low and gravelly and occasionally broken as if he weren't used to talking. "Jim." He shook his head and sipped his coffee. "How to explain if you weren't there?"

Rosie put his hand on the man's shoulder. "Nam?"

Jim nodded.

"Trinity, 3rd Marines," said Rosie, tapping his chest.

"Huh." Jim looked up and met Rosie's eyes and offered his free hand to shake. "Eleventh Cav, halftrack commander. Two tours. Medical Discharge."

It was as if the men were speaking a different language, but Casey knew not to interrupt.

"He served in the Army," Rosie translated for the women. He turned back to the man. "Small tanks that cleared paths in the jungle. Rough duty."

Casey returned to the kitchen to warm up what was left from dinner. Minutes later, she came back with a full plate and cutlery.

The man's eyes bulged when he saw the food. They sat in silence while he devoured the meal. He didn't refuse when LouAnne swapped his empty

152

plate for pie. "Mighty thankful," he said, licking his lips. "Didn't think you'd see me with the storm and all. I was so cold. I couldn't stay outside another night."

"We bought the caboose two years ago. Where have you been all this time?" Casey asked.

"Lived rough for a bit. Worked a farm a year or so and then found this address through the caboose sale record. I wondered if anyone had been able to open the safe, so I hitched down here. I've been using the empty rooms over the garage at the big house until the people moved in."

That explains why the sighting of Hobo at the caboose and the rental coincided, thought Casey.

"I was safe there for a while and could take a little money at a time from the safe. Until last week." He glanced at Isabella's new collar. His face cracked into a smile for the first time as he looked to Casey. "Thanks for taking Isabella."

"What happened over there?" Rosie's voice was gentle. "Why are you living rough?"

Jim shifted in his chair and was silent for a long minute.

"I was trail sweep after a firefight. Bodies everywhere. Heard screaming and ran to a hut where four of ours were taking turns with a young local woman. I ordered them to stop. 'Spoil sport,' my sergeant said and shot the girl in the face." Jim swallowed hard and closed his eyes for a moment. "Then he turned on me, laughed, and shot twice." Jim touched the side of his head and his chest. "They found me in a pile of bodies when they counted up the day's kill. I don't remember anything till I was Stateside in the psych ward at the VA. Been a long road home."

"Why 'better off dead'?" asked Rosie.

Jim shook his head. "Long story."

Rosie fetched another log and fed the stove. They watched it catch fire and waited until he spoke.

"When I could talk about what had happened, no one wanted to listen. Some didn't believe me. But finally, I was interviewed by a reporter at a local paper. I told about my experience and about the 'kill boards' that tallied who had killed the most people that was used for rewards. Not just enemies. The saying went, 'If it's dead and Vietnamese, it's VC.' Vietcong. But these were innocent young girls.

"The reporter contacted the Army to corroborate the facts. Army brass swooped in and suppressed the story for damage control. There had already been too much bad press on our conduct in the war. I was treated as a whistleblower. They scuttled the article. Sarge was their new poster boy, a high school football star, now a decorated war hero, running for mayor. I was a threat to him and to the Army."

"How long were you in the hospital?" asked Rosie. Casey refreshed the coffee as Cap regrouped. Telling his story was hard work and he seemed to be tiring.

"First, they saw to my wounds, and later I was treated for serious anxiety issues. The counselors did what they could to get me to forget the horrors and concentrate on the future. When I was discharged, I retreated to our old family camp up in New Hampshire by the river. One night, coming back from fishing, I watched three men douse and torch it. Nothing I could do, outnumbered with only a handgun.

"I paddled my canoe downstream. A vagrant charged me $10 for his license, and I became James Jones. No body was found in the fire, so they knew I was still alive. A little later, I discovered the caboose. I contacted my brother Alex, and he brought me money and clothing. They must have followed him. Found out where I was."

"Sorry for so many questions, but one more. Who is the dead body in the woods?" asked Rosie.

Jim shook his head. "A vet I met in a soup kitchen. He stayed with me in the caboose a while. Jerry. Don't know his last name. I gave him some clothes. One morning early, he walked into the woods to do his business. I heard a shot. Must've been a sniper. Dead center forehead. No way to identify him. I ran.

"My brother Alex was convinced I was dead. He claimed the body and had it buried. Even posted an obituary. It's for the best." His voice rose. "I'm officially dead unless you resurrect me. Alive, I'd be a danger to family and...to Emily." He nodded to the picture Casey had shown him.

Rosie had been studying Jim as he spoke. "Could be what you say is true. Or could be you tell a good story. What's your full name? Why should we believe you?"

"Fair enough. Captain James Ferguson." He removed his cap and pushed his hair aside, uncovering a long scar on his scalp. He shrugged off Rosie's coat, unbuttoned his shirt, and bared another hideous scar from a gunshot wound in his shoulder.

Casey winced. "What's the sergeant's name?"

"Wilson. Sergeant Bennet Wilson. Butch for short."

Chapter Thirty-Six

J im's revelation of Wilson's name convinced Casey that the man was indeed Hobo. The hour was late, and with rain still pelting down outside, Casey had a decision to make. She rose and gathered bedding from the storage area under the loft and asked Rosie to help set up Jim overnight in the caboose.

"You sure?" Rosie asked.

"Yes. It's too late to find another place. He should be safe. I think Wilson was convinced that there was nothing left in the safe that could help him locate Jim."

As Rosie walked Jim to the door, Jim turned. "Thank you." Casey tossed Rosie the keys to the caboose, and they ducked out the door.

LouAnne was already brewing more coffee. When Rosie returned, they sat around the table. Although the decision was Casey's, her friends' opinions were important. For the next hour, they discussed Jim's story and Casey's experience with Wilson, the contents of the safe, and the fact that there was now a dead man bunking in the caboose. Casey was amazed that he had managed to live above the garages at the White House undetected, although no one had been living there for over a year. LouAnne liked the idea of having a strong man around because Casey was so vulnerable living solo in the station with no close neighbors.

"How about I call him a distant cousin who is out of work, maybe laid off, and I need to hire someone to do maintenance. You know, mow, trim, do the garbage, clean the gutters…the things my real cousin Jackson took care of when he lived over the garages."

They mulled over this idea for a bit. "Where would he stay?" asked LouAnne.

"I guess in the caboose, for now. I doubt that the Kennedys would want him to live on their property. I feel bad that Jim's money is held by the police, where he can't get it unless he wants to join the living again. He seems to think that if he's alive, his brother and Emily will also be endangered."

None of them had any idea if Jim was breaking any law or if his brother Alex or lady friend knew he was alive. They agreed that until they could come up with a better plan, Jim was better off dead. Casey's experience and everything Jim said about Wilson and the other members of his military company, convinced them that Jim would be a target if he reappeared.

"As soon as we can figure out how to do it, we need to get Jim far away from here," said Rosie. "Wilson's dangerous and has already been here twice."

"You're probably right, but I watched Jim when I gave him the photograph. He doesn't want to leave Emily behind," Casey said. "I think that photo went to Vietnam and back. Sounds like he was also close to his brother."

LouAnne rose. "Low profile for him for sure. See if he'll agree to work for his board."

Casey walked them to the door.

"Take care, girlfriend," LouAnne said as she and Rosie both gave her a hug and left.

Casey walked to the window of the kitchenette and looked over at the caboose where there was still a light shining. What had she agreed to? She believed Jim's story and felt it was the right thing to help him, a man who had been attacked and severely wounded and spent years in rehab at the VA. But he was a target, so endangered that he had willingly become a non-person, someone living under the radar. She wasn't as convinced as LouAnne that having him around made her safer. More like the opposite.

The Army brass and the people at the VA didn't want to hear his story. Why did she and her friends? There were always two sides to a story. He could be a sicko who she just foolishly invited into her life. Somehow, she didn't really believe that in her gut, but she could feel the muscles in her chest tighten in anxiety. So much for the simple, idyllic life in a quaint little railroad station. She called her fur friends up to the loft. Under the covers, she listened to the rain pound on the roof, unable to let go of the new worry, practicing the breathing exercises she'd learned in prison to release tension.

Chapter Thirty-Seven

Saturday, 11/5

The next morning, Casey carried two steaming mugs of coffee to the caboose and was surprised to see Jim sitting on the metal steps and pulling on his heavy work boots. He accepted the coffee with a smile and invited Casey to join him inside where they could sit at a pull-down wooden table.

Jim got right to the point. "What's the verdict?"

"We believe you and agree with you that you're better off dead, at least for now." She sipped her coffee before continuing. "I'm sorry that the police have your money and gun, but there's nothing to do about that unless you want to be resurrected. As a temporary solution, would you consider helping me out with maintenance in exchange for room and board and a base salary? I can offer you what I'd pay a contractor to do mowing and trimming around the White House and the A-frame. You'd have to agree to keep a very low profile. There's no guarantee that Wilson won't return if he learns you're here."

"Believe me, I know how to lay low," said Jim. "That's very generous of you."

"I could use the help, and I'd feel a bit safer with another pair of eyes around here. Speaking of which, you need to know that the new tenant has installed a camera under the eaves at the station to check on my comings and goings and my visitors." She pointed through the caboose window to the overhang above the front door. "I don't believe the camera range extends to the caboose, but you're being watched any time you enter or leave the station."

"That's very strange. Why not take it down if it bothers you?"

"Good idea. With you here, I think it's time to trash it." She was tired of Fisher's intrusive behavior and also thought it would be best if he weren't asking questions about the new man, Jim. She looked at him with a critical eye. "Do you have any other belongings to bring inside?"

"I have two other shirts and another pair of jeans and underwear, but they're rather…"

"Leave them outside the door. I have a washer-dryer in the station. I'll collect them when I bring you soap and a razor. Don't take it personally, but you could use a little cleanup. If you'll let me, I'll cut your hair. Wilson will still recognize you, but you won't stand out like a mountain man in Welton. When you're ready for breakfast, come on over to the station."

"I really can't thank you enough."

"We'll see what you think after the haircut." Casey carried the mugs back to the station and was surprised that Isabella followed her inside. "You my dog or his?" Isabella wagged and led Casey to her bowl.

Minutes later, the phone rang. Casey considered blowing it off, but then dutifully picked up after four rings.

"What was all the commotion last night? Who were those people?" Of course, it was Fisher.

"Friends and a…cousin. Why do you care?" Casey's normally polite manner was fraying. She didn't wait for an answer. "I'll be showing the maintenance man the equipment shed behind the White House today, so don't be surprised if you see us on the property. We'll set up a convenient mowing and trimming schedule with the Kennedys soon." She hung up and launched the phone into the cradle.

Next, she set about collecting a razor and soap, shampoo and a toothbrush and extra towels and took them to the caboose. She swapped the toiletries for the dirty laundry that Jim left outside the door and returned to the station.

While the clothes were in the washing machine, she retrieved a stepladder from the storage area under the loft and set it under the eaves over the front door. She donned a pair of gloves and carried a set of pliers and clippers as she climbed up the three steps. With a couple of hard tugs, she wrenched the camera from its lodging, clipped the wires, and dropped it to the ground. With a satisfied grin, she grabbed a hammer from her toolkit and smashed the offending machine to bits.

She jumped to the side at laughter behind her.

"Didn't waste any time," said Jim. His damp hair wet the shoulders of a clean shirt. Without whiskers, he was a nice-looking man, if rather gaunt with high cheekbones, a straight nose, and heavy eyebrows.

She waved the heavy clippers. "Ready?"

He backed off a step before he realized she was teasing.

Inside the station, she set him up in a chair in the kitchen area and wrapped a towel around his neck. "Just a trim, a hippy tail, or short?"

"Short."

"Okay." She bit her lip and took aim, clipping away, doing her best with regular scissors. "This is just temporary. Once we get you situated with clothes and the like, you can get a real haircut." She made sure to leave shaggy dog bangs in front and side to cover the scar on his temple. Neither talked much. She was concentrating, and he seemed naturally reticent.

Casey stood back to survey her work. She stifled a smile with a non-committal shrug. "There's a mirror in the bathroom over in the corner. See what you think." As he walked away, she whispered, "Forgive me." She heard him chuckling in the bathroom. Time for breakfast. Maybe she could make it up to him with food. She fried up a hearty breakfast of bacon and eggs and toast as Jim wandered around the station.

Casey called him to the table. "After we eat, we need to go shopping for a few necessities. This afternoon, I'll show you the equipment shed behind the White House. How's that sound?"

Jim nodded agreement. He was too involved in chowing down to speak.

Over the next few hours, they drove the Muttmobile to several locations. At the first stop, they focused on spending Loretta's largesse on clothing—a winter coat and shoes and personal items. Then they dropped by the dump and picked up a few dishes and pots and pans, and a stool. Next, Casey purchased bedding for the caboose as well as a new coffee maker and cutlery at a home goods store in Welton. When the Muttmobile was full, they returned and unloaded before making one last trip to buy groceries for both Casey and Jim for the week.

They agreed that they'd done enough for one day and that Jim's introduction to the maintenance equipment could wait. Casey left Jim to arrange the new goods in the caboose and returned to write in her journal. She decided against including Jim's history in case the notebook fell into the wrong hands. She made a new entry for "Caboose expenses" and recorded the personal items they had purchased for Jim under a "Miscellaneous" category.

Casey was aghast at the dent the expenditures made in her savings. She would eventually be reimbursed for Jim's maintenance work, but in the meantime, she might have to consider working another party at the A-frame.

Chapter Thirty-Eight

Sunday, 11/6

The next morning, Casey looked out the front window of the station. Petey rode around the parking lot wearing Jim's new Red Sox cap. Jim sat on the metal steps of the caboose with Isabella at his side, cheering on Petey as the boy navigated an obstacle course they'd made from stones and bricks, his very own bicycle rodeo.

At the ding of a timer, she removed sticky buns from the oven, a favorite from her childhood, and now fuel for a growing boy and a recovering vagrant.

When the phone rang, she waited until she heard the caller's voice on the answering machine before deciding to let it go. Fisher's insistent voice demanded she give him a call. He was probably pissed off that she'd offed the camera. She'd ignore him for a while. She vowed not to jump every time he ordered. He could cool his heels. She had a life. Well, she was developing one.

A Welton police cruiser rolled to a stop at the edge of the drive. Fortune got out and waved to Petey and then stopped abruptly when he noticed Jim sitting on the metal steps of the caboose. Casey intercepted him as he walked toward the station.

He greeted her with a warm smile and a question in his eyes. She waved Petey and Jim over. "You've met Petey, and this is my cousin Jim." Fortune bent and shook hands with Petey and then straightened to shake with Jim.

"Mike Fortune, Welton police."

"Come on inside, everyone. I've just baked sticky buns." Casey led the parade of men, boy, and dog into the station.

"Smells great!" exclaimed Fortune. They sat around the dining table while Casey served buns all around, and coffee for the adults. After not one but two buns, Fortune addressed Casey. "I have news and a question for you." Jim seized the opportunity to bow out and challenged Petey to a game of cards in the caboose.

"Busy woman," Fortune commented, watching them leave. "Thought your relatives were in Ohio."

"Some are, but Jim comes from New Hampshire." She didn't offer any further explanation.

After a few seconds of silence, Fortune leaned forward and spoke. "First, news. The gun from the safe is military issue as we suspected, but we have no way to trace ownership. The autopsy determined that the body found in the woods was killed by a rifle shot to the head. Fingerprint analysis identified that the man who was living in the caboose was Captain James Ferguson, the fellow you called Hobo. His brother Alex Ferguson claimed and buried the body."

Casey nodded as if the information were new to her. "Any clues as to who might have killed him?" she asked.

"No. The New Hampshire police are investigating."

"Sad. So sad." Casey's reaction was honest, although she was withholding information about Jim's appearance. She looked up at Fortune. "Did you serve?"

"I was lucky. Pulled desk duty in Germany in 1968."

While I was in prison. "And now, your question?" Casey was eager to change the subject.

"Do you have contact information for Chauncey Cunningham, the man I met here last week?"

"No, sorry. I think he may be up in Maine interviewing with a friend."

Fortune frowned and studied her. "No phone number?"

Casey shook her head. "I've only seen him twice recently—both times he was passing through on his way north or south." *I don't know which because he was lying.* "Why? Is everything okay?" She paused for a moment. "He said his father was dying," she added.

"Nothing serious. I checked his license plate after leaving last week," Fortune admitted with a sheepish grin. "I'm rather protective of my friends. Authorities in North Carolina would like to speak to him about a legal matter." Before Casey could ask another question, he added, "And no, they didn't explain."

"Now I have a question." Casey screwed up her courage. "What's the punishment for prostitution in Massachusetts?"

Fortune sat back, eyebrows raised, eyes wide.

Casey laughed. "Your expression is priceless. Not to worry, I already have an honest job managing the rental property. A friend asked me to find out."

"Sure. A friend with questions. Well, I'd have to check. It depends on who is being charged. They penalize pimps more than prostitutes, usually a combination of fines and prison time." The radio on Fortune's belt squawked. He apologized and walked outside to take the call. Casey watched him retreat, appreciating his rear profile and his air of confidence.

Moments later, he poked his head inside. "Gotta go. Thanks for the buns. Delicious."

Yes, delicious buns.

She walked to the caboose, knocked, and entered, interrupting Jim and Petey, hunkered over a serious game of cards. "Detective Fortune just confirmed the identification of the man..." she glanced at Petey, "...who lived in the caboose was Captain James Ferguson." She quickly headed off any questions with, "Who's winning?"

Petey scowled and pointed to Jim.

Chapter Thirty-Nine

Agnes

Monday, 11/7

Agnes stared at her toenails and decided she wasn't the Frisky Fuschia type. She'd just had her first-ever pedicure at the spa. How they babied you! Oiled and trimmed, and a leg massage. The latter had made her nervous and a bit self-conscious at first, but it felt so good she finally relaxed. Maybe a burgundy. Didn't really matter unless she wore open-toed pumps. Yes, with straps. Not too high because she still was uncertain with the heels.

The shrill ring of the telephone interrupted her reverie. She looked at the machine and waited for the answering machine to kick in. She had no desire to speak with Casey, and there weren't many others who had her number.

"Hello, this is Blair from Welton Real Estate calling. I have an update. I think—"

"This is Agnes Dempsey." She interrupted with a curt identification, thinking that it gave her control of the conversation.

"Oh, good to speak with you. May I call you Agnes?"

"Miss Dempsey is fine." Now Blair could speak her peace.

"Right. I thought you'd like to know that Mr. Kennedy contacted me and asked me to investigate properties—including yours—with similar acreage in the Boston suburbs. He may have a prospective investor looking for land to develop."

"Interesting. Did he give you a timeframe?"

"He pressed me to get back to him within a week or so. Size, valuation, zoning, existing structures, sales history. He sounds serious. He offered to pay me for a report."

Agnes tapped her new nose. "That's the same information I've asked you to find. I'm assuming you'll share the report with me."

"Well, if I do, I'll ask for an exclusive listing if you decide to sell. It's a lot of work."

"I'll consider it." Agnes ended the call without making a commitment. She sat back and considered a few alternatives. Would she even need a real estate agent if she could secure a private deal with Kennedy? The real estate commission on the sale of the White House properties would be huge. She shouldn't give that greedy agent time to get her hooks into him.

She glanced at her toes. No time to change the color now, she had to move fast and strike while the iron was hot, or whatever that saying was. She flipped open her address book, called the airline, and booked the next flight into Boston. Next, she dialed the Kennedys' number. When Loretta Kennedy answered, Agnes was annoyed and abrupt. "Tell Mr. Kennedy that Agnes Dempsey called and will be back in town at the end of the week." Finally, she fished out the business card of the man who had flirted with her on her last trip and considered contacting him. At the last minute, she thought better of it. All in good time. Unload the property first.

Chapter Forty

Fortune

Fortune answered the doorbell and escorted Anita into the living room. She sat and patted the couch next to her, but he chose a seat across from her over the coffee table.

"How've you been, Mike? I've only seen you twice since I got home. I was hoping we could spend some quality time together." She leaned back and crossed her long legs. Elegant as always, she'd come in cashmere with pearls, wool slacks, and some fancy brand of Italian flats.

He'd recognized her expensive signature perfume the minute he entered the room and was pleased that he couldn't remember what it was called. God, she was a beautiful woman. Beautiful and calculating. He sipped his beer while she did the lower-the-head-and-raise-the-eyes slowly ploy. Not going to work, sweetheart.

When Mrs. Fortune joined them, Anita rose and leaned forward to give her former mother-in-law a kiss on the cheek. Mrs. Fortune ducked aside at the last minute and asked if she would prefer coffee or tea.

Anita offered a naughty smile. "Either the sun's over the yardarm, or it's five o'clock somewhere. I'd love a glass of wine."

"I don't have any open. How about iced tea?"

"Sure, thanks."

After Mrs. Fortune left the room, Anita reached into a large designer bag and pulled out a handful of brochures which she spread out on the table facing Fortune. "These are a few of the schools my parents are investigating for Davey—most of them here in New England and two in France. They're willing to pay full tuition and board plus travel expenses, as you will see inside where I've added the prices in the margins. These are top-notch institutions—"

"We've already discussed this. I'm sure they're the very best money can buy," replied Fortune. He didn't lean forward to touch the brochures. "That's very generous of them." He let the topic hang. No way would he make this conversation easy for her.

His mother returned with a glass of tea and cookies for Anita and a cold beer and a smile for her son and then retired without a word.

Anita continued with her program. "As I told you before, that's why I came home. To select Davey's school, and of course, to see you. I've missed my son. And you."

"Shouldn't have left, but that's a separate issue." He sipped his beer and then placed the bottle on the coffee table, using a brochure as a coaster. "I seem to remember mentioning that Welton's public school system is—"

"Yes, yes. We both know how good it is. But the private schools offer so much more in terms of valuable contacts for the future, and an excellent placement record for college admissions."

"But they don't offer a parent."

"We didn't think you'd agree right away. Dad has hinted that we should hire a lawyer to sue for custody of Davey on the grounds that my family can offer so much more than…this." Her hand gesture indicated the house.

"Uh-huh. Good luck with that. You're a single woman living in France with her lover." Fortune couldn't keep the derision from his voice. Ha! He'd scored a frown and a downturned mouth, detracting from his ex's perfect portrait. "Why don't you marry him? You'd have a much stronger suit." Fortune stood to show their conversation was over. "I have to pick up Captain from training."

Anita pouted. "I was hoping we could go for a drink." She stood and walked to him.

"There is no 'we,' Anita." He walked a few steps toward the front door and then turned back to her. "Are you and Phillipe no longer together? Are you seriously considering returning to the States?" It would mean another emotional adjustment for Davey if she relocated.

"Only if there's something to come home to." She spoke in a breathy voice laden with longing.

Listen to her words. Always transactional; not unconditional. Would she consider returning if they got back together? Really? Or was she just trying to soften him up with a little fling. What's her game plan? He suspected that if he caved and sent Davey off to school, she'd be on the next plane to France. Follow the money. "I take it Daddy has given you an ultimatum: 'No more perks unless Davey goes to private school.'"

Anita's voice hardened as it followed him to the door. "Our legal counsel thinks we have a strong case. Nice as this little place is and as kindly as your mother has been, you're still a single working parent with a demanding job. You can't compare it to what my parents will give him. I don't need to remind you that we have joint custody."

He turned and in two strides, he was in her face. "No. You wanted an answer, and that's it. He's a little boy. He needs to live with a parent, not in a school. If you start throwing lawyers around, I'll be forced to respond, which I really do not want to do."

"Oh, come now, Mike. You know the mother always has the upper hand in a custody case."

"Not if she's unfit." He let his words sink in before continuing. "Not if the mother abandons her husband and child and leaves the country to live as a rich man's mistress in France.

Anita gave it one last shot. "For Davey's sake, I beg you, Mike, consider."

"For Davey's sake, Anita, no." He left without another word.

Chapter Forty-One

Casey

Tuesday, 11/8

C asey watched Jim screw a basketball hoop and backboard onto a long vertical two-by-four that he'd fastened to the platform end of the caboose. He had Petey holding tightly to the wooden beam, thinking he was helping, although it was safely secured. Man and boy worked well together. Earlier, Casey had given them rakes to clear leaves from the parking lot, which was now a basketball court, or at least half a court. She also asked Jim to move a few large tree logs into a circle where they could make fires in the evening.

She enjoyed having a strong, willing helper around, one who could do the heavy lifting. Jim earned his keep the day before on the riding mower around the White House, A-frame, and carriage house. She'd need to hire a professional outfit to cut down the high grasses of the fields, but that could wait until spring.

Time to water Agnes' plants and check for mail at the carriage house. As she and Isabella walked up Station Road, she reaffirmed her determination to make things work despite her discomfort with the Kennedys. It was an unusual arrangement, but her whole life had been a series of crazy events.

At the top of the hill, she was surprised to see the gate open. Kennedy definitely would not like that! She could expect a scold from Fisher. She frowned at an unfamiliar car in the drive next to the carriage house and picked up her pace. Could Agnes be back? She was about to insert the key, when a blonde middle-aged woman opened the door. She looked like the classic wealthy matron. The woman stared down at Casey with an expectant expression. Casey backed up a few steps, confused.

"Well?"

Ah, the voice. Beautifully made up, Agnes had lost a few pounds and was toned up. Her mousey, dishwater hair had been highlighted and professionally coiffed, and her nails manicured. But the voice was one thing Revlon couldn't alter. Casey looked closer. By far the biggest shock was the classy new nose. The hatchet had been reduced to a normal, appealing straight nose. Amazing changes in less than a month, with only a little telltale swelling under the eyes and in the cheeks. Agnes was stunning, if not beautiful. Her lace-up shoes had been discarded for Italian leather pumps. Mary's tailored suit looked tailor-made for her.

Casey managed a smile. "You take my breath away. When did you get back?"

"This morning. Why are you here?"

Glad to see you, too. "To water your plants. I wasn't expecting you."

Agnes remained in the doorway, not inviting Casey inside. "I'll be back for a while anyway. I may take a cruise in November." Spoken like a rich matron who owned three very valuable properties. "How are things with our tenants?"

"Very strange. I'd like to speak with you about a few matters."

"Not now. I've an appointment in Boston and a lunch."

"Did you get my messages?" Casey persisted.

"You worry too much. Just do what you must to keep them happy. You're certainly being paid enough." Agnes backed up but then turned abruptly. "Did you take my nail polish?"

Casey raised her hands, displaying short, unpolished nails, eyebrows raised as if confused. *Yes, but I'll let you wonder a bit.* She edged sideways and glanced into the sitting room where a copy of *Penthouse* was lying open on an ottoman. She suppressed a smile. "I moved the bills and records for the

White House to the station for convenience, because I'm managing them now. I couldn't find a copy of the rental agreement, so I can't tell if they're paying correctly."

Agnes didn't comment.

"I also found a copy of a letter Mary wrote to her stepson, Worthy. Very interesting. Even with her failing eyesight, she had unique strokes in her script." Casey paused to let her words sink in. Agnes' eyes narrowed. She was paying close attention. "You do remember that I have been teaching a course in handwriting analysis in Cambridge—"

"I don't place any stock in that stuff. Why you waste your time is beyond me." As she backed up to close the door, she added, "If you're going into town, pick up—"

"No plans for town today." *No plans anymore, anyway.* "Call when you have a moment." Casey offered a plastic smile, whistled for Isabella, and was off. She walked slowly back down Station Road, her mood arcing from surprise to disappointment to frustration. So much for any partnership or coordination with Agnes on the management of the property. She hadn't expected the woman to become her best buddy, but she seemed openly hostile. The comment about Mary's writing stopped her cold for a moment. Although Casey's comment about Mary's writing was true, she'd found the writing in Mary's desk over a year ago. Good. Let Agnes stew on it a bit.

On the positive side, Casey did have two new friends. Little Petey delighted her with his energy, curiosity, and laughter, and she enjoyed the company of the largely silent but kind and helpful new occupant of the caboose. She wasn't sure what to think of him staying there or how long he expected to be there. She didn't have references or history or anything other than the man's incredible story. An orphan and a hobo.

Deep in thought, her reverie was interrupted when she reached the bottom of the hill by shouts of two young voices and two men. Jim and Petey were challenging another man and boy about Petey's size. As she drew closer, she saw a police cruiser parked off to the side and recognized Fortune and Davey.

They paused the game when she came into view and walked over to greet her.

"I was hoping you and Petey would be here again this afternoon," said Fortune.

Davey walked forward with a shy, "Hello."

"Hi, Davey." Casey smiled at the smaller Fortune, who sported his father's dark hair and eyes with lashes any grown woman would die for.

Casey gestured toward a large pile of dry leaves at the end of the parking lot that the fellows had raked earlier. She'd love to burn them in the pit and throw in chestnuts and wait for them to pop the way she'd done with buckeyes in Ohio. "Can we burn leaves in Welton?" she asked Fortune.

"You need a permit from the Fire Department. I'll call it in."

"Thanks. I'll get a fire started. I have the makings for S'mores." Casey walked over to the circular fire area Jim had created earlier. She felt Fortune's eyes as she gathered twigs and sticks for kindling. Soon the pounding of the ball on the drive and the voices of the players resumed.

Fifteen minutes later, LouAnne and Rosie drove up in the van they used for the battered women's shelter where they worked. They piled out and joined the fray, dwarfing the wide-eyed little boys. Casey called Petey and Davey over. "Petey, why don't you show Davey how to open the safe." Davey's jaw dropped, and Petey's eyes lit up. They disappeared inside the caboose in a flash. Casey smiled, wondering how many times Petey would try to open the safe before he got frustrated. She'd changed the combination to the last three digits of her Social Security number when she left Loretta's payment inside.

Casey lit the fire and sat back as relaxed as she'd been in a long while, listening to the background noise of the basketball game. Using a sharp knife from the kitchen, she whittled the ends of sticks for marshmallows. The instant Rosie realized there was food in the offing, the game was called, and the players and boys joined Casey around the pit. Marshmallows were burnt to a crisp, dropped into the fire, and a few captured and sandwiched with chocolate inside graham crackers. The adults watched the boys and swapped stories around the fire. Jim was reserved but friendly and didn't miss any chocolate.

CHAPTER FORTY-ONE

All too soon, they heard the clanging of the bell from atop the hill.

"That's Petey's signal it's time to go home," explained Casey.

Petey's mouth was sticky and smeared with ash and chocolate, and his fingers looked positively gooey. His mouth turned down as he returned the Red Sox cap to Jim and ran up the stone steps to the White House.

"We should go, too. I think we wore Davey out." Fortune rose and signaled to his son.

"A tired boy is a good boy," said Casey.

"One of the tenets I live by," agreed Fortune. "Thank you for a great afternoon." He offered Casey a warm and genuine smile. "Nice to see you all," he said to the others as he bundled Davey into the cruiser and was off.

LouAnne grinned at Casey. "Whooooie!" She waved her hand as if she'd been burned. "You go, girl!"

Casey couldn't help but turn crimson. Quickly, she headed off any further comments from LouAnne by tossing the keys to the Muttmobile to Rosie. "Dump closes in a half hour. Down Church Street to the right. Can't miss it. There's bound to be something your outfit can use in the swap shop. I saw a desk and a set of pots and pans you could use at the shelter."

"They let us in?"

"Yup. You're driving a car with a genuine Welton sticker."

"Maybe get your cop friend to escort us les' they think we stole it."

Casey watched them drive away and then joined Jim by the fire. They sat in silence for a few minutes, enjoying the fresh fall air and the scent of the burning logs mixed with sugar.

"Thanks for the basketball rig," she said.

He nodded. "I like your friends. I guess it's okay to be around the cop. He doesn't seem overly curious."

"He has no reason to question you. You don't mind being dead?"

"The alternative is a second death. The government doesn't want to hear my story, and my unit would prefer me underground. I could use some peace." He hesitated. "I think the cop likes you."

"Ha! A cop and an ex-con. Exonerated or not, oil and water." Casey could tell by Jim's startled expression that Jim had no idea what she was talking about. "You shared your scars. I'll share mine." She showed him her arm and then filled him in about her years in prison, and also let him know that she and LouAnne had been cellmates. "Bunch of misfits. We've all had some chaotic years. I could use some peace as well. I'm glad you're here."

She gathered the remnants of wrappers and boxes and retired to the station. She was about to turn in when she noticed the blinking light on the answering machine. Damn! She'd forgotten all about the earlier call from Fisher that she'd blown off. Now there were three messages. Too late to call back now.

Chapter Forty-Two

Wednesday, 11/9

In the morning, Casey punched the button on the answering machine.

"Call me." Fisher's rude voice demanded.

She punched it again. "Call me immediately!" Fisher again at a higher pitch.

The third message was Agnes' whine. "Why don't you answer the phone?"

Just as Casey began dialing Fisher's number, the doorbell chimed for a full five seconds, followed by pounding on the door. Casey put down the phone and peered through the peephole. Lovely new Agnes scowled back at her.

"Careful there, you'll wreck your manicure," said Casey as she opened the door. Agnes stepped forward, but Casey didn't move from the threshold. "How may I assist you?" she asked in a sweet voice.

"You can answer the phone. I received a complaint from that Kennedy lawyer saying you were unresponsive." Again, Agnes advanced, but Casey didn't budge.

"The lawyer said you've been entertaining questionable friends and that a young man is staying in the caboose."

Questionable? Meaning black? How would Fisher know that? Another camera?

"Who are these people?" Agnes continued.

None of your business. "I'm not on call twenty-four hours a day."

"You won't be on call at all if you don't fulfill your duties and change your attitude."

Casey changed tack. "We've never discussed my responsibilities. Perhaps we can do so now. I understand that I'm to maintain services for the White House properties."

Agnes glared at Casey. Casey smiled back, maintaining eye contact.

"What if there were an emergency? You're to do whatever they want you to do—"

"I'm not gallivanting off to a spa, nor am I a servant. Mrs. Kennedy expects me to serve drinks and dinner. And babysit. Not part of the deal," broke in Casey.

"Find a caterer. A babysitter. How hard can that be? I'd rather not be bothered, but I could easily replace you with a reliable maintenance company. With your history, you'll be hard pressed to find another sweet deal like this one. I'm giving you fair notice. Do your job."

"Yes'm." Casey backed up and shut the door. She watched Agnes raise her chin and stomp five steps to a shiny new black sedan. The woman couldn't be bothered to walk down the lane. Or she wants me to see her fancy new wheels.

"Get a broom," Casey fumed. But Agnes held all the cards, and both she and Casey knew it. Nothing Casey could do but call Fisher and apologize. She lifted the receiver and dialed. One ring and a pickup.

"Hello, this is Casey. Sorry, I—"

"Call Mrs. Kennedy now. You have her number." Click.

Casey chucked the phone, her euphoric mood from the afternoon shattered by demanding masters. She fixed a smile on her face. Someone had told her that it was hard to be angry while smiling. It wasn't working. Before dialing, she took a few long breaths to bring down her heart rate and encourage an attitude adjustment. She needed the job.

Loretta answered on the third ring. "I'll need your help again Saturday. Come to the pool and we can discuss arrangements."

"Now?" But Loretta had already disconnected. This time, Casey scored by tossing the telephone into its cradle from two feet away. She was wearing ratty jeans and a sweatshirt, but she'd be damned if she'd change. "C'mon, Bella. The other Wicked Witch crooked her finger."

She worried her way up Station Road. What did Loretta expect this time? What was Casey willing to do? Could she refuse to serve when the men arrived? Heck, she was already on camera the once. It would probably be too cool in the evening to be outside where the camera was. If she wrote her thoughts and activities in her journal, would that be defense enough if the Kennedys were charged with a crime? Casey didn't even know if anything illegal was happening.

She walked through the gates and past the carriage house to the A-frame, entering through the back way leading directly into the pool area. Loretta sat in the sun on a lounger nursing a tall drink. She beckoned for Casey to join her. Casey turned her head away from the camera and walked to the table in Petey's corner and waved for Loretta to join her there. Loretta shook her head and pointed to the chair next to her. Casey ignored her, took a seat at the table, and waited.

Loretta rose and approached Casey. "What's your problem?" she asked, clearly irritated. She raised her glass for a sip but didn't offer Casey a drink.

"I prefer not to be on camera."

Loretta sat back and studied Casey and then looked down as if considering how to respond. Her voice lowered to a near whisper. "I understand." Her tone changed from preemptory and rude to soft and almost apologetic. "But I need help. William won't let me hire an outside catering service, and Olga refuses to serve."

"That doesn't explain the camera."

"I know." Her tone was confidential. "But the less you know, the better. William isn't a good man. He doesn't care about you or the girls or what they do. He wants to capture a few of the men on tape. That's already too much information." Loretta twisted her wedding band. She took a long drink from the glass before continuing. "Please, I know you're confused, but Petey and I need your help."

Now it was Casey's turn to study Loretta, who seemed to be genuinely distressed. "None of my business, but if you're unhappy, why stay? Why not get into one of those fancy cars and drive away?"

"It's not that simple." She covered her mouth with her hand. Casey glanced

179

at Loretta's face and frowned. Heavy makeup covered what looked to be a swollen and bruised cheek.

Loretta followed Casey's eyes. "Yes. He's violent." She rolled up a sleeve, revealing a deep bruise on her arm.

Casey could barely make out her next words.

"He says he'll kill me and Petey if we try to leave. And I need money to escape. He controls the accounts. The men here pay in cash, so..."

Casey got the drift. "This arrangement is far from a normal escort service," she said. She chewed her lip, considering the offer. Plenty of reasons to refuse, including arson, abuse, possible prostitution, and suggestions of blackmail.

Loretta reached out and took Casey's hand. "I've had to be cold and bitchy for show on camera, so I know why you dislike me. But for Petey's sake, please, please help me." With tears welling in her eyes, Loretta whispered, "I'm afraid. William doesn't trust me."

He shouldn't, and I'm not sure I should either. Casey looked down at Loretta's hand atop hers until Loretta removed it. They sat in silence.

What could Casey do? It would be hard to convince anyone that she had no idea what was going on, and she'd been paid an outrageous sum for an afternoon and evening of light labor. Petey frequented her caboose regularly, so authorities would assume she and the Kennedys were friends. Loretta was a woman in trouble, asking for help. What she did wasn't Casey's business. Not her problem. But she had become quite fond of the little boy. And she sure could use the money.

"Just one more night," begged Loretta.

"What do you need?" Casey acquiesced against her better judgment.

Chapter Forty-Three

Thursday, 11/10

The next morning, Casey rose determined to protect herself but not to overthink her situation. After two cups of coffee, she'd convinced herself that one more evening at the A-frame serving dinner wouldn't hurt anything and, indeed, would garner another five hundred dollars.

She was delighted when LouAnne called, but had to demur when Lou asked her to dinner Friday night. "Agnes returned yesterday," she explained. "She and Fisher are on my case for not being responsive. Agnes threatened to replace me with a maintenance service. I'm afraid I'll have to lie low for a bit. I need the job."

"Nasty. Well then, how 'bout we bring dinner to you? Maybe you could invite that cute cop and the fellow who's staying in the caboose. Not the harridan, though."

"You won't believe Agnes' physical transformation. The best makeover money can buy. Except for the voice and the personality, she's a handsome fifty-something, claws and all. And..." Casey hesitated, "I agreed to serve dinner at the A-frame Saturday. I didn't have much choice. Off camera, Loretta is totally different—a rather nice lady who needs money in order to leave her violent husband. She showed me a few ugly bruises."

"Huh. Interesting development. Guess money can't buy it all. I wouldn't worry about serving, 'ceptin' for the camera. You be careful, girl.

Something's off there."

Casey hung up and fussed about, decluttering the small space. Should she invite Fortune to dinner? She didn't have a home phone number. For that matter, where did he live? Casey stewed until noon when Jim showed up at the door.

"Any chance I could use your phone for a short call?" he asked.

"Sure, no problem. Rosie and LouAnne are coming to dinner tomorrow night if you'd like to join us," she added. He gave a thumbs-up. She left to give him privacy and drove to a local nursery where she purchased topsoil and bulbs to plant around the front of the station.

Delayed alarm bells began ringing in her head. *Who could Jim be calling?* He was supposed to be dead. None of her business. But he'd promised to lay low. She dallied and worried and worried and dallied all the way around the nursery and finally told herself to stop. Let it be. She bought a planter and fall flowers for the platform and a hanging spider plant for inside her new home.

Home. She loved the sound of it. She drove back to a home of her very own. For the past year, she'd been barely scraping by without resources to invest in enhancements to the station. Now with the promise of a new salary, she could spruce it up a bit. She unloaded the Muttmobile and set about repotting flowers in the planter. Soon, she was sweating and covered with dirt. Take a load off, girl. She fixed herself an iced tea and surveyed her progress.

Oh no! She heard a car approach. She entered the station and peered out the front window. Fortune's cruiser coasted down the road. Why was she always such a mess when men appeared? She flicked her hair from her face as he got out of the car and opened the door to greet him.

"You've been busy, I see," he laughed.

"What's so funny?"

"I'd wipe the dirt from your face if I had the nerve," he teased. He tried to suppress a grin without success. "Actually, I came to invite you to dinner Saturday night."

Wow. "Rats." Casey bit her lip. "I have to work for the Kennedys Saturday

182

evening." She had to wipe her nose with her hand, and he began laughing in earnest. She looked down at her blackened fingernails. Her turn to screw up her courage. "You met LouAnne and Rosie. They're bringing dinner here tomorrow. Any chance you could join us? Jim will be here as well."

"Plenty of chaperones," said Fortune. "Sounds good. What can I bring?"

"Nothing. But you could help me with something. I bought a hanging plant, but even with my stepstool, I'm not tall enough to affix the screw to the ceiling."

"Sure." Inside, she noticed that Jim had left a note of thanks and a five-dollar bill by the phone. Must've been long distance. She showed Fortune the hardware to hang the plant and watched him mount the stool and easily twist the screw into the ceiling. She handed him the plant and then backed up and admired both the plant and the hanger.

"Thank you," she said.

He got down and approached her. "Anything else I can do for you?"

Oh yes. Casey blushed and looked down. Maybe her face was so dirty he wouldn't notice.

He turned to admire his handiwork and slipped his arm around her waist.

She took in a sharp breath. "Aren't you going out with the real estate lady?" she blurted.

"Not anymore." He drew her close with a frown. "You have altogether too many eligible bachelors hanging out around here." He looked into her eyes and raised his brows, asking permission. "You're trembling."

"Uh huh."

"Me too." He leaned down and—

His beeper squawked. Both of them laughed from nervous energy.

"Duty calls. I'll catch you later."

"Promise?"

"Promise."

She was still trembling when he walked out the door.

Chapter Forty-Four

About an hour before LouAnne and Rosie were expected to arrive for dinner, Rosie called from a pay phone and had to cancel. They'd been rear-ended at a stoplight, and the van had to be towed. That left Casey with a cop and a hobo for dinner guests and no food. She rushed out and bought steaks and potatoes and salad fixings, red wine, and some ice cream. Not very inventive, but the best she could do on the spot. She was spending money like she had it.

Fortune arrived first with a bottle of wine. Casey told him about the change in plans for the evening. She handed him the corkscrew and asked him to do the honors. She had a fire going in the woodstove and had lit coals in a small portable grill on the platform for the steaks. The potatoes were greased and baking in the oven. They settled in chairs next to the stove.

"How did you say Jim was related to you?"

"He's a cousin."

"Mother's or father's side?"

"Why do you ask?"

"I'm interested in everything about you."

"Well, let's see. You know I'm from Ohio. Both of my parents are dead. I have one older brother and a great aunt. And Agnes. I guess I have to include her. She's Mary's adopted sister."

"How long have you been in New England?"

"Three years. As you know, I went back home to Oberlin for a year after release from prison to finish my degree before coming East."

"And that's how you came to be here with your Aunt Mary."

Casey was trying to remember how much Fortune knew about her background. He had been on the Welton force during the cataclysmic events that resulted in the death of two women when Chance was posturing as her Aunt Mary's stepson to garner his inheritance.

Fortune watched her for a moment. "That whole thing with Mary's stepson was a horrible mess, but you seem to have survived the ordeal. At the time, I think the state police were interested in speaking to the fellow who was here visiting you recently. Cunningham, you called him."

Casey nodded but didn't comment.

"Your father was the priest, right?"

"How do you know that?"

"I'm a detective. But he died before you arrived."

"Yes, I would have loved to have met him. By all reports, he was a very special soul."

"So, is Jim related to the Dempseys?"

"No. And it's my turn to ask questions. Where do you live?"

"Here in Welton with my mother and Davey on Summer Street. She's a godsend, helping me with Davey during the day. That's why I'm a cop in Welton. I had other aspirations, but necessity and mother got together. And I know you're curious but don't want to ask—my ex, who you met in the restaurant the other day, lives in France with a rich financier." He let that sink in before asking, "You every marry?"

"No. My best friend married my man while I was in prison."

Insistent banging on the door interrupted his interrogation. Casey frowned. Jim wouldn't be rude, and she'd left the door unlocked. Her question was answered when Agnes stormed into the room and marched over to Casey.

"Did you order this?" She slapped the copy of *Penthouse* magazine on the side table, almost toppling Casey's wine.

Casey had seen the magazine on Agnes' table. Agnes had had it for days and was using it now as an excuse to interrupt Casey's party. Casey picked it up, made a face as if surprised at the racy cover, and turned it over. "It's addressed to Occupant, President's Lane."

"Did you order it?"

Casey shrugged and raised her hands in innocence. "Must be for Mr. Kennedy."

Jim picked that moment to enter with Isabella. Casey rose to pour a glass of wine for him. As she passed Fortune, he whispered, "Naughty girl."

Agnes stared at Fortune while addressing Casey. "I thought you were supposed to be serving dinner for Mrs. Kennedy."

"Tomorrow evening."

The scowl of Agnes' well made-up face deepened as she examined Jim. "Are you the man staying in the caboose?"

Jim looked up at her but chose to sip his wine rather than answer. Agnes turned to Casey. "You do know that the property isn't zoned for anyone to live there."

"Oh, but it could be. For now, Jim is staying as my guest and helping me with maintenance. Jim, meet Agnes Dempsey, owner of the White House properties."

Agnes dismissed him with a nod and cycled back around to Fortune. "I recognize you. You're from the police. Is there something wrong?"

"Not that I know of, but I haven't started grilling yet." He awarded her a first-class smile.

"I'd invite you to join us, but I only bought three steaks," Casey added. She picked up the magazine. "Don't forget this," she said, leading Agnes to the door.

When the door closed, Fortune chuckled. "Nicely done. I didn't recognize her until you mentioned her name. What a transformation. Appearance anyway."

"It's the 'anyway' part that's a little tough to take." Casey agreed.

Casey explained to Jim that LouAnne and Rosie weren't coming. "It's just us chickens," she said.

"I understand you're Casey's cousin?" Fortune asked Jim.

CHAPTER FORTY-FOUR

"Mmm hmm. Second, I think. Not sure how that works exactly."

"Mother's or father's side?"

Jim looked to Casey, who jumped in to answer. "I think we're related somehow through my great Aunt Mae. Her family was from New Hampshire."

Silence.

Fortune studied. Jim. "Marine or Army?"

How can they tell? Rosie also had the same sixth sense.

"Army. You?" Jim said, staving off the next question.

"More wine?" Casey rose and filled glasses all around. "How do you like your steak?"

Fortune opted for medium rare, Jim for medium. "And rare for me," said Casey. "You mentioned that you're doing the grilling honors? I've got the coals going on the platform." She handed Fortune a platter of meat and utensils.

Once Fortune closed the sliding door behind him, Casey turned to Jim. "I'm sorry. I hope you're not too uncomfortable eating with a detective."

"He asks a lot of questions."

"Well, say you're out of work—you make up the kind of work—and I offered you a place to stay and temporary employment." They made small talk about other chores and things that needed to be done on a regular basis until Fortune returned with the food. Casey added potatoes and salad, and they settled down to dinner.

Fortune's next question was about Petey.

Casey filled him in. "Mrs. Kennedy said his parents were killed in an accident a few years ago. I don't know the details, but she did say she was his aunt and that she and her husband hadn't wanted children."

"Poor kid. I can see why he loves coming down here. He likes both of you. And he's in love with your dog." The second half of the statement was directed to Jim just as he was sneaking a morsel to Isabella. Fortune raised his eyebrows in question. "You've got a great bond with the pup."

"She's a sweetheart."

"No other family?" Fortune asked Jim.

"I have an older brother, Alex. Or I should say, had. Must be careful talking to a policeman."

"Gone? Died?" Fortune prodded.

"Well, he was declared dead...by mistake. And because of some dicey circumstances I won't go into, he prefers to remain dead. We even buried a homeless man in the family plot to convince his detractors."

Casey watched Jim carefully. He was probably trying to figure out the legal implications of a wrongful burial, but he was playing with fire.

"Quite a story. Now, I'm curious," said Fortune."

"You're a policeman. I'd hate to think the family committed a crime trying to do a good deed."

"Would probably be best to clear it all up. Maybe not for your brother. Doesn't sound like there's malice on your part, but deception is always frowned upon. Be happy I'm not an officer in New Hampshire, or I might feel obliged to investigate. I'd much rather have another glass of wine."

Jim eagerly uncorked the second bottle. "Where are you from?" he asked Fortune.

"Welton. Davey and I live with my mother on the other side of town."

"Do you like police work?"

Casey enjoyed watching Jim grill Fortune.

"I wouldn't recommend it for everyone, but I've always been interested in forensics, and I love dogs. As a detective, I've found a good position here, at least for now. Half my time I spend training with K-9 dogs, the other half in more mundane matters."

"You have your own dog?"

"German Shepherd named Captain."

"Ice cream?" piped up Casey.

They gobbled down bowls of ice cream and polished off the remains of the second bottle.

"Thanks for including me," said Jim. Isabella trotted behind him to the door. He gave her the hand signal to stay and looked up to find Fortune watching him as he left the station.

Fortune sank back into his chair. "So, he's the hobo who lived in the caboose before you purchased it. Lt. Colonel James Ferguson. And the man found murdered in the woods rests in the Ferguson family plot."

Casey glared at him. She felt like a fool. He'd been playing them all along.

Chapter Forty-Five

C asey cleaned their plates with an attitude. Fortune had known all along who Jim was and was toying with them to see how much they'd say.

Fortune followed and encircled her from behind. "Let's start over. I made you a promise earlier." He kissed the back of her head and turned her to face him. "I keep my promises."

Moments earlier Casey would have melted into his embrace, but now she was too pissed off to respond. She pulled back, tortured by the possibility that she might have compromised Jim. Had she made a dreadful mistake by exposing him to a cop?

Fortune's face clouded. "Not interested?" Clearly, he didn't like being rebuffed.

"All too interested, I'm afraid, but I need to talk with you." She led him back to the fire, determined to clear the air. Maybe if Fortune knew how great the threat to Jim was, he'd understand why Jim needed to remain dead. He already knew his identity. She decided to share Jim's story. "You knew all along who he was."

"I do my homework."

"Do you know his story? What he's been through?"

Fortune shook his head.

While Casey recounted Jim's story about being targeted by soldiers from his unit in Vietnam who wounded him and left him to die, Fortune maintained a stoic expression, offering an occasional nod, or "Go on," but giving her few clues about his reactions. "The Army refused to hear his story because it's bad publicity." After she finished, he remained silent for so long, Casey asked him what he thought.

"Do you believe him?" Fortune answered with a question.

"Yes. Rosie checked with the VA and confirmed his medical discharge and history. Jim also showed us his scars from head and chest wounds he received from friendly fire. He told us that his brother Alex helped him with clothing and money while he was in the caboose. He suspects that's how the man, Wilson, from his unit, found him—by following Alex." She paused. "What do you think?"

"Not sure."

Casey didn't know how to gauge Fortune's reaction. The silence between them became more prolonged. She mentally recounted the exchanges between Fortune and Jim.

"You already knew his identity even before you came tonight, didn't you?" she asked, unable to keep the accusation from her voice.

He leaned back. "I'm a detective."

"I'll take that as a yes. Why did you lead us along?"

"I wanted to see where you stood."

"Huh. 'Where I stood.' Just a little test of my moral fortitude." Casey clenched her jaw.

"I need to know if I can trust you. You weren't exactly forthcoming." A defensive note entered Fortune's voice. "Don't get too attached to this man, Casey. You may not know what you're dealing with. If I can figure out who he is, his sergeant should be able to do so, too."

"I told you. Wilson knows the safe is empty and that Lt. Ferguson is buried in New Hampshire. He has no reason to return."

"Can't you see? I'm just trying to protect you. These are desperate and dangerous men. One already shot a hole in your car." Fortune leaned back and crossed his arms. "I swore an oath to uphold the law."

Casey could kick herself. "I should have known better," she whispered. When she spoke next, her voice broke. "They'll kill him. Do you understand me? Kill him. They already burned down his house and murdered a homeless man by mistake. He doesn't have a chance if he's exposed. He's the one who needs protection."

"Did it occur to you that I may not have a choice?"

"But you do. Look into your heart, and you'll know what's right."

Fortune didn't reply.

"We make many tough choices in this life. Don't expose him."

"You may be asking me to ignore my duty." His frown was a plea for understanding.

Her voice rose. "I'm not asking you to do a damn thing! I'm begging you—"

"You're crossing a line, Casey."

"So be it." She walked to the door. "Black and white doesn't work for me. Jim is a good man who served his country." She wanted to hug the man and claw his eyes out at the same time. "What are you going to do?"

"I don't know." His expression was tortured.

"Let me know what you decide." She opened the door and turned away so that she didn't have to watch him leave.

Chapter Forty-Six

Saturday, 11/12

Casey banged around the station the next morning second- and third-guessing her actions—and the lack of them—from the night before. Fortune wanted to be able to trust her, but he had been leading them along, knowing Jim's identity, toying with them to see how much they'd disclose. The more she thought about it, the angrier she got. Why couldn't Fortune check out the sketchy people in the White House and leave the tortured vet alone? She knew the answer. He was interested in her. Claimed to be "protective." He should protect Jim, not even think about exposing him. Not everything was black and white. She was angry, yes, but so disappointed in her heart of hearts.

What a bust! Chance and Fortune. Quit dragging your toenails, girl. Her mother's voice spurred her into action. She grabbed a trowel to finish planting the bulbs she'd purchased earlier in the week. By mid-morning, she was covered in dirt. She realized that she'd been waiting for Petey to appear, and that she'd grown used to his morning visits. Jim joined her and helped her dig holes for the daffodil bulbs and then asked if he could take the Muttmobile for a few errands.

By the time she'd showered and changed, it was time to go up to the A-frame to help Loretta with her company. At least the weirdness of that situation would distract her from obsessing about Fortune, wondering if— admit it—hoping that something would come of it, and thinking about what he was doing today. She still didn't know that much about him. She'd enjoyed hearing about the K-9 training with his dog Captain. Cool it, Casey. There's a very good chance—bad choice of words—you never will learn more about the man.

Think about Loretta. Was she a conniving bitch, a madam, or a desperate housewife doing all she could to escape an impossible situation? Casey opened the desk and withdrew the note Loretta had left her at the White House. She placed it next to Kennedy's list of responsibilities, where he'd written in a few extra requirements by hand during her initial visit at the White House with Agnes.

A cursory glance at the writings side by side told her why Loretta feared her husband. His script was blunt, heavy and angular without so much as a twist, curl, or loop to lessen the powerful, egoistical personality. No generosity, lightness, or humor.

Next to it, Loretta's writing was diminished by comparison.

Casey didn't see any tremor or worry traits in her writing, emotions Loretta had shared with Casey at their last meeting when Loretta had said she feared for her life if she tried to leave Kennedy. Well, the woman was imaginative, smart, and in control, signs that could make her a good actress. On the other hand, maybe a current writing would show she was barely holding it together. There was only so much this small writing sample could tell her.

What a mess. For Casey, an uncomfortable, subservient, but very lucrative mess. She walked up the road, through the gate to the A-frame.

The scene was similar to what she'd experienced before, except indoors, with the same ladies sitting around the circular fire pit, talking and primping, and Petey sitting at the dinner table at the side, engrossed in a jigsaw puzzle. Loretta greeted her and gave her the menu, substituting shish kabob for steak, but otherwise, the dinner she'd prepared before. Casey served drinks and snacks and listened as best she could to their conversations. Apparently, the women were awaiting the men who were finishing up a round of golf.

When she joined Petey at his table, he was quiet and withdrawn. "I missed you this morning. I was planting bulbs." No response. After a few moments of the silent treatment, Casey quizzed him directly. "What's wrong, sport?"

"Nothing," he mumbled. He didn't look up from his puzzle, but Casey could tell he wasn't concentrating on the pieces.

"Talk to me," she said.

He looked up and glanced toward Loretta, and looked down again.

He seemed afraid. Of what? Of Loretta? Casey studied the puzzle for a moment and found an outside edge piece. She moved to a position where her body blocked Loretta's view of the boy. "Try this." She handed him the piece to put in place. "Is Aunt Loretta mad at you?" she asked in a low voice. He nodded his head yes.

"What happened?"

He glanced up at her. "I heard them fighting. Uncle William kicked me out of the room. He was really mad. Yelling. I was scared he would hurt her."

"She seems okay now. Why are you afraid of her?"

"Later, she came to my room. She said I shouldn't go to her room to spy on her, but I wasn't. I just wanted to get the key to the bike lock."

"Why did she take the key? Doesn't she want you to ride the bike?" Had she caused the poor boy trouble by providing him wheels?

"She said I shouldn't be friendly, that you were a convict and Jim was a homeless bum." He looked down again with tears in his eyes. "I said it was a lie, and she asked if I'd seen the scar on your arm you got in prison." Casey was about to explain when Petey's eyes practically bulged out of their sockets.

Loretta stood directly behind Casey. "Time for dinner, Peter. Go with Olga. I'll speak with you later," she said in a steely voice. Olga stood in the doorway to the A-frame, waiting. Petey began collecting pieces of the puzzle to put in the box.

"Leave it," Loretta demanded.

Petey hung his head and walked to the door.

Before Casey could challenge her, Loretta's demeanor shifted. She sat down quickly. "We're going to have to leave. Very soon," she said in a confidential voice. "I'm preparing him for disappointment. He won't be able to return to see you or take anything with him. You aren't supposed to know this. I can't tell him to say goodbye, lest he give away our plans. He's already brokenhearted about the last move. I'm trying to protect him."

"By taking away what little joy he has?"

"Try to understand, Casey. Kennedy is a violent man—" Loretta placed her hand on her cheek to draw Casey's attention to the bruise that was artfully covered by makeup but still visible at close quarters.

Casey winced. "No camera this evening?" Casey asked.

Loretta didn't move her head. "Look under the hood above the fire pit," she whispered. The inside telephone rang. "Our guests will be arriving soon. Please help me. Please. This last time."

Loretta rose, put a smile on her face, and joined the ladies. Moments later, they left the room to dress for the evening.

When the men arrived, Casey noted that Kennedy didn't accompany them. About a half hour later, Loretta's friend Paul appeared.

As the evening progressed, Casey noticed the same pairings from the week before. This time, Loretta was much more effusive and handsy with handsome Paul, who was responsive to her overtures, leaving Casey no doubt as to her intentions with the man. The couple stayed in the kitchen area well out of range of the camera. Following dessert, the other couples sat around the fire pit with cordials. Santa walked outside to smoke his evening cigar. Laura and Colonel Mustard were the first to venture upstairs.

Casey was ready to leave but looked around for Loretta for confirmation that her job was completed. Loretta was missing for a few moments before reappearing. She beckoned for Casey to join her in the kitchen.

Casey really wanted to see little Petey one more time. "I know you think you're protecting Petey, but would you let him come down tomorrow morning for one more visit? One last spin around on the bike? Please? I promised him we'd make cookies. I've helped you. Do this for me. It would mean a lot to both of us."

Loretta considered for a moment before responding. "Okay." She handed Casey a tote filled with bags of leftover appetizers and desserts and an envelope for her evening's work. "There's a little something on the bottom…

for me for safe keeping," she said as she escorted Casey to the door. Casey didn't understand what she was talking about, but was eager to leave.

She walked slowly to the station, tired and dispirited. She hoped Petey would be okay. Tough on the little guy to keep moving around, but she understood Loretta's decision to leave.

Inside, she unloaded the food to put it away and found a packet at the bottom of the tote. With trepidation, she removed it and set it on the counter, dreading what she imagined the contents would be. Contents for "safe keeping." Loretta hadn't sealed the packet. She probably realized that a curious Casey would open it. Casey stared at it, resisting the urge to peek inside for as long as she could. Oh, what the hell.

Ten thousand dollars. Escape money. Now what should she do? Return the tote to the A-frame? Would Loretta still be there? Hide the money and risk taking it to Loretta at the White House in the morning? Put it in the safe with the cool five hundred she'd earned for her services and decide what to do in the morning.

This was serious. Before she was just on camera serving. Now she had the proceeds from what she was pretty sure was an evening of prostitution.

Chapter Forty-Seven

C asey awoke, worrying about what to do with the money. She brewed a pot of coffee and placed calls to LouAnne and Loretta. She left a message to please call with the former but hung up when Loretta's machine answered. What could she say? Come get your money? Where is Petey? She didn't want to give away Loretta's plans. Too bad Loretta felt she had to leave, but the bruise on her cheek provided a compelling reason to go. Did he know about the man Casey called Paul Newman? Kennedy was violent. Loretta needed to protect herself and Petey.

Casey sure would miss the boy. She turned up the radio and sang along with Simon and Garfunkel to distract herself and dispel a feeling of impending disaster. What was her problem? She had friends, a home, the semblance of security, and a good-paying job. Just her luck, the tune was "Bridge Over Troubled Water." She cracked two eggs into a bowl and mixed them with butter and brown and cane sugar while she waited for Petey to arrive and help her make chocolate chip cookies. She pulled aside the kitchen curtain, hoping to see him as he came down the stone steps from the White House.

When she glanced out the window, she was surprised to see a man emerge from behind the caboose. From a distance, dressed in jeans, checkered shirt under a jacket, and a baseball cap, he looked a lot like Wilson. She hadn't heard a car approach, but then the music was blaring. Thank goodness Jim had asked to use the Muttmobile overnight. He hadn't said why he needed the car, but she didn't want to pry. He had promised to purchase mulch and to pick up an umbrella for the platform when he returned.

Casey wiped her hands on a towel. She didn't like the idea of that man loitering around the caboose. She and Isabella walked outside and approached him.

He eyed her and smirked.

Casey knew the man was looking for a reaction and controlled her expression. "What do you want?"

"Stopped in to see Jim."

Casey didn't respond.

Wilson kicked one of Jim's muddy work boots that he'd left by the stairs of the caboose. "Someone's wearing his boots. Way too clunky for your little feet." He looked up at the basketball hoop attached to the end of the caboose and then at her. "No offense, but you're a bit short for stardom in the sport. I bet you didn't construct this backboard."

Damned if she'd answer the man's questions.

He bent over and picked up the basketball, dribbled, shot, and missed. He got the rebound and threw hard at Casey.

She refused to be cowed. After ten years of practice in the prison yard she was over eighty percent at the free throw line. She scowled and landed a perfect bucket.

Wilson walked around the hoop. "Who rigged it up for you?"

When she didn't respond he checked out Petey's bicycle. "Bet the bike belongs to that little boy who visits."

This time, Casey couldn't mask her surprise. He must be watching the station, probably from the road.

One side of his mouth turned up in an ugly smile. He opened his jacket to expose a pair of small binoculars, confirming her suspicion. He nudged Petey's little backpack with his foot. "Where's your dog car?"

"Time for you to leave." Casey had had enough.

"I'm warning you. James Ferguson is a dangerous man with severe psychological problems. He needs help. He's been spreading lies about our Army unit to cover up atrocities he committed in battle. Some of the men are determined to stop him. Turn him in before someone gets hurt. You're harboring a criminal." With that parting shot, Wilson walked up Station Road, where he must have parked his car.

Why was he on foot? Probably because he knew she'd hear a car approach. So, sneaking up, looking for Jim. She was glad Petey wasn't here when he came. But where was Petey? She placed yet another call to LouAnne and one to Loretta. Neither answered. She left an urgent message for LouAnne, but again hung up, not knowing what to say to Loretta.

She didn't want to admit she was frightened, but she slipped the small spray canister of Mace into her coat pocket just in case Wilson returned. She was pretty sure he would. What would have happened if Jim had been here when Wilson showed up? She couldn't tell if Wilson was armed, but she bet he was. There are two sides to every story. It was true that Jim had been in the psych ward at the VA. Could he be a threat? Much as she disliked Wilson, she shouldn't discount his advice.

Nothing Fortune could do. No one had threatened her or stolen anything. She'd had an unwanted visitor wander down Station Road.

Petey hadn't come to visit, and Loretta hadn't claimed her money. Casey forced herself to finish baking the cookies while she mulled over the money. She really didn't want it in her safe. Where to hide it? In Petey's backpack? With Agnes? In the Muttmobile? In a safe deposit box? No, then she'd be claiming it as hers. Somewhere off her property. She had to get rid of it!

She'd give Loretta another day, and then if she didn't come for the money, Casey could leave it at the A-frame.

Chapter Forty-Eight

Monday, 11/14

Now that Agnes had returned, Casey decided it was time to formalize their agreement regarding Casey's salary and benefits. As an employee, she needed a firm, signed contract. She had nothing. No job description. No contract. From Agnes, or from the Kennedys. She'd made all the arrangements foolishly without any paper cover. Time to get some formal documentation.

She loaded up a plate of cookies as a peace offering for the Gorgon. As she walked toward the carriage house, she combed her memory, trying to figure out when Agnes had first expressed her dislike for Casey. Interesting, it was immediate, the moment Agnes met her. Well, the feeling had been mutual.

At the door to the carriage house, Casey heard a woman laughing. She'd never heard Agnes laugh before. Well, the sound was more like a nervous titter, but if she added more volume, it might sound convincing. She pushed open the door and entered, hoping for a positive reception.

Oops! There was Agnes, all smiles and new teeth, holding a wine glass, sitting on the couch close to—could it be?—Kennedy? With his arm around her shoulders. She backed away only to be jostled seconds later by a surprised Kennedy on his way to the door. He slowed when he recognized her. "We meet again," he said with a look meant to undress her. What a creep.

When Agnes saw that her new guest was Casey, her powdered nostrils flared, and her red mouth turned down at the edges.

Casey couldn't help but gape at the new woman before her, astonished by what a little surgery, makeup, fine fabric, and Mary's jewels could accomplish. And amazed at how quickly a lovely image could turn sour. She responded with the best version of a smile she could muster and offered the plate of cookies.

Agnes straightened her skirt and regained her composure. "We need to talk," she said, taking the plate of cookies and leading the way to the dining room.

Those were supposed to be Casey's opening words. She followed Agnes, now on guard for whatever the woman had in store. They took seats at the dining room table.

"I've decided not to renew the agreement on the White House property. I'm giving you fair notice that your fat salary won't continue after December. Time to polish your resumé...such as it is."

Casey considered retracting the cookies. Hadn't Kennedy signed a lease? "I haven't seen anything written about the rental arrangements."

"Because it's none of your business."

"What's your plan?"

"That's none of your business either, but you'll find out soon enough. William and I have been approached by someone who builds retirement communities and low-income units. The town may be amenable to his proposal to develop this property because it's parked out here by the train tracks. He says there's growing pressure from the state for towns to provide low-income housing units."

"But what about zoning?" Casey asked.

"40-B overrides local zoning laws where less than twenty percent of housing is affordable. The goal is to allow working families and seniors to remain when otherwise priced out of the conventional housing market in suburban and rural areas." Agnes sounded like she was reading a brochure, and indeed she was. She picked up a paper and continued, "The 1969 Massachusetts Comprehensive Permit Act, called 40-B, provides relief from exclusionary zoning practices."

"Welton will fight the program tooth and nail with lengthy appeals."

"Not my problem. The developer can appeal forever once he purchases the property."

"You won't mind having multiple units in your backyard?"

"Won't be my backyard. The carriage house is part of the proposal."

"Where are you going?"

"Far away from this town, all the horrible memories…and you."

Blindsided by the direct attack, Casey leaned back in her chair. After a few moments silence, she decided it was time to clear the air. "Why do you hate me? I've never done anything to you."

"Because you're a gold-digging tramp. Mary's little pet. She could never spare a thought for her own sister. Along you come, claiming you're Jed's daughter. He, a revered priest. Sullying his name and memory, suggesting he would be involved with the likes of your mother…a married woman who already had a child. There's no proof of your claim of parentage. I have no problem believing you're an illegitimate child. Your mother could have slept with—"

Casey jumped to her feet. "Keep my mother out of this!"

Agnes rose and stood face-to-face with Casey. "Or what? Touched a nerve, did I? Maybe because you're just like her? You had an affair with a married man in Ohio, seduced your cousin Jackson here, and tried to snag another married man, the one who is still sniffing around. Oh, don't get me started."

"How could I seduce my cousin Jackson if I'm not related—"

"When I think about it, you could be related to Mary, but not through dear Jed. Because Mary was also a tramp. Slept with her boss and broke up the perfect couple. Wrenching an innocent little boy from his father, for money and sex. She was already living high on the hog when she sold our family home. My home! Pricking her fingers and whining about her diabetes, as if she wasn't always the center of attention."

Agnes's face twisted into the picture of rage; eyes wild as she continued her rant.

"She and Vera. Vera was the worst! She slept with British soldiers and caused the ruin of our family. Father and two brothers slaughtered because she whored around. We had to push her around in her wheelchair, change her diaper, and spoonfeed her. She should have died. Instead, she produced the other bastard, Jackson."

Casey backed out of reach, aghast as the white-hot hatred poured forth. "Calm down or you'll stroke out." Gradually, Agnes' features rearranged into her new normal, petulant and vaguely nasty expression. They both sat down, glaring at each other.

After a moment of silence, Casey continued in a normal tone of voice. "No one in your family or mine had an easy time of it. Listening to your litany of woes, I almost feel bad for you." Casey paused to let the feeling pass. "You seem to think the world owes you because you didn't get your share. But as my mother always said, 'Life is short, and it sure isn't fair. Get over it.'"

Agnes seemed to have momentarily lost her voice.

"Things are different now, Agnes. You're healthy and secure with a lovely cottage and rental income, and even a new, improved face. You probably made a killing on the sale of the Chatham house. No friends, though. Maybe you should get a cat." Casey shook her head. "On second thought, stick to African violets."

When Agnes didn't respond, Casey continued. "I think I understand why you're still nasty. Mary and Vera are dead. Jackson moved out of reach. I'm the only target left. You've disliked me since the day we met. Think that will ever change?"

"Get out."

"Not before we talk about your tenants. I think they may be involved in some dicey business in the A-frame. They have cameras spying on—"

"What they do is none of my business, and for sure, none of yours as long as they pay."

"I should remind you that your new friend Kennedy is a married man. You're not just nasty, you're a nasty hypocrite."

"One more word out of you, and you're fired."

"No. This time, I get the last word. I quit." Casey slammed the door on the way out.

Chapter Forty-Nine

Casey argued with herself all the way down to the station. She'd just quit a job that paid handsomely, one that she was good at, making arrangements and managing the affairs of the property. Had she blown it in a fit of pique? Maybe Agnes wasn't the only one with a new nose job. Casey may have just cut off her nose to spite her face.

But she disliked everyone associated with her job: Agnes, Kennedy, the help Olga and Vlad and, most times, Loretta. She had no job security, no job definition, no protection whatsoever. Life was too short.

Agnes planned to sell to a developer anyway and was going to fire her the second there was an agreement. Casey almost smacked her forehead. Of course, Kennedy arranged the deal. Why else would he waste time with a middle-aged shrew. He wanted the property.

Casey hated the idea of months, maybe years of disruption in her little Eden. Having the property next door divided and ripped asunder for a myriad of housing units to create a mini-city atop the hill. Imagine the number of cars coming and going. The noise. Children overrunning the caboose, using it as their playground. Maybe the town could forestall the construction, but Agnes made it sound inevitable. The property was the perfect, out-of-the-way place to park unwanted units of unwelcome residents.

Halfway down the hill she spotted the Muttmobile in the driveway. Jim had returned. Time to warn him about the visit from Wilson.

As promised, Jim had purchased mulch to cover the area where they had planted bulbs. He'd already spread the brown cover over the area and to her surprise, planted a small shrub next to the front stoop. The door to the station was open, and she could hear sounds from the platform at the rear of the building. She walked through and popped her head out the back door to greet him.

Jim had been working hard in the sun and had shed his shirt, exposing his long, skinny frame and the ugly scars she'd seen earlier. He'd carried in and set up the base for anchoring an umbrella that would provide shade for the table.

He smiled a greeting and cranked a lever, raising the umbrella. She produced cookies and iced tea and asked him to sit for a moment and cool off. He plopped down across from her and took a few long gulps of iced tea. "Thanks," he said, wiping his brow.

"And thank you. This is great. The front looks good, too, with the bush and mulch."

"It's a red azalea." He smiled, obviously pleased by her reaction.

Casey paused a moment. She really didn't want to burst his bubble, but the reappearance of Wilson couldn't be ignored. "Wilson came again this morning. He's convinced you're still alive. He may have even seen you, because he's been watching the place from the road with binoculars."

Jim tensed and set down the cookie he was about to eat. "I'm sorry that I've exposed you to this. He's an evil man." He rubbed his eyes and continued. "I thought I had more time. You must have wondered what I've been up to, borrowing the Muttmobile this week. I've been to see my brother Alex and Emily, the woman in the picture that was in the safe. Alex really believed the body he claimed was me, but now that he knows the truth, he could be in trouble. We'll have to move fast."

Both of them started at the sound of a car pulling up to the station.

Would Wilson return so soon? "Quick! The loft." Casey grabbed Jim's glass as he dashed inside and climbed the spiral stairs to the open sleeping area above the living room. She dumped the glass in the sink and rushed to the door.

As Casey watched through the window, a man in a baseball cap got out of the car and then opened the passenger door. Out bounded a very large

German Shepherd. Fortune leashed the dog, approached the station, and rang the bell. Although she was greatly relieved that he wasn't Wilson, Casey was still leery of Fortune.

When Casey opened the door with a cautious smile, Fortune seemed nervous. "I try to keep my promises. At least those that you'll let me keep." He gave a sheepish smile." I said I'd stop by with Captain."

Isabella leaned against Casey's leg, watchful.

Casey offered her fingers to the big dog for sniffing. Captain responded with a paw, and they shook. Isabella inched a few steps forward, head low, still cautious of the huge dog that dwarfed her. "He's eaten, hasn't he?" Casey asked with a stab at levity.

"Friend, Captain." Fortune dropped the leash. Captain lay down in front of Isabella so that their heads were at the same level. Two minutes later, they were circling in the sniffing dog ritual, tails awag.

Casey wished that making friends were that easy for humans. "Beautiful dog."

"He passed his exams this morning with flying colors and is now the county's official K-9 unit."

Casey heard the obvious pride and affection in Fortune's voice. Captain's ears pricked forward, and he glanced up at his master. He knew they were talking about him.

"You wanted to know where I stood with Jim, so I thought I'd fill you in on a recent development that affects him."

Casey nodded. She hadn't asked Fortune to look into either Chance or Jim. She wished he wouldn't do so much investigating. With Jim, it could lead to trouble.

"May I come in?" he asked, frowning when she didn't invite him in.

"Sure." She backed away and ushered him inside, but remained standing.

"Jim needs to know that there's an exhumation order for the body buried in the Ferguson family plot."

"How can that be?"

"Apparently, there's some question about the identity of the deceased and how he was identified. There's a challenge from the mother of a homeless man who has been searching for her son. She found out that a man wearing an M1965 Vietnam jacket frequented the local soup kitchen. Her son lived in that make of military issue jacket, and the man found in the woods also wore that jacket. It was still recognizable, a waterproof, polyester cotton and nylon field jacket, size small." Fortune watched her closely as he spoke.

"But earlier, when questioned, Alex said his brother wore a size large. Now the mother wants to compare dental records. She's hired a lawyer who filed the claim."

Casey nodded and was about to tell Fortune about the visit from Wilson when Captain's hackles rose and he let loose an ear-splitting barrage of barking, his attention riveted on the loft.

Fortune wheeled to the threat, hand on his holster, following the dog's alert.

"Stand down, Fortune. It's Jim."

Jim peered down from the loft.

"Quiet," Fortune commanded. Captain stopped barking but maintained his alert posture. Fortune took in the scene from Jim's bare torso to Casey and back.

It took a moment for Casey to realize how it must look. A half-naked man in the loft, and her acting nervous and guilty.

Fortune's voice was hard as he addressed Jim. "Now you know where you stand." He then looked down at Casey with eyes full of disappointment and anger. "And I know where I stand," he said. "You move fast. I misjudged you." With a snap of his fingers, he and the dog were gone.

Chapter Fifty

"Goddam it!" Casey howled. The only decent, eligible, sane, single man she'd met in years now considered her white trash, a "mistake in judgment." There was a simple explanation if she could get him to listen to her. A very big if. But right now, she had more pressing problems.

Jim practically crept down the spiral stairs from the loft. "I'm so, so sorry I've messed things up for you. I'll leave as soon as I can warn Alex and contact Emily."

"Need the car?"

"Just the telephone, please."

Casey left to give him privacy. Outside, she picked up Petey's little backpack and unlocked the caboose. Time to move the money. Or was it? She sure could use the extra cash now that she was unemployed. No! She quashed the temptation. It wasn't hers. What was she thinking?

It wouldn't do to have anyone—Fortune, Wilson, or even Jim—find over ten thousand dollars in the safe. Agnes would love for Casey to get caught with a pile of money. She jammed Loretta's cash into the pack and made her way back up the hill, this time to the A-frame. Later, she could move what was left of her salary money to a safe deposit account.

She rang the bell. No answer. She rang it twice more before opening the door with the universal key and the code she'd established for the A-frame. Inside, she hollered a loud "Yoo-hoo!" to make sure she wasn't interrupting another tête-à-tête.

When no one responded, she rushed through the building to the door to the pool. She had been late scheduling the pool closing which wouldn't happen until the end of the week. She cracked open the door a few inches. Silence. No one. She skirted along the outside wall of the A-frame to stay out of range of the camera until she reached the corner table where Petey had usually played under an umbrella. She left the backpack on the seat of his chair and pushed it under the table. Casey could leave a coded note for Loretta.

She retraced her steps to the door, careful to avoid the—but when she looked down, there was no tiny red blinking light. The outside camera was gone. Strange. She needn't have worried about being taped. Now she noticed other things that she'd missed in her haste to dump the backpack. Everything was in order. Absolutely nothing out of place. The towels were laundered and folded; lounge chairs lined up. The grill scoured clean. Inside, there were no glasses or dishes in the sink or on the counter. The dishwasher was empty. Nothing at all in the fridge. The place was spotless. As if the parties had never taken place. No camera hidden under the hood.

Now she was curious. Upstairs she found the same story. Beds made. No used soap bars or partially used bottles of shampoo in the bathroom. Empty drawers and cabinets. Nothing in the waste baskets. She looked for holes, places for cameras around the bedrooms but didn't find anything.

Had Kennedy shut down the operation? Or was Fisher the one responsible for the cameras? Was Loretta okay? Petey hadn't shown up to play or make cookies as promised.

Was she doing the right thing, leaving the money? It was an awful lot of money to leave unprotected, but what else could she do? She could get caught snooping. Time to leave.

When she got back to the station, she called and got Loretta's answering machine again. "Petey left his backpack here. I stuffed it with the things he'd been storing in the safe and left it in his corner at the pool."

What was happening with the tenants? The scoured A-frame suggested a dramatic shift, but Casey had no idea what it meant. She should wash her hands of it all. The Kennedys were too sketchy by half. But she worried about little Petey. He was so vulnerable.

Everything was moving too fast. Unbelievable. In less than a week, she found herself unemployed again, threatened by some crazy man who shot up her car with a rifle, witness to some sex blackmail scheme—and she'd dumped a small fortune in a child's pack by a pool. She needed to settle down and put her life together.

Chapter Fifty-One

Fortune

Fortune pounded the steering wheel as he drove up Station Road. What a fool! Protecting a sweet and helpless damsel in distress. Well, she had other ideas. Harboring the homeless vet. More than that. The image of Jim's naked torso in the loft was too much. She'd already taken the guy to her bed. His earlier euphoric mood evaporated, smothered by a wild mixture of rage, jealousy, disbelief, embarrassment, and disappointment. Loss. He'd felt so hopeful after their first encounter. Then he'd been uncertain and frustrated when Casey had asked him to disregard Jim's illegal status, showing no understanding or appreciation for Fortune's position and responsibility. And then, within a day, was fooling around with the man.

She had no judgment. She was interested in that pretty face, the Southern jackass Cunningham, and now she was a sucker for Jim's sad story. He'd been so wrong about her. Seemed all she wanted was sex. So did he, but not with just anyone who came along.

Would she have even said anything if Captain hadn't sensed movement in the loft? He hadn't thought she'd be the type to sleep around. Wholesome Ohio girl who baked cookies and rescued animals and befriended lonely little boys. Okay, two sides to every story, but he wasn't interested in learning more sordid details. She was no more trustworthy than Anita who'd broken up their family to screw around with a rich French playboy.

Time to cool off before dealing with that mess. He had to take Captain home before he met with a family divorce lawyer to explore his options for gaining sole custody of Davey. Fortune and his mother had had a long, heart-to-heart about Anita and her parents' request to send Davey to a private school. They agreed it wasn't just about school, but about control.

Her parents had never accepted Fortune as a suitable husband for their precious daughter or father to their only grandchild. Fortune was convinced that she wouldn't have married him if she hadn't been caught out. Theirs was the classic shotgun wedding. She was on the rebound from an Ivy League lover, using Fortune to taunt the other man who hadn't had the common sense to bow his knee to her every wish. Maybe he'd been the smart one.

Fortune had to admit he and Anita had had a glorious first year, at least he thought of it that way. Anita was beautiful and intelligent, quick and fun to be with, and sexy as all hell. But his life as a cop and her pregnancy soon sent her into a spiral. His friends were other cops and townsfolk, not society types. Handsome wasn't enough fun for her. She wanted a party.

He wasn't up to snuff, and it turned out, she lacked the mothering instinct. After Davey was born, she got restless and wanted to party. She liked having a child, but not caring for one. He didn't doubt that she loved Davey at least a little, but he didn't trust her to guide and protect him the way he and his mom would. The grandparents wanted an heir, but only if they could control and direct his destiny with their money and influence.

He was sick of the endless back-and-forth negotiations, power plays, and pseudo-seduction ploys. Thank God for his mother, the one woman he could trust. Poor Davey couldn't help but be vulnerable to his mother's appearances. Her only regular visits were during the Christmas holidays with her parents in Welton and two weeks in the summer at her family compound on Martha's Vineyard. Those were probably the times when Phillipe had to be with his wife and children in Nice. Fortune wondered if the man even knew that Anita had a son.

Regardless, it was unfair to toy with a little boy's emotions. Last week, Davey admitted that he didn't want to go to Martha's Vineyard with Anita.

He'd rather play baseball with his friends at home.

He steeled himself for the meeting. He'd done enough research to realize that only twenty percent of fathers achieve sole custody, and that the legal process could either be quick and painless or take up to several years and cost thousands, depending upon the agreement between parties. He was torn because he was saving his thousands for college for Davey.

He had a few good arguments on his side. She had abandoned Davey at age five to live abroad with a playboy. Fortune offered a solid home with him and his mother in a town with an excellent school system. A father with a good-paying, responsible job, and a doting grandmother with a lovely little house. He continued to rehearse his lines as he drove. He tried to erase the image of Jim in the loft, but it kept interrupting his concentration. Why was everything such a goddam mess?

Chapter Fifty-Two

Casey

Tuesday, 11/15

Casey spent the next morning thinking about what she needed to do to extricate herself from the job. The accounts for various services would need to be transferred to Agnes. She'd already created a list of service providers with phone numbers and contact names. Kennedy and Fisher would need to be notified of the change. Agnes would have to hire an individual or company to maintain the property. Keys. What else? Codes. Bank accounts and records of transactions for taxes.

In a way, she was relieved to be rid of the burden of the Kennedys. Demanding, rude, involved in some really dicey enterprise, violent—there was nothing to recommend the arrangement except for money and Petey. Did Loretta get her message? Or was the money still sitting under a beach umbrella by the pool? There was nothing more she could do. Time to figure out exactly how much she'd saved and how much she would need. The real estate taxes were low for the station because the railroad maintained the title to the land, and the assessment on the building by itself was low, but she still had living expenses.

For work, she sure wasn't going to get any positive recommendations from Agnes, Kennedy, Fisher, or even Loretta. What to do? How about handwriting analysis? She was still associated with the Cambridge Center for Adult Education. She was signed up to teach another course, but it wouldn't begin until the first of the year. There must be other places where she could teach. It would be a great way to meet folks who were likely to believe in the power of graphology. A good marketing tool. Also, she could work parties and cruises, although it would be a rather shallow application of the skill. Her prison time gave her some street cred because she knew about criminals, and many employers were interested in using graphology to screen potential bad apples in the hiring process.

She was free to do anything. Play tennis, walk in the woods, sketch, paint, take a class herself. She found herself smiling for once, instead of pacing and frowning and worrying about the next unreasonable demand. She'd meet new people. Make a few friends. Maybe even go on a date. She was still young and healthy with her wits about her.

Free of everything—including Fortune. Her bubble popped. Should she leave him a message? Would he believe her? Not likely. She remembered the disbelief and disappointment in his eyes when he left.

Yup, she was free for sure. No man. No job. No prospects. Free as a bird. The phone jangled.

Before she could say a word, Fisher demanded, "Send the boy home."

"He's not here. I expected him yesterday morning, but he never came. I left a message with Loretta—"

Click.

Casey looked inside the caboose, but no Petey.

Back inside the station, she returned to her list, but her concentration had evaporated, replaced by worry about the boy. She picked up the phone and dialed Fisher back to ask how long Petey had been gone, but Fisher didn't pick up. Cryptic as he was, he usually answered. Loretta hadn't answered either. What was going on?

Casey put on a jacket and walked a quarter of a mile up and down the tracks calling for Petey. She returned to the station and began to worry in earnest when someone pounded heavily on the door.

Through the peephole, she saw the great bulk of Vlad, Kennedy's bodyguard or whatever he was. She opened the door.

217

"Where's the boy?" he demanded.

"I just told Fisher. He's not here. What's happening? How long has he been missing?"

Vlad shouldered her out of the way and marched through the station. He opened every closet, searched the bathroom, climbed up to the loft, and turned on the light illuminating the back of the platform.

Casey was no match for the giant, even if she could get to the Mace in her jacket. She angled toward the phone in the kitchen. Vlad's large paw reached over her shoulder and pulled her away. "No police. Unlock the caboose."

"He's not there."

"Open it."

Vlad was strangely impersonal, intent on his mission. Casey took her key ring out of her jacket and led him to the caboose, although she knew that the boy wasn't there. Vlad entered and looked through the railcar, opening everything. He climbed up to the cupola. He got down and yanked open the storage closet. "What's in here?" Casey shone a flashlight into the area where the safe was. Vlad eyed the safe but said nothing.

Casey followed him out of the caboose. He scowled at her, stuffed himself into the driver's seat, and drove off without a word.

Casey heard the phone ringing inside the station, but by the time she reached it, Agnes' voice on the answering machine was demanding that she call immediately. Casey deleted the message with a flourish of her wrist. She didn't work for her anymore.

Petey was missing, and Loretta didn't answer the phone. Casey had to assume that Loretta had found the backpack and had taken off with the boy. She could only pray that it was true. If it were, Kennedy was undoubtedly desperate to find Petey and had sent Vlad to look for him.

She rejected the idea of reporting Vlad to the police for his intrusive behavior. She had let him into the station and the caboose. He was rude and pushy, but he hadn't hurt her or taken anything. Besides, if Loretta had escaped with Petey, Casey didn't want to get the police involved and foil Loretta's plan.

Casey locked and bolted the door and then retired to her rocker. No car. Jim had taken the Muttmobile again. He said he had a plan and just needed one more trip to arrange things. Although she asked what he was going to do, he demurred, saying it was better for her not to know. She had to wonder if he trusted her because of her connection with Fortune. He could be planning to disappear again.

No boy. If Petey really were missing, would anyone let her know if he was found or if he came home? No matter what she did, she had no idea if she would be taking the right action. What would Fortune do? Her thoughts spiraled into fits of worry and crashed with the realization of her helplessness. Try to relax and hope for the best. Meditate. Do the breathing exercises. The soothing motion of the rocker helped, and her eyelids grew heavy.

Ring! Must be dreaming.

Ring! Riiiiiing! Casey's eyes opened wide. Doorbell! Heavy pounding. Casey retrieved the can of Mace from her jacket before approaching the door. When she looked through the peephole, she was astonished to see Agnes' magnified eyeball peering back at her.

When Casey opened the door, Agnes rushed in, disheveled and out of breath. "Why don't you answer your phone? Some brute just searched my house without my permission, looking for a child. What is this about? What have you done?"

"The brute is Vlad, your good friend Mr. Kennedy's right-hand man. He came here, too." Although she was glad that Agnes wasn't injured, Casey rather liked the idea of Vlad pushing her around. She might begin to realize what Casey had to deal with.

"Call the police! This is unacceptable!"

Casey gestured toward the phone. "Feel free to call."

Agnes frowned.

"Did he touch you? Hurt you?" Casey asked.

"No, but he barged right in and pushed me aside."

"Was anything broken?"

"No."

"Was anything stolen?"

When Agnes didn't respond right away, Casey prompted her. "Did he take anything?"

"The magazine."

Casey suppressed a smile. "Your copy of *Penthouse*."

"Not my—"

"Did you let him in?"

"Yes, but—" Agnes sputtered for a moment and then plopped down in a chair, uninvited. "What are you involved in?"

"Nothing. Our neighbors are looking for their little boy."

Casey took the opportunity to retrieve the lists she'd made earlier in the day and place them on the table before Agnes. "Calm down. There are a few more details I'll have to deliver to you later when you write me the final check for this month, but I think these pages summarize most of what you will need to know right away."

"You can't just dump all this on me." She pushed the papers aside.

"Sure, I can." Casey refused to budge.

"I can't believe you're doing this to me after all I've—" Agnes cut her whine short. She must have realized the folly of her approach.

To Casey's surprise, the woman began to whimper.

"Don't leave me in this mess, Casey." Agnes' voice was getting younger and more pathetic by the minute.

Casey nudged the papers closer. "You'll be fine. You have days before the accounts accrue to you. Best contact that maintenance company you spoke of earlier. I'm sure they'll be happy to hear from you."

Agnes sobbed. "But, but…I was planning to travel next week."

"Sorry. Can't help you."

Chapter Fifty-Three

Seemed she woke every hour on the half hour through the night worrying about one thing or another, mostly Petey and what to do for a living. And dreaming about Fortune and the disappointment and disgust in his eyes when he left. When the sun rose, she gave up and crawled down the loft stairs to the kitchen for coffee. She looked out the window and saw that the Muttmobile was parked in front of the station. Jim must have returned late at night and hadn't wanted to disturb her.

She poured two mugs of coffee and walked to the caboose. "Yoo-hoo, it's Casey," she called. Moments later, she heard Jim unlatch the door. He was groggy but offered a big smile as he accepted the coffee and pulled down the folding table for them.

"Good morning," she began.

"You know the woman in the picture that was in the safe?"

Casey nodded.

"She said yes," he beamed.

"Congratulations! I wondered what you were up to. That's wonderful news."

"Thank you." He sipped his coffee. "She waited for me for years. After I was released by the VA, I disappeared, thinking I'd be no good to anyone. When Alex identified and buried the homeless man, he thought it was me, that I was dead. She did, too. But when I called him, he immediately got in touch with her. It's a miracle."

Casey had never seen a person glow before. Although she hated to ruin his rosy mood, she needed to get down to business. "What are you going to do?"

"I'd hoped we'd have a little more time. Wilson must know about the exhumation order. That's why he came here again. I'll pack up my things this morning. Emily plans to come by this afternoon, and we'll take off."

"I have a little money to help you. Let me get it." Casey went to the storage closet and opened the safe. She retrieved the yellow envelope containing $500 and handed it to him.

"This sure will help. You'll be okay without it?"

"I'm fine." Truth was her cash reserves were perilously low.

"I hope it's okay to take the car this morning. I need to get a few supplies for our trip and then make a quick pass by the dump. I've seen packs and bags in the swap shop." He walked her out the door and surprised her with a hug before leaving in the Muttmobile.

Casey returned to the station and refreshed her coffee. Thank goodness, he'd be getting away. And getting away with his old love. The sooner the better. Wilson had already tried to kill him three times, once in Vietnam and twice in New Hampshire. She carried her mug out the sliding door to the table and umbrella Jim had set up on the platform and sank into a chair. She hoped Petey was far away with Loretta, or, if he'd run off, that he'd come home soon.

So many thoughts swirling about. What on earth could she put on her resumé? She needed to make a list and buy a few groceries and dog food, but Jim had the car. Was Petey okay? Where was Loretta? Could she trust her? Casey was running on empty without sleep. Her chin rested on her chest, and soon her eyes closed.

A sharp blow to her head toppled her out of the chair onto the platform. She was conscious for a few seconds, long enough to feel blinding pain and see the ugly smirk on Wilson's face above her before she passed out.

When she came to, she was outside, propped up on the metal stairs at the front end of the caboose. Her hands were tied in front of her with heavy twine. Her head pounded from the blow, and she had a hard time focusing.

Wilson paced to and fro close by. When he walked past her to glance up the lane, she saw a gun tucked into the back of his pants. On the way back to the caboose, he noticed that she was conscious. "Now we wait." He made what she assumed was a smile.

"I told Jim about your visit. He left this morning. He's not coming back."

"But he is. He's got your dog car. I saw him drive off this morning."

"You've been following him."

"Clever girl. Now shut up." He walked to the end of the caboose and stepped behind it into the shade.

Casey craned her neck and saw Wilson's pickup parked out of sight behind the caboose. Jim could return any moment. How could she warn him? She'd call out, but would it be too late? Wilson had a gun and the element of surprise. She faded in and out, blinded by the pain in her head and the direct sun overhead. Huh. That meant it was already noon. She'd been out a while.

If Wilson had been watching, why didn't he attack Jim earlier? Because of her? Wilson might think she could call for help or even intervene with a weapon. He'd waited and neutralized her.

Too soon, the Muttmobile drove down the lane. As the car neared, Casey screamed, "Look out!" at the top of her lungs, but Jim couldn't hear her above the noise of the engine. When he got out, Wilson emerged from the shadows and pointed the gun at him. "Afternoon, Ferguson."

Jim froze, eyes wide with shock.

"I've been waiting for you. Good move, burying that homeless man." Wilson moved closer. "But now it's time to bury the right person in that grave."

Jim cast his eyes about and backed toward the Muttmobile. "Won't work, Wilson. I told the police about you."

"Sure, you did," said Wilson. "That's why you're planning to run off with your honey."

Casey frowned. How did he know about Jim's love? Easy, he'd been following him. Not hard to spot the Muttmobile.

"I've been watching your brother's house."

Jim took another tack. "Why bother killing me? I'm already dead."

"Because I can't trust you to keep your yap shut. Shouldn't have contacted the Army and spoken to the press."

"You'll go down for murder."

"Nah. This is how the story will go. You accused me of war crimes. I had to find you to clear my name. And then you, the crazy vet who'd spent time in the loony bin at the VA, drew a gun on me. Self-defense."

Casey slumped to the side to distract Wilson. A sharp object pricked her arm, and she gasped aloud. She looked down to see what had hurt her. It was the same three-pronged gardening fork they'd been using for planting bulbs that she'd threatened Wilson with before.

At Casey's cry, Jim moved toward her.

Wilson whirled and placed the cold gun barrel against Casey's temple. "One more step, she's dead."

Casey closed her eyes, waiting.

"What did you do to her?" Jim asked.

Wilson glanced at Casey. "Just a tap on the head. Although now I think on it, she'll have to go." He turned and pointed the gun at Jim.

Casey gripped the fork handle in her tied hands.

"But you first." Wilson chuckled. He seemed to be enjoying himself. He stepped forward and aimed.

Casey screamed and launched herself forward, using the full force of her body to bury the prongs into Wilson's neck. The momentum of the collision caused Wilson to stumble forward, howling in pain. He shook her off. She landed hard on her side, unable to move.

Jim grabbed Wilson's gun hand, bent it back, and slammed it against the side of the caboose. The gun flew out of Wilson's hand and skittered across the drive. Both men dove to the ground for it, but Jim was closer and got there first. He rolled out of reach, stood, and aimed at Wilson.

Wilson rose, breathing hard. He gripped the handle of the tool and wrenched the prongs from his neck with a howl, releasing a stream of blood. He took a few steps backwards.

"Far enough, Wilson. One more step, and I'll shoot."

"You're no killer, Ferguson. You left all the killing to us." Wilson took two more steps backwards.

"You're not listening."

Wilson smirked and stepped—

Bang!

Wilson screamed and grabbed his left leg, sinking to the ground.

"Turnabout, Wilson. For what you did to me."

Casey stared in horror at the manic bloodlust in Jim's eyes. He was going to kill Wilson! "Don't do it, Jim," she begged. "He's not worth it." But Jim was beyond listening, his eyes fixated on Wilson.

Time slowed down as Jim advanced on the man who had shot him and left him for dead under a pile of bodies. His breathing became labored, and his hand shook as he pointed the gun between Wilson's eyes.

A red VW bug lurched down the lane toward the station, but Jim didn't react, he was so intent on Wilson.

A petite blonde jumped out of the car and ran toward Jim.

Had to be Jim's love. "Stop him, Emily!" yelled Casey.

Jim panted over Wilson, his eyes glazed. As Emily approached, she spoke in a low, calm voice. "Easy now, Jim." She drew closer. "Slow down. It's all over." Another step. "Take a deep breath." She inserted herself between Jim and Wilson and placed her palm on Jim's chest. "Back away." She waited for him to step back and then held out her other hand. "Give me the gun." After a long moment, Jim's eyes left Wilson and met hers. He surrendered the weapon and collapsed to the ground, head in his hands, moaning.

Emily rushed to Casey. She put the gun down and untied her hands. "Hold the gun while I call for help," Emily said. She entered the station and returned moments later, out of breath. "The phone cord's severed."

"Wilson must have cut it after he knocked me out," Casey said. "You'll have to drive."

Emily glanced at Jim, who was rocking side to side. "If I do, he's in no condition to help you. Will you be okay?"

Casey nodded. What choice did she have? Wilson was in the middle of the parking area, holding his injured leg. She struggled to get up. "Help me to the tree."

Emily led Casey to the tree at the edge of the parking lot. She handed her the gun before rushing to her car. As she turned it around and drove off, Casey sat and tried to get her bearings. To her surprise, Wilson had managed to crawl toward her and was about ten feet away.

"Far enough."

"Whaddaya going to do, shoot?" Wilson smirked and kept moving.

"Why not?" Casey pointed the gun just to the right of Wilson's good leg and pulled the trigger. Wilson screamed. He wasn't hit, but he didn't move again. The explosion ricocheted inside Casey's injured head. Her eyes blurred. "As I said, far enough." She leaned back against the tree and rested the gun on her knees. "Now we wait."

Focus. Count to a thousand. She bit her lip until she tasted blood.

Chapter Fifty-Four

Fortune

A servant opened an enormous carved oak door at the front of the mansion and ushered Fortune through an atrium into a formal sitting room where Anita's parents and their daughter were waiting. Fortune dreaded the meeting, but it was past time for them to clear the air in person. No more dinners here, lunches there, and he-said, they-said, she-said conversations. Although his mother was a pivotal player in the family drama, Fortune was glad to spare her from the meeting. She was at home with Davey. They'd set the time in the afternoon so there would be no question of food or drinks or socializing.

Once he was seated, Anita's father leaned back and crossed his arms. "You called the meeting."

So much for niceties. Not even a polite hello. Fortune looked to Anita, who avoided his eyes. She was the one who had arranged the get-together, but if she didn't want to speak first, he was willing to open the discussion. "Anita told me of your plans to send Davey to a private school and said you had gone as far as securing a place for him with a few of them. She also indicated that if I didn't agree to the arrangement, you would consider legal action.

"While it's a very generous offer, I don't believe it's in Davey's best interest. He's already experienced a great deal of trauma and disruption for a child. He's also not old enough to make this decision for himself. He's happy and healthy. Private school might well be an option for his high school years, whether a day school or a boarding arrangement. We'll have to see when the time comes. But he's too young now."

He turned to address Anita. "You've been relentlessly badgering Davey to leave here, either to go visit you in Europe, to go away to school, or more recently, to go on vacation for a month at your family compound on Martha's Vineyard. The pressure is tearing him apart because he wants to please you, and he also wants to please me and Mom and stay here. Last night he was crying, and I asked what was wrong. He admitted that he didn't want to go to the Vineyard. He wants to stay home and play baseball with his friends. I convinced him to go for a week. That's long enough for everybody. That's all you get."

"That's not for you to say," objected Anita. "You can't just make a unilateral decision. We have joint custody."

"Yes, we have joint custody, but you don't have a home or a means of support or a stable lifestyle. You jet about Europe to join Philippe, who doesn't seem inclined to divorce his wife and leave his children to make a life with you."

His statement elicited an audible intake of breath from Anita's parents.

Fortune turned to them briefly. "You didn't know the man was married with a family?"

Anita also appeared to be shocked.

"You didn't think I knew? You underestimate me. I'm a detective." He was just getting started with Anita. "Does Philippe know you have a seven-year-old boy?"

Anita glared at him but remained silent.

"I didn't think so. You appear at Christmas and for a month in the summer, probably when he vacations with his family. That's your business. I'm asking you to let up on Davey. Give him space." He paused to let his words sink in. "I have two important jobs—to be a father and a detective. I do not have time for this, and I've run out of patience. If you don't stop your cajoling and demands, I'll submit a petition to the court for sole custody."

"You wouldn't!" Anita exclaimed, truly surprised. Her father struggled to rise from the couch in protest, but his wife pulled him back down, shaking her head.

"I met with a family divorce lawyer who said that under normal circumstances, I wouldn't have a chance, but when I described your abandonment of Davey at age five and your current living arrangements, he changed his tune. He thinks I have a case."

No one spoke for an entire minute.

He faced Anita again. "I loved you once. More than you'll ever know." His voice broke but he continued. "Part of me will always love you. But *we* are over. Finished. No more flirtatious games or suggestions that you might return if I do your bidding. I've moved on.

"I do not want to take legal action. A public court battle that airs all the dirty laundry of our failed marriage isn't in anyone's best interest. We need to minimize the effect of our failures on our son. He needs both a mother and father and grandparents who can be civil and who will respect his needs."

Fortune's beeper squawked. He moved to turn it off, but when he saw code 10-71, he abruptly rose. "Emergency. Gotta move." Code 10-71 meant shots fired. As he raced to his cruiser, he called dispatch for the location.

"The old Church Street rail station."

Chapter Fifty-Five

Agnes

A gnes sat at her desk in the study at the carriage house, staring at the papers Casey had unloaded on her the night before. How was she supposed to make sense of all this? The numbers swam before her eyes. She'd felt good about giving Casey a piece of her mind until the girl up and quit. The realization began to sink in how little Agnes knew about the property. She had no idea of how to hire a maintenance company or even what one did. But how hard could it be to find out? That real estate agent probably knew a slew of them. She dialed Blair, and the woman's efficient voice answered on the first ring.

"Agnes Dempsey here. I'm thinking of hiring a maintenance firm to take care of the White House properties. Would you have any recommendations of companies in the area?"

"I could look into that for you. What all would you like the company to do?"

Everything. "Oh...just the normal things, you know, fix things that break, arrange for mowing and the like." She heard a loud popping sound outside like a truck backfire.

"What kind of maintenance do you need? Weekly? Monthly? Are you thinking of a landscaper or a cleaner to come regularly, or a general contractor for electrical repairs or to take care of plumbing problems? There are many types of maintenance."

"Let's put it this way. I want a company that my tenants at the White House can call whenever they have a problem they can't fix themselves. If the company doesn't have the expertise in-house, I would expect it to subcontract a firm that does."

"An all-inclusive service, then." Blair was quiet for a moment. "That could be quite pricey."

Those were not the words Agnes had hoped to hear. "What does 'quite pricey' mean?"

"Well, I can't say without more details. I'd need a list of particulars. May I ask what you're paying Miss Cavendish to care for the properties currently?"

How does she know I'm using Casey? Agnes hesitated. "No. I don't think she would appreciate me discussing her salary publicly." A second loud bang outside. Strange. Could someone be hunting? In Welton?

Distracted, Agnes didn't know what to ask next, so she changed the subject. "Have you been able to come up with comparable listings yet?"

"Sorry, I haven't had time to draw up a report yet. I'll try to have something for you by the end of the week. I've been trying to reach William Kennedy, but he must be out of town. As I mentioned, he's also interested in the report."

Yes, and you want an exclusive listing from me before delivering it. Agnes was relieved that Blair hadn't been able to reach Kennedy. She didn't want Blair butting in on her real estate dealings with him.

Their conversation was interrupted by approaching sirens. "Something must be happening on Church Street. Call me with your recommendations." She hung up. The sirens became so loud they sounded as if they were in her backyard. Agnes hurried outside and turned up the road towards Church Street just as a police cruiser with strobes flashing and siren blaring screamed down Station Road. Two more police cars followed.

What on earth could be happening? Agnes bit a nail before she remembered it was coated with expensive polish. "Dammit!" She automatically crossed herself at the transgression. She hoped there wasn't an emergency to do with the missing boy. And if she were honest, and she might as well be, she hoped nothing was amiss with Casey. The girl might still prove useful.

231

Agnes returned to the carriage house but kept her ears peeled while she paced and worried.

Kennedy hadn't called again as he'd promised. What if he didn't buy the property? She'd have to hire some "pricey" firm to replace Casey. Or would she? Think about it. The White House job had been perfect for Casey. She needed the job. Ever since Mary died, she hadn't been able to find anything other than temp work, and that Cambridge handwriting thing that couldn't pay very well.

Another niggling thought crept in. Casey was suspicious of the note Agnes had used in court to be appointed Power of Attorney over Mary's affairs after her first stroke. So far, Casey hadn't challenged it, but she'd been dropping hints.

Mary died intestate as far as anyone had been able to determine. Casey was sure there had been a will, but no one could find it or locate a lawyer or notary that had drawn one up. That's because it was handwritten. The informal will that Agnes had found in the desk left the properties to her niece and nephew, Casey and Jackson, with no mention of Agnes—her own sister! Nothing at all. So unfair. Agnes had destroyed it in a fit of pique. She knew she could have convinced Mary to do the right thing and change her will in the end, but the end had come too soon.

When neither Casey nor Jackson had made an objection or alternative claim, the probate court had appointed Agnes, the closest family relative, the fiduciary guardian and executor of the estate. Everything was okay unless Casey could prove that Mary didn't write that first note that had given Agnes initial financial control. That would be forgery and would unravel everything. Agnes needed to keep Casey occupied with maintaining the properties while she arranged a quick sale. Once finalized, a sale would be very difficult to reverse.

Time for a new plan. Agnes needed to regain control. When Casey brought her the final accounts as she'd promised, Agnes would ask her to stay on for the next six months or until the property was sold, whichever happened first. She'd be doing the girl a favor, giving her plenty of notice and time to find gainful employment. That plus some kind of apology for her outburst might work, although they both knew they'd never be buddies.

More sirens approached, and again Agnes walked outside. Two ambulances turned down Station Road. Someone was hurt! What if Casey was injured? Or died? Unbelievable. What is the girl mixed up in now? Should she investigate? Nothing she could do, but she was dying of curiosity that felt like the excitement and dread when approaching an accident on the highway.

She returned to the carriage house and changed into slacks and walking shoes. Wouldn't make sense to drive. There were already a lot of vehicles down there. She walked past the gate toward Church Street. As she turned down Station Road, she had to step aside when an ambulance raced past her, back up to Church Street, sirens blaring and lights flashing. Moments later, a police car followed and slowed as it came alongside her. The officer rolled down his window. "Stop. The road is closed. The area is a crime scene."

Crime scene? It hadn't occurred to her *she* could be in danger. Those popping sounds really could have been gunshots! She hurried back to the carriage house and locked herself in.

Chapter Fifty-Six

Fortune

Fortune arrived at the station within minutes, followed by O'Malley and another cruiser. Jim was rocking back and forth on the ground, holding his head with a woman beside him. Another man was lying halfway behind the caboose, not moving. A bloody garden tool lay in front of the caboose. No gun in sight. Casey sat on the steps of the caboose, a gun resting on her knees.

O'Malley walked to Jim and pushed the woman aside, while the other policeman ran to the man by the caboose. When Fortune approached Casey, she didn't move. She stared toward the man by the caboose, eyes glassy, blood dripping from her lower lip. He bent over, touched her shoulder, and took the gun out of her hand. "Talk to me," he said. She didn't move or react to his presence. He checked her neck and felt a pulse, and then rushed to the cruiser to call for multiple ambulances.

What the hell had happened here? The injured man had a gunshot wound to his thigh and was losing blood from a three-pronged injury to the back of his neck. That explained the garden tool with bloody tines. An officer worked to staunch the bleeding while waiting for help to arrive. Jim weaved from side to side, and Casey was out. The only one in any condition to give a statement was the woman.

When Fortune approached her, she introduced herself as Emily, Jim's fiancée. She was trembling so hard she could barely speak. Fortune entered the station to get her a glass of water and immediately noticed that the telephone had been ripped off the wall.

"Don't hurt him!" Emily cried outside.

Fortune rushed back with the water. O'Malley had flipped Jim onto his stomach and handcuffed his hands behind his back. "Can't you see he needs help?" Emily knelt beside Jim, stroking the back of his head, murmuring to him. O'Malley ignored her, yanked Jim over, and forced him to stand. He shoved him forward and walked him to the rear door of his police car.

"Not so rough there, officer," commanded Fortune. "We don't know what the score is here." O'Malley didn't respond and lowered Jim's head into the car.

Fortune helped Emily to her feet and gave her the glass of water. Although she was crying, she was the only coherent person on the scene. "If you can, tell me what happened." He spoke in a low, calm voice.

"Jim and I were leaving this afternoon. I came to pick him up, and that man Wilson was on the ground, wounded. Jim was holding a gun. It wasn't his—he doesn't have a gun anymore; the police took it. Jim and Wilson had been fighting, and Jim was…"

She either couldn't continue or didn't want to say more. Fortune waited before prompting her. "Then what?"

"I took the gun from Jim, and he collapsed. Casey was on the ground, hurt. I helped her up walked her to the tree and gave her the gun. The phone was out, so I drove to town for help." At this, she broke down into sobs.

"That's enough for now. Wait for me in the car over there for a little while."

Two ambulances arrived at the crowded scene. Medics efficiently loaded Wilson and Casey onto stretchers and into the ambulances. With ear-splitting sirens, they left the scene for the hospital. O'Malley drove off with Jim in the back seat of the cruiser.

Fortune and the other officers stayed at the scene until the crime scene crews arrived. Fortune bagged the gun carefully and then found two ejected shell casings, one in the middle of the parking area and the other beside the tree where Casey had been sitting. Looked like either Jim or Casey had shot the injured man. He also collected the bloody tool.

He'd tried to warn Casey that she was dealing with two very dangerous characters, both war vets, one with a history of mental illness, and the other who had shot Casey's pumpkin and car. The image of Jim in the loft flashed through his mind. Was Jim sleeping with both Emily and Casey? And what was with the phone, ripped off the wall?

Casey looked so much smaller and more vulnerable than normal, probably because she was usually in constant motion. She could be a damsel in distress, or she could be one of the dangerous characters, who was now a candidate for a second, longer prison term for attempted murder.

Chapter Fifty-Seven

Casey

Thursday, 11/17

No cat. Scratchy sheets. Casey opened her eyes, winced at the bright lights, and tried to focus. Everything was white and beeping. Something was wrapped around her head. A woman in a lab coat approached the bed. "Good morning." She took Casey's hand and placed fingers against her wrist to take her pulse. "How are you feeling today?"

Today? What day? She was in a hospital bed. She tried to sit up but was constrained by the sheets.

"Relax. You took quite a rap on your head. I'd like to ask you a few questions." The nurse pressed a button, and the back of the bed raised Casey to a sitting position. She held two fingers in front of Casey. "How many fingers?"

"Two."

"Follow my finger." The nurse moved her hand about. "What's your name?"

"Casey Cavendish."

"Who is the President of the United States?"

"You really don't know?" Casey was tiring of this routine. "Okay. Jimmy Carter."

The last she remembered she was sitting against a tree holding a gun. "Is Jim all right? Did they arrest Wilson?"

"I'm sorry, hon. I don't have any answers for you. For now, it's important that you get some rest. The doctor will be in to see you in a little while."

After breakfast, the doctor appeared, declared her alive, and said they'd keep her another day for observation. When she shook her head to object, the pain was excruciating. "You have a hard head, but you took quite a blow. We need to make certain you're okay before we can release you. Get some rest."

Sleep. Sounded good, but when she closed her eyes, her mind wouldn't cooperate, swirling with negative thoughts. Why was she plagued with violence? How had she earned so much rotten luck? Was she in control of anything? She'd been framed and sent to prison. She found a new family and lost it. The gift of a caboose came with an unsolved murder and crazy violence from the Vietnam War. She wasn't the cause of any of these horrible situations, but had landed smack dab in the center of them, buffeted and injured.

So depressing. She had the station, but she longed for a home. She wanted a family, but that was beyond her reach. Men just wanted sex. Heart, hormones, and hope had aligned with George in Ohio, and his betrayal had crushed her. Would she ever trust fully again? Her prospects were grim. The only man worth his salt was Fortune, and he thought she was a tart.

She had two good friends in LouAnne and Rosie, but they were busy with a new venture and were expecting a baby. Poor Jim. He finally was functioning and had found his old love, only to be brought low by that monster Wilson. Would anyone believe Jim when he claimed self-defense? Casey pictured Jim in her mind's eye as he rocked back and forth with his head in his hands.

Loretta? She was a strange woman, not a pal, operating a brothel in the A-frame. Children? Casey'd loved George's daughter Gabby, and now Petey. She liked Fortune's boy Davey, too, but kids were not for her without a partner.

And family? A brother and a great aunt in Ohio. Agnes, for Christ's sake.

Even employment was a major challenge. A BA in history. Teaching? Who wants their children to learn from a woman who spent ten years brushing shoulders with criminals? Go back to school and learn a trade? How to pay for it? Handwriting, maybe. But it would take time developing a clientele.

She'd done everything right, and it all turned to shit. The more she thought, the lower she got. Even that worried her. Mary had confided in her that her father, the priest, was manic depressive. It could be hereditary. Was she on a downward spiral headed toward catatonia? Maybe that would be a blessing.

"You have fifteen minutes. Miss Cavendish needs to rest and recover."

Officer O'Malley strode into the room and sat in a chair opposite Casey's bed. He frowned at the nurse who had followed him but nodded his assent before she left the room.

He looked at Casey and shook his head. "Once again, you're at the center of a violent scene." He took out a notebook. "Tell me your version of what happened at the station yesterday."

Casey was disappointed that Fortune had relegated the debriefing task to O'Malley, but not really surprised. She spoke slowly, beginning with Wilson's prior visits to the caboose looking for Jim. Then she recounted the events as best she could from when Wilson knocked her out to her last memory, leaning against a tree holding a gun on him. She hoped she made sense.

He followed her words and took notes while she spoke. "That it?" he asked.

"Yes. Do you have questions?" His challenging manner suggested that he didn't believe her.

"Loads of 'em. Your story doesn't match Sergeant Wilson's, and given your history, his is more believable." O'Malley flipped shut his notepad and started to rise.

"I wasn't telling a story," Casey objected. "What did Wilson say?"

O'Malley settled back down. "Wilson said he was following Jim because Jim had accused him of the rape and murder of civilians after a firefight in Vietnam. Wilson is running for public office as a decorated veteran and needed Jim to retract his accusations prior to the election.

"Wilson said that you were woozy, and your hands were tied when he arrived. Jim was going to take off with your money. He tried to reason with Jim, but Jim wouldn't listen. Jim pulled a gun and shot him in the leg. Wilson thought he was dead for sure, but the girlfriend came and talked Jim down. He collapsed. The girl gave you the gun and drove to the police. You shot one round to keep Jim from attacking Wilson again, and then we came."

Officer O'Malley gave her a smarmy smile. "Now, would you like to revise your story?"

"No. You've got it backwards. Wilson attacked Jim." How could she convince this pile of lard that Wilson was lying through his teeth? Clearly, O'Malley wanted to believe Wilson. "I gave the money to Jim. He was going to leave with Emily. Wilson came and drew a gun on Jim." She was becoming more and more upset when the nurse entered and ended the interview.

Casey's mind whirled. She was confounded and blindsided by Wilson's version of events. Was she in trouble? Was Jim? Who would people believe—an ex-con with a head injury and fuzzy memory, a veteran who was in recovery from serious bouts of anxiety and paranoia, or a decorated veteran and family man who was running for public office? Other members of Wilson's military company would deny Jim's allegations which would of course, also incriminate them.

The nurse took her blood pressure and frowned. She left and returned shortly with a few pills. "You really need to sleep. I'm sorry that the officer got you so riled up." She pulled the blinds and left the room.

Fifteen minutes later, the pills and the quiet beeps won out over her crazed thoughts, and she dozed off.

Chapter Fifty-Eight

L ater in the morning, Casey awakened when another woman was wheeled into the room. For the next few hours, she serenaded Casey with moans and groans and a running commentary about the ineptness of the hospital staff. She was hard to ignore. Casey asked an aide to pull a screen between their beds closed, but the effect only muted the woman's higher notes.

Outside the door, yet another woman's penetrating whine bombarded her senses. The nurse gave a new visitor instructions to be brief and not to upset the patient.

"I'm her aunt. I need to speak with my niece."

Casey closed her eyes and willed her eyelids not to twitch, playing possum, but she couldn't protect her ears.

"A fine mess you're in now. It's the company you keep—criminals, crazy hobos. Just when I need your help, you're in the hospital. I haven't been able to reach that nice Mr. Kennedy, and now the real estate agent is badgering me for details about the property that I have no way of providing. Are you listening?"

Apparently, Agnes hadn't noticed that Casey's eyes were closed. Casey groaned and rolled to the side, effectively blocking one ear. The annoying voice faded in and out. "...need a pest-control man to remove squirrels in the attic...keeping me awake at night with their noise...when are you coming...you need to fix your telephone..."

Did she just say she had squirrels in the attic? Casey fought hard to suppress a smile.

"That nasty Mrs. Kennedy came looking for you, all upset, wondering where you were. She needs your help. I told her you were in the hospital but would be back soon and could help her. You're still working for me until the end of the month, so you need to respond."

Couldn't Agnes see the bandage around her head?

"She said their little goose was missing. What on earth is she talking about? She wants you to come to the White House as soon as you can."

Did she say, "their little goose was missing?" Pay attention. Casey opened her eyes. Loretta and Kennedy called Petey their Little Goose. Casey sat up, fully awake. "Is Petey still missing?" she asked.

"Who is Petey?"

"Loretta's little boy. The one Vlad was looking for when he barged into your house."

"How would I know?" Agnes' voice took on a petulant tone. "What on earth happened at the station? There was an awful ruckus."

Just then, there was a tap on the door, and Fortune walked in. "I'll need a moment with Miss Cavendish," he said, dismissing Agnes. Agnes rose with a whiff, her new nose bent out of shape, and marched out the door.

Miss Cavendish?

He didn't sit. "Officer O'Malley is writing up your statement. When you're more rested, I'd like to go over it with you."

"Did he tell you what I said?"

"Yes."

"Do you believe me?"

"Frankly, I don't know who or what to believe. I've come to advise you, once you leave here, you are to stay at the station until we clear up all the details."

"I'm under house arrest?"

"You could put it that way."

Look me in the eye, dammit! "Have I done something wrong?"

"Did you discharge the gun?"

"Yes, but I aimed wide on purpose to warn Wilson not to crawl any closer. It was self-defense. He was the one who attacked Jim."

"We'll need to revisit that claim with all parties involved. Shooting toward an unarmed man could be construed as anything from reckless endangerment to attempted murder."

Jesus God, he was cold! "At least let me know how Jim is."

"Jim has been transferred to the VA."

"Have they found Petey?"

Fortune frowned and met her eyes for the first time. "Found him? I didn't know he was missing."

Casey was torn. Should she tell him about Loretta's plan to escape with Petey? No. "Kennedy's handyman, Vlad, came to the station and to Agnes' house searching for him, and just now, Agnes said Mrs. Kennedy was looking for him."

"When did he go missing?"

"I don't know. When is now? I don't know what day it is."

"I'll look into it." At the door, he turned for a last word. "I'm sorry you're hurt. The station was open, so I fed Isabella and Little Mother." With that, he was gone.

"Damn! Damn! DAMN!" Casey felt like she could explode in frustration.

The nurse rushed into the room. "Calm down!" She took Casey's wrist. "You need to rest and not get all riled up."

"When can I go home? When is the doctor coming?"

"I'm sorry, but the doctor is seeing to a number of emergencies. He said to hold you over until morning." She produced a small cup with pills. "Take these and try to relax."

Not as if she had a choice. Casey downed the pills and tried to relax, but it wasn't easy with all the foreign noises and bustle of the hospital.

Chapter Fifty-Nine

C asey had to wait until mid-morning the next day before the doctor declared her alive and fit to go home. She was about to call LouAnne to beg a ride when the nurse popped her head into the room. "It's time to get ready to go. Your ride is here."

My ride?

LouAnne sauntered into the room and over to the bed, shaking her head. "Hey, girlfriend. Lucky you got a rock-hard noggin." Her words were teasing, but she held Casey's hand and searched her eyes. "Doctor says you can go if you behave. We'll take you home and get you settled."

After the nurse gave her final instructions for release, an orderly came for her with a wheelchair, insisting she ride down the hallway, into the elevator, and all the way to the door. Rosie gave her a peck on the cheek and wheeled her to their van. He drove them to the station and then left on a mission.

They were greeted at the door by a little dog with a full-body wag, and a cat who looked annoyed. LouAnne settled Casey into her rocker and then fixed her soup and a sandwich. "We went out for groceries this morning. That local store is expensive! Now, tell Lou everything."

Little Mother jumped into Casey's lap, demanding attention. Casey petted her while she recounted both versions of events, hers and Wilson's.

LouAnne listened intently with an occasional interjection. When Casey finished, LouAnne tried to lighten the mood. "I passed that handsome cop

244

on the way into your room. He's the one who called us."

"Huh. I wondered how you knew where I was. Guess he knew I'd be checking out before I did. I don't think he believes me. And he thinks I slept with Jim."

"No way."

"Way. He saw a shirtless Jim hiding in the loft when he came by with his dog. We thought the person at the door would be Wilson."

"But now he's met Jim's girlfriend…"

"Makes it even worse." Casey bit her lip again, where it was already sore. She wouldn't cry, but it sure was unfair.

"You sweet on that handsome cop?"

Casey chose not to answer. "And little Petey is missing. His mother was looking for him."

"How long?"

"I don't know."

"Sure hope he's okay."

Just then, they heard two taps of a horn. LouAnne went outside and spoke with Rosie. "Girlfriend, you gotta get the door," she shouted.

Casey rose slowly and held the door open. Rosie and LouAnne hefted a sofa bed out of the rear of the van and up the three steps into the station. They moved a few pieces of furniture around and set the bed against the far wall.

"No way you're climbing up to that loft," said Rosie.

"I don't believe you guys!" said Casey. She got some sheets and a blanket, and they made the bed.

"We'll check out the caboose and look up and down the tracks, just in case there's a little boy hiding. Now you listen to Lou. Bed rest. No catting around. You need a good week of peace and quiet." After very gentle hugs, they left.

"Move over, you two," Casey said to the furballs. She sank into her new bed fully dressed. Little Mother curled up next to her, and Isabella settled at her feet. Wonderful quiet. No beeps, carts rolling around, voices in the hallway, nurses appearing at all hours. Just as her eyes began to close, she heard a car pull up outside. Moments later, the doorbell rang.

She dragged herself to the door and was surprised to see Fortune through the peephole.

She opened the door and gestured for him to enter.

He didn't smile but nodded at the sofa bed. "Good idea."

"LouAnne and Rosie," Casey said.

He took in her black eye and puffy cheek and the knob on the side of her head. He grimaced. "You look awful."

Not what a girl wants to hear, but at least he was speaking to her.

"May I?" he asked, pointing to a chair.

Her turn to nod.

He sat and took out a notebook. "Two things. First, I got a call this morning from an officer in Charleston, South Carolina, asking if I had heard or seen anything more of Chauncey Cunningham. I told the officer, I'd ask you if he'd surfaced again." He waited for her response.

"He breezed through last week, but didn't come in."

"Did he say where he was going? Do you have a number or an address for him?"

"I think somewhere up north, and no, I have no contact information. Why are they looking for him?"

"What was he driving?"

"The green Jaguar."

"What day was this?"

"I don't know. I've lost contact with the days."

"Okay. I'd like to clear up a few points from the statement you made to O'Malley."

"Sure, but not until you tell me what is going on with Chance."

"The Jaguar was abandoned in northern Maine. According to the officer, Cunningham is a suspect in the embezzlement of funds from his family's business. The police didn't start looking for him until the family discovered the theft a few days ago. I called Granger, and he thinks Cunningham's probably somewhere in Canada by now. He had a big head start."

Fortune studied her for a moment. Casey wasn't really surprised. Chance was a very smooth, sketchy character. He hadn't been charged with a crime when he impersonated Mary's son-in-law, but he wasn't honest either. Now, apparently, he'd crossed the line and was on the wrong side of the law.

"You will call me if he shows up again?" Fortune asked.

"What are your questions about my statement?"

"You didn't answer me."

"See how it feels when people don't answer your questions?" Casey stared at Fortune to make sure he got her point before adding, "Yes, I'll call you."

Little Mother took this moment to jump down from the sofa bed and saunter over to where Fortune was sitting. Uninvited, she jumped up into his lap.

Surprised, he petted her. She curled up in his lap with a loud rusty purr.

"Wilson claims that Jim knocked you out and was about to take off with your money when he arrived. Jim had $500 in his wallet when we searched him."

"I gave the money to Jim earlier that morning. He and Emily were planning to leave, to get away from Wilson, and I wanted to help them. He took my car to run errands to prepare for their trip and didn't return until I was tied up and sitting on the steps of the caboose."

"So, Jim didn't knock you out."

"No. When I came to, Wilson was the only person here. He had a gun and was waiting for Jim to return."

Fortune pushed Little Mother off his lap in order to make a note of her comment before continuing. "Emily said Jim was holding the gun when she drove in, and that Wilson was on the ground, wounded. I assume that Jim shot Wilson."

"That's right, but only in self-defense." Casey described how Wilson walked past her, aiming the gun at Jim. "I distracted Wilson by hitting him from behind with the garden tool. They fought, and Jim came up with the gun."

"*Distracted?* You hit Wilson with the fork with your hands tied?" Fortune sounded skeptical.

Casey placed her wrists together, rose, raised them over her head, and brought them down hard, struggling to keep her balance as she demonstrated her move.

Fortune winced. "I get the picture." He paused for a moment. "Why did Jim shoot Wilson?"

"Wilson kept walking forward, challenging Jim, who held the gun. Jim told him to stop, but he didn't. He taunted Jim, saying he didn't have it in him to shoot. He was wrong."

"Emily said she took the gun from Jim and gave it to you. Did you fire it?"

"Yes. I told you yesterday. Wilson didn't think I'd shoot either when I told him to stop. I aimed wide." Casey met Fortune's eyes. "Do you believe me?"

Little Mother made another pass at Fortune by jumping nimbly into his lap. He stroked her gently before answering Casey's question. "I want to, but I also don't want to get your hopes up. Jim has a history of mental problems and had to be subdued a number of times in the VA hospital. He's still traumatized. Pretty out of it. Without his account, it will be your word against Wilson's."

Fortune put the kitty down on the floor and picked up his notepad. "Wilson has a strong following and a solid reputation. He claims that Jim is bitter and deranged. Two members of Wilson's Army unit deny Jim's accusations. A representative from the Army admitted that Jim had been wounded by friendly fire and found in a pile of bodies, still alive when they were counting the number of enemy dead."

Casey was determined to convince Fortune. "You know how Wilson had been stalking Jim and was threatening me—I even drew a picture of him—and how he shot my pumpkin. He's the crazy, violent one. You can test the bullet I dug out of my car to see if it matches the rifle in his pickup truck. For that matter, if they have the bullet that killed the vet in the woods in New Hampshire, they could test to see if it matches Wilson's rifle."

Fortune started to write, but Little Mother refused to be denied. She leaped up again, planted her hind legs on Fortune's lap, and her forepaws on his chest, and nuzzled his chin. He grinned at her and nuzzled back.

Casey shook her head at the brassy feline.

Fortune held the kitty in his arms as he stood. "I'll call the phone company to get a repairman in to fix your phone." He placed Little Mother on the table, retrieved his notebook, and headed for the door. "Don't go anywhere. Take care of yourself."

Casey wished she were a cat.

Chapter Sixty

After Fortune left, Casey wandered around the station at a loss for what to do. Fortune said to stay put, which she interpreted as house arrest while the police investigated the wildly dissimilar accounts of what had happened between Jim, Wilson, and her.

She had no job. No duties. And certainly, no pressing social engagements. She'd transferred most of the records for the White House properties over to Agnes, although Agnes probably wouldn't know how to interpret some of the details.

She was really worried about Petey. Vlad had barged into Agnes' place and the station days ago looking for him. When she visited the hospital, Agnes said Loretta had been to her house looking for Petey, so clearly Loretta and Petey hadn't made their escape as of yesterday. Casey wasn't supposed to drive, and the phone was out of commission, but she could walk up to the White House to see if Loretta was still there and, if so, find out if she'd found Petey. The doctors said to take it easy, but how hard would it be to walk up the hill? She was a little unsteady, but she could go slowly.

She donned a shirt and jeans and began the trek up the stone steps to the White House. She had to stop and rest every so often, catch her breath, and check her balance before continuing. Finally, she reached the top of the steps and walked across the circular drive to the White House. The sheer size of the building still cowed her. This is where rich and famous people lived. But she reminded herself, her Aunt Mary had also lived here, albeit in the servants' quarters. She rang the bell and waited. She rang again and then, when there was no response, knocked hard. She expected Vlad or

Olga to answer the door.

She knew the alarm code to enter. But should she? Agnes had passed on Loretta's instruction for Casey to come to the White House as soon as possible. That sounded urgent. Casey used her key, turned the knob, entered and punched in the numbers to stop the alarm. She'd only been inside once since the Kennedys' arrival, and then it was with Agnes for a short meeting with Kennedy. She'd been so hopeful then, eager to meet her new neighbors, but Kennedy's gruff reception, demands, and handwriting put a damper on her positive expectations.

Now all was quiet. "Anybody home?" she called out. No response. Where could they be? Loretta said Kennedy often traveled, but Vlad and Olga stayed close to home as did Loretta. She walked through familiar rooms still arranged with the furniture and décor from when Mary and Vera had lived there. It felt like time travel being here again amidst the same trappings she'd known before.

As far as Casey could determine, nothing of significance had been changed or added. Even if the place had been rented furnished, wouldn't there be some signs of occupancy? No new Kennedy wedding pictures graced the sidebar. No magazines or knitting lay on a table. Nothing. No personal touches.

In the library, a few notebooks, pens, and loose papers on the desk were signs that someone occupied the place. She tried the drawers of the desk, but they were locked. She shouldn't be snooping, but this was very strange. The house was like an empty mausoleum.

In the rear servants' quarters where Mary and Vera had lived, there was no sign of Vlad or Olga. At all. Beds were made, closets and drawers empty. No toothbrushes, towels, washcloths, or shampoo. Every sign of occupancy was cleared out and cleaned up. *Seriously* strange. What had happened? Where had they gone?

In the kitchen she found a half-full pot of coffee and a mug in the sink. She touched the side of the pot. Cold. Probably breakfast coffee. There was food—cheese, butter, milk, juice and the remains of something that looked like lasagna—in the fridge. In the breakfast nook she found oranges and bananas arranged in a bowl. Half a bottle of wine corked on the counter and a few dishes in the dishwasher suggested someone was still here.

How long had she been snooping? Was she pressing her luck? She'd already quit her job, so she couldn't be fired. She'd say she'd come to find out about Petey and was worried when no one answered the door. But that wasn't a good reason to have her nose in the fridge.

Dare she? In for a penny. She padded up the stairs to the second floor. At the top, she had to decide which way to turn, east or west. Mary's old room was in the east wing, so Casey turned left. Yes. She'd guessed right. The adult Kennedys used the rooms at the end of the hallway. The master bedroom was clearly Loretta's haunt. The walk-in closet was packed with expensive clothes and multiple pairs of shoes. A vanity was chock-a-block with creams, lipstick, eye makeup, and perfumes. A pair of slacks and a sweater were draped over a chair. Hairbrushes, a pill container, and soaps crowded the sink in the bath. So, it was fair to assume that she hadn't left.

Kennedy's room across from Loretta's was immaculate, almost regimental by comparison with suits lined up, and jackets, slacks, and shirts neatly arranged in his closet. Loose change and cufflinks lay on the bureau.

She walked down the hall to Petey's room in the west wing. Again, clothing was strewn all around, but there were very few toys. Casey would expect a rich kid to have all manner of expensive games and sporting equipment, models, boy stuff. She looked but didn't find his backpack or sneakers. If Olga was taking care of him—or had been—she was doing a lousy job.

Enough. How long had she been inside? She was really pushing it. She rushed downstairs, careful to reset the alarm before she closed the door. Phew! Good to be outside. She walked around the house to the garages. There were three bays. A shiny black Mercedes sedan occupied the first. The second and third bays were vacant. Casey remembered when the Kennedys had arrived, they'd come in a parade of two cars and a van.

Looked like Olga and Vlad had left in the van. Kennedy could have taken a cab to the airport for one of his trips. Loretta had spoken to Agnes recently, worrying about where Petey was. Had Loretta found the backpack and left with Petey after Casey talked with Agnes? Maybe. One car was missing.

But probably not. Casey had just seen her clothes and makeup in the master bedroom.

Could be Loretta was at the A-frame. Casey was tired and confused but determined to find out. She walked down President's Lane and turned down the drive to the A-frame. Once again, no one answered the door when she rang the bell and knocked.

She offered a loud "Yoo-hoo!" to announce her presence. No response. Inside, the place was immaculate and empty. Time to see if Loretta found the backpack. Casey opened the door to the pool. It looked like the pool service had finally come and closed the pool for the season. The filter was off, and the tarp stretched the length of the pool. They should have stored the pool furniture. Casey reminded herself that it was no longer her job to tailgate service providers.

She walked to the far corner table where Petey had played under an umbrella while the adults frolicked. Huh. No pack. Either Loretta or Vlad and Olga or the pool service people had found it. Casey sank into a chair, none the wiser. What else could she do? She rested and mulled over what she'd seen. She'd hoped that Petey had come home, Loretta found the money, and that they had lit out for parts unknown, but what she'd just seen at the White House suggested otherwise.

The sun felt good on her face. She closed her eyes. Her head ached but the pain was nowhere near as bad as it had been a few days ago. The doctor said in a month or so, she'd be like new.

The sound of a door closing jarred her awake. Disoriented at first, it took a moment for Casey to regain her bearings. She listened carefully but didn't hear any other sounds. Once again, she noted that the pool service had done a substandard job. They should have lowered the water level below the skimmer, and the tarp had wrinkles in it when it should be taut.

Oh no. On the far side of the pool, it looked as if some poor animal had nosed under the tarp and been caught. Casey walked over and bent down, hoping she was wrong. She had to tug hard to lift up the edge. The smell was putrid. She held her breath and yanked.

Kennedy stared up at her with bulging, sightless eyes. A large kitchen knife protruded from his neck.

Chapter Sixty-One

Casey dropped the tarp and staggered backwards. She fell into the grass, gasping and heaving until nothing remained in her stomach. After she caught her breath, she heard footsteps behind her. A shadow blocked the sunlight. She looked up and was surprised to see Loretta peering down at her with a concerned expression.

"I'm *so* sorry you had to see that." Loretta reached a hand down to help Casey stand. She guided her to a pool chair. "Sit for a moment. Do you need some water?"

Casey shook her head no and instantly regretted the motion. She was confused. Loretta knew her husband's body was in the pool.

Loretta pulled up a chair and took a seat close to Casey. "Are you sure you're okay?" Her eyes traveled over Casey's face and her black eye. "I heard about the horrible mess at the station from your aunt." Her voice lowered, and she continued. "I planned to come down to the station after I'd done a few errands today to check in on you. It looks like you took quite a hit."

Errands?! Her husband was under the tarp with a knife in his throat!

Loretta nodded her head as if to acknowledge the horror on Casey's face. "We've had some violence here as well." She waited for Casey to speak, but Casey had no words. "You knew that my husband was a cruel man. I told you about him earlier. And you know how I planned to escape with Petey and the money from the parties."

There's a dead man twenty feet away. "What happened?" Casey asked in a feeble voice.

"Fisher found out my plan somehow. Maybe because of something you

255

said to him? I don't know how." Again, she waited for a reaction, but Casey was speechless. "Anyway, he alerted William. Are you following this?" Loretta leaned forward and looked directly into her eyes.

Casey nodded very slowly. Kennedy was dead, but where was the boy? "Where is Petey? Has he come home?"

"Your aunt brought him to me this morning."

Casey closed her eyes. "Thank goodness."

"Your aunt's not a very pleasant woman, but I suspect you're aware of that," Loretta said with a wry smile. "She caught Petey in her kitchen stealing food. He'd been hiding in her attic."

Loretta was chattering away as if the situation was normal. "Ah, the squirrels," muttered Casey as she tried to make sense of the surreal scene. Agnes had complained of squirrels in the attic.

"Squir—"

"Why did he run away?"

"He saw the fight between me and William. He freaked and ran."

Casey frowned and glanced around. "Where is he now?"

"Playing in the caboose. He's okay, but still a bit traumatized. When I was sure that you'd been released from the hospital, I took Petey down to see you. Understandably, he's too frightened to return to the White House or the A-frame. You weren't home, but your car was still there, so I guessed you were on your way to the White House. Your cute little dog was delighted to see Petey. I left the two of them together, did a few errands in town, and came up here."

So, that's why there was one car in the garage. Loretta had the other, and Vlad and Olga had left in the van. "Thank God he's back. I was worried when Agnes said your Little Goose was missing. Why do you call him that?"

"That's William's nickname for him. It's because of Petey's trust fund. We manage the money. Frankly, that's how we could afford to rent the White House."

"But why did you need more money by giving parties?" Casey asked.

"You know what they say, you can never have too much. We were both happy with the arrangement. I made money, and William used the tapes."

"Blackmail," muttered Casey.

"Let's call it leverage. The tapes were useful in delicate business negotia-tions."

"Why not divorce him? You'd probably get custody of Petey."

"Not an option. I told you before that he's a very jealous and violent man. He threatened to kill me if I tried to leave him or looked at another man. When he found out…" She hesitated.

"…you were having an affair…," said Casey. She swallowed hard to dispel a second wave of nausea. "What happened? Who stabbed Kennedy?"

Loretta frowned but then nodded acknowledgment. "William and I had a tremendous fight. You saw the bruise on my cheek." Loretta pushed up her sleeve, revealing a new purple bruise on her arm. I feared for my life."

Loretta was silent for a moment, watching Casey. "I thought William had left on his weekly trip to New York and that it was the perfect time to escape. He fooled me. I took Petey and went to the A-frame to collect the money and tapes. I was standing right here when I heard a car in the drive. I looked over the fence and saw William. I ran inside and called Vlad for help on the intercom.

"William entered by the pool gate, and we argued. He yelled at Petey to get in his car and stay there. He was out-of-his mind crazy screaming. He chased me inside and hit me across the room. I thought for sure I was going to die. I dodged around furniture, made it to the kitchen, and grabbed a knife. William caught me and gripped my arm so hard I dropped it. He hit me again, and that's when Vlad appeared.

"He overpowered him and got the knife and…" Loretta lowered her eyes and gestured toward the pool. She put her head in her hands as if to dispel the memory. She paused for a few moments to regain her composure. "Olga helped roll him into the pool and cover him. They hosed the blood off the pool deck. And now they've taken off."

"Why would Vlad defend you?"

"You need to understand. Vlad and Olga hated William. They were illegals, and he held that over them, treating them like slaves. Vlad came to me and said it was time to go because William had ordered him to install a bomb in my car. William promised them the van and plenty of money and told them they could pick up new identity papers and airline tickets from Fisher in Rhode Island."

Casey had seen violence in the heavy strokes, deep slashes, and sharp angles in the man's writing, but a *bomb*? Casey couldn't believe it. "That sounds like the plot of a B movie."

"Not as strange as you might think. We received a number of bomb threats in Rhode Island that we reported to the police. And then there was the arson. An explosion would fit right in.

"Vlad was no fool. He realized William would try to frame him. Vlad had been involved in arson and explosives activity in Eastern Europe. He knew they'd be deported the second the police started asking questions. Vlad was defending me, but still, he stabbed Kennedy. He knew they had to run."

Unbelievable. But then again, Casey glanced across the pool, there was a man-sized bump in the tarp.

Casey closed her eyes, trying to think. Vlad had come looking for Petey before the whole mess with Wilson. So, that was when Loretta and Kennedy had the fight, and Kennedy was stabbed. But the A-frame had been completely scoured clean when Casey had left the backpack with the money at Petey's table. Was that before or after…? Before. The pool was still open. Casey struggled to keep the timeline straight.

Clearly, Loretta was still here because she had to find Petey. Besides, with no more Kennedy, there was no reason to run. But why was the body still in the pool? "Have you called the police?"

"I will, but I needed to give Vlad and Olga time to get far away, and I was focused on finding Petey and calming him down. Now that he's back, I can make the call." Loretta stood. "Enough for now. You must be exhausted. Let's get you situated back at the station. You've had quite a hit on the head." She helped Casey up, put her arm around her waist, and steered her toward the door. Casey looked back at the lump under the tarp.

"Before I make the call, though, I'd like to store a few things in your safe." Casey stopped. "What things?"

Loretta walked over to a storage bin where they kept beach towels and pool toys. She opened the lid and withdrew Petey's backpack and a tote bag. "The money we earned. It was good of you to bring it up to me. Now I don't need to run, but I'd rather the police didn't discover our little side business." Loretta continued walking toward the door.

Casey didn't follow her. The last thing she needed in her safe was the ill-gotten gains from a prostitution ring and tapes that would probably be used for blackmail. "You have plenty of places to hide things."

"Probably, but what's more secure than a safe? I'd feel more comfortable if you do me this one last favor."

"Sorry. I'd rather not."

"Don't be sorry. It's not a big deal. Just for a little while until all this blows over."

All this blows over?

Casey's astonishment at Loretta's casual statement must have shown on her face, because Loretta quickly added, "You don't need to worry. I'll share some of the money with you. After all, you're on a few of the tapes." Loretta smiled and took her arm to encourage her.

Casey withdrew her arm and backed away. She didn't like being used. Offering her money and reminding her she had been recorded sure smacked of manipulation. Her voice, feeble with shock earlier, gained strength. "No."

Loretta turned abruptly. "No? Oh, but I think yes." Her tone changed from soft and comforting to controlled, her eyes narrowed, and her facial expression, so understanding seconds before, was now set in hard lines.

Despite her fogged brain, the instant change in demeanor wasn't lost on Casey. "No," she repeated.

"Huh." Loretta set the backpack and tote down on the deck and retraced her steps to the far side of the pool. She lifted up the tarp. Crouching, she gripped both hands around the knife in Kennedy's neck, turned her head aside with a grimace, and yanked. The body bobbed up and down in the water as Loretta re-covered it with the tarp. She stood holding the long carving knife for a moment and then slowly approached Casey. As she drew near, she brandished the blade in the air with a smile. "Yes, was the correct answer. Grab those bags and move!"

Chapter Sixty-Two

Casey backed away, shocked by the changes in Loretta. She'd seen traits of manipulation and control in the woman's handwriting, but not violence. But who knew what one would do in desperate circumstances?

"You don't think I'll use it, do you?" Loretta's smile was ugly. She lunged forward and swiped, slicing Casey's arm.

Casey gasped and grabbed her injured limb.

"Now, pick up the damn bags! One in each hand. For balance," ordered Loretta. Casey did as she was told. She glanced down and saw that the tote was crammed with plastic cartridges, undoubtedly tapes.

"Move!" Loretta pricked her in the rear with the point of the knife.

At any other time, Casey could probably overpower Loretta with a sharp turn and a few feints and kicks, but she was in no shape to make any quick moves. In contrast, Loretta was in good shape, wasn't injured, and was determined. They walked through the gate in the pool fence and down the path. Every few steps, Loretta encouraged Casey with a prick. Casey walked slowly but had to keep moving.

"Turn right," Loretta said as they reached the intersection with President's Lane.

"Where are we going?"

"The caboose, of course."

"Why? Petey's probably on his way up here."

"Wrong. I locked him and that cute little puppy of yours in the storage closet." Loretta poked her again. "I said, turn right."

Why right? So that they wouldn't pass the carriage house and be seen by Agnes. Loretta said that she'd just returned from errands and left Petey in the caboose. She must have locked him in and then driven back to the White House. When Casey wasn't there, she walked down to the A-frame. Now, Loretta had no intention of plodding all the way down to the station. She'd get the car.

Casey's mind ran in circles trying to figure things out. If Loretta had Petey and his trust fund, plus a backpack crammed with money and the tapes, why did she need Casey? Loretta thought she knew the combination to the safe. Even after she'd put the goods in the safe, then what? She wouldn't entrust her treasure to Casey. And why bother to hide anything?

Casey struggled to put the pieces together. She was missing the point. Without Kennedy, Vlad, or Olga, she and Fisher were the only ones who knew about the money, the tapes, and the cameras. She would want to hide the evidence. Now that Kennedy was dead, Loretta would control the trust fund, but earlier, Loretta had said. "You can never have enough." She still wanted the money from her parties. Maybe she assumed she could ensure Casey's silence because Casey appeared on the tapes serving the guests, had accepted money, and had the evidence in her safe.

Why lock up Petey? Loretta said he was afraid of Kennedy, but he could have run away from her. For sure, he'd fear her now. Poor kid trapped in a small, dark, stuffy place. At least he was with Bella.

Was there anyone who could help? Agnes was the only one around. Vlad and Olga were gone. LouAnne wasn't likely to make another visit to check on Casey today. Fisher was in Rhode Island, and Kennedy was definitely incapacitated. She couldn't imagine Fortune was about to pay a social call. Would Agnes help? Could she? Irony of ironies, Casey had to pin her hopes on Agnes and try to get to the carriage house.

Casey pictured Loretta brandishing the knife at the pool. Right-handed. She remembered some of LouAnne's prison advice. Go toward your attacker, not away. Casey slowed her pace and hung her head. With a low moan, she pretended to stumble and faint and fall backwards. Loretta stopped short, giving Casey a second to twist about and swing the backpack into Loretta's knees. Loretta screamed and sliced, but Casey jumped aside. With all the power she could muster, she buried her fist into Loretta's stomach.

"Oooof!" Loretta staggered, lost her balance, and fell on her back and the knife sailed into the brush beside the road. Casey turned around and willed her legs to move downhill toward the carriage house. At first, she tried to run but almost fell. She had neither the balance nor the stamina to keep up the pace. How far? About a football field. Mind over matter. Loretta would lose time searching for the knife.

She moved in fits and starts. Move. Breathe. Move. Breathe. Keep going. Halfway there. She bent over and had to stop. Her legs were rubber. C'mon, girl! Her lungs burned, and her heart pounded against her ribs. For a second, she dared a look backwards. Loretta was up and running, knife flashing in her hand.

Fifteen yards more. She forced one foot in front of the other. Footfalls and hard breathing behind her. One more effort. Could she make it? Push!

"Agnes! Help! Agnes!"

She banged into the door as it opened to a startled Agnes. "Help me. She'll kill me!" Casey begged as she staggered through into the hallway.

"Casey? What on earth—"

In the kitchen, she fell against a table. Up or down? Attic or cellar? No time. She couldn't climb stairs. The cellar door was in front of her. She opened it, ducked inside, balanced on the top step, and closed the door just as Loretta burst into the house. Casey stood stock still in complete darkness.

"Where is she?" Loretta demanded.

"What do you think you're doing—?" answered Agnes.

Footsteps ran from one room to another and then back into the kitchen.

"Don't be cute. Where's Casey? I saw her come in." Loretta's heavy breathing sounded as if she were standing right beside the cellar door.

Silence.

Casey heard a loud smack. "One more time. Where is she?"

"Okay, okay. Don't hurt me. Put that down. Please."

Loretta must be threatening her with the knife. Casey held her breath. Would Agnes give her away?

"She's...she's...probably in the attic." Casey followed the sound as they moved across the kitchen through another door to the stairway that led up to the attic. A set of single footsteps returned to the kitchen. Casey froze. She gasped as the cellar door opened. Agnes leaned forward and flicked on the light. "Hurry. Door's in the corner." She waited for Casey to reach the bottom step before plunging her back into darkness and closing the door.

Casey groped her way slowly in the cold and musty cellar, bumping into unknown objects, toward the far side of the cellar. A faint light came from a high, dirty window, probably an old coal chute, but it was enough for her to keep her bearings. She felt a surge of déjà vu, remembering the cellar of the old inn where she had grown up. She was careful not to knock things over, catching something—a lamp?—at the last second before it toppled to the floor.

Finally, she reached the three steps up to the outside door. She pushed upward, but it didn't budge. Would it be locked? She pushed harder. She was losing blood and strength. On the third push, the old door screeched and grated and opened out onto the backyard. Had Loretta come down from the attic? Could she hear the noise? Didn't matter. Casey had to move.

Where to go? Church Street? Or the caboose? Either direction, she had no way to defend herself. Her only hope was the can of Mace in the pocket of her jacket hanging on a peg inside the station. Think! Loretta would expect Casey to take the Station Road because she was in bad shape, and it was downhill. Instead, Casey decided to return to President's Lane and retrace her steps up to the White House and descend the stone steps to the caboose and station.

She was at the back of Agnes' house. As she ducked under an open window on her way to the front of the house and the road, she overheard voices inside.

"You lied. Where did she go?"

"She ran past me. I assumed the attic."

Silence.

"Never mind. I can see where she went," said Loretta.

"Oh my god, is that blood?"

"Yes." Loretta's voice softened. "You understand, don't you? I didn't mean to hurt you or your niece, but I'm desperate. She kidnapped my little boy! Casey's dangerous. She was in a knife fight with William. He's dead and she's injured."

"No! I don't believe you."

"I'm telling you the truth. His body is in the pool."

Casey kept moving, but she was weakening, and the going was slow. The sun was low. Where had the day gone? She'd started late in the morning, and all that snooping had taken time. She turned to look behind her and was surprised to see Loretta leave the carriage house and run uphill on President's Lane. Casey'd guessed wrong! She fell into the bushes.

Moments later, Loretta raced by her without slowing down or looking to the side. Now what should she do? So tired. She forced her eyes to stay open, struggled into a sitting position, and then stood by leaning against a tree.

How long? Minutes later? She didn't know. Time didn't make sense. A black Mercedes roared down President's Lane and stopped at the intersection to the A-frame. Loretta got out. For a few minutes, Casey couldn't see what she was doing, but then she reappeared with Petey's backpack and the tote Casey had dropped. Loretta got back into the car. Casey crouched down as the car passed. Loretta didn't slow down. Casey stood and watched the car turn right at the gate. Loretta could be headed out to Church Street, or she could turn right again down Station Road to the caboose.

What were the chances Loretta would leave Petey? Zero. He was now her golden goose, no longer shared with Kennedy. She'd go to the caboose for him. Casey pictured the poor, terrified little boy locked in the storage closet. Was the flashlight in the closet? When had she used it last? Most likely, she'd left it under the sink. Thankfully, he had Isabella, but he had to be terrified in the dark.

Casey struggled out of the brambles to the road and began the haul up the road to the White House steps. Tough going. She took off her shirt and wrapped it around the wound on her arm to staunch the bleeding. She forced herself forward, thinking of little Petey's sweet smile and her dear little dog. C'mon, Casey girl. Don't wimp out now! Loretta killed Kennedy, or was it Vlad? Loretta knew about the body. She'd left Petey in the caboose so that she could find Casey. Still didn't make that much sense. Surely Loretta could find a place to hide the bags.

Wait a minute. Loretta told Agnes that Casey had killed Kennedy. Was there any way Loretta could convince people that Casey had some motive, some reason to kill him? Wilson was trying to frame her for shooting Jim in the knee, and Fortune said she could be charged with firing at an unarmed man. She'd already been framed and sent to prison for an earlier crime she didn't commit. Did she have a big sign on her forehead, "Kick Me" or "Sucker"? Maybe she was preordained for prison stripes.

Casey reeled at the top of the stone steps leading down the steep embankment to the caboose and station. She reached for the railing and sank to the steps, dizzy and weak. She'd never be able to navigate the stairs. Unless… She inched forward and lowered her bum to the next step. One step at a time. She groaned and plopped down to the next and the next. When she was halfway down, she could see the parking area and a shiny black Mercedes. Loretta had come for her Little Goose.

There was no reason for Loretta to hurt either Petey or Bella. She'd parked them there for convenience. So, why was she still there? Clearly, Loretta wanted her. Casey's mind spun as she butt-bumped to the bottom. She gripped the railing and stood. Her jacket hung on a peg inside the station door.

Get the Mace.

Chapter Sixty-Three

Agnes

Agnes collapsed into a chair in the kitchen, her whole body trembling in shock. She listened to Loretta trundle down the cellar stairs searching for Casey. Moments later, she heard the creaking of the rear cellar door as it opened and then bang as it closed. Evidently, Casey had escaped out the back, and now Loretta was chasing her.

Could it be true, William dead? No! He was right here in her living room last week. He wanted to purchase the White House properties. He was healthy and vital and handsome. He couldn't—but that woman—his wife—claimed Casey killed him in a knife fight. Casey wouldn't be in any shape to fight a big man like William. Agnes rubbed her cheek where Loretta had struck her. Loretta was crazy with that bloody knife. Out of control one moment, solicitous the next.

It didn't make sense. Agnes had just caught the boy stealing food from her refrigerator that morning and had handed him over to Loretta. Casey was only released from the hospital this morning. How could she have killed William? Why would she kidnap the little boy?

She looked at the trail of blood leading to the cellar door. Nothing made sense, but something awful had happened. The image of Casey lurching into the house, hurt and desperate, crying, "She'll kill me!" replayed in her mind. Why would Casey be up here and not down at the station? To visit Loretta.

Agnes had passed on Loretta's request that Casey come to the White House as soon as possible.

Agnes picked up the phone and dialed 0 and asked the operator to connect her to the police.

"Welton Police. Please state your name and location."

Agnes was so flustered she could barely speak. "Mr. Kennedy has been killed. His wife is chasing my niece—"

"Slow down, ma'am. Please state your name and address."

"Agnes Dempsey, President's Lane. Please hurry." Agnes gripped the receiver so hard her hand hurt.

"I'll connect you to an officer who can help you."

Seconds later, "Officer O'Malley. How can I help you, Miss Dempsey?"

"Mr. Kennedy is dead, and his wife is—"

"Where is Mr. Kennedy?"

"I…I…don't know."

"How do you know he's dead?"

"His wife said Casey killed him in a knife fight."

"Where is Mrs. Kennedy?"

"She left. She's chasing Casey with a knife. Casey's hurt."

"Calm down now, Miss Dempsey. You're not making any sense. Miss Cavendish is in the hospital."

"No. She was just here. I hid her in the cellar."

"So, Mr. Kennedy is dead, and Mrs. Kennedy is chasing Miss Cavendish with a knife. Do I have that right?"

"You don't believe me, but there's blood on my floor."

"Okay, ma'am. We'll send somebody to check it out."

Agnes didn't know what else she could say to convince the officer, so she hung up. What would she do if William really was dead, and Loretta caught up with Casey? Hard to believe she'd protected the girl, but she needed her. Agnes looked down at the blood and shuddered. She hadn't prayed in a long time. It might be a good time to start.

Chapter Sixty-Four

Casey

There was a light on inside the caboose, so Casey could assume Loretta was inside. Casey'd be a sitting duck or total fool to enter without the Mace. She'd have to skirt around the car to get to the station door. Isabella would have greeted her if she were free. No sounds from a small boy. According to Loretta, she'd left Petey and Bella inside the storage closet. No one peered out of the windows of the caboose, just the light shining through.

She sat for a moment, paralyzed with indecision. This wasn't even a very subtle trap for her. Go back up the Station Road to Church Street or the carriage house? Agnes had surprised her by leading Loretta to the attic and turning on the light for Casey to descend the steps. Would she help her again? Admit it, Casey, you don't have the energy to make it back up the hill. It was probably a mistake to return to the station, but nothing she could do about it now.

She gathered what was left of her energy for a push to the station. She forced one foot in front of the other, telling herself to pick up her feet. She struggled to the Muttmobile and leaned into it for support, leaving fingerprints on the hood. Once again, she searched the area for any signs of life or disturbance. Nothing moved or looked out of place. The front door of the caboose was ajar. Casey couldn't remember if LouAnne and Rosie locked it after looking for Petey. Doesn't matter, Casey girl. You're not thinking. The door was open for Loretta, and it's open now.

One last push, and she was at the station. She unlocked the door and punched in the code to disarm the alarm. Seconds later, a piercing high tone sent a message to Loretta pinpointing her location. "Damn!" She carefully reentered the correct number, and the infernal noise stopped.

Inside, she collapsed into a chair and caught her breath. The cut in her arm wasn't that deep, but it hurt like hell and was bleeding. She shuddered to think that the same blade that had been lodged in Kennedy's putrefying body had also sliced her arm.

She unwound the shirt that she'd wrapped around her arm. She located scissors in a drawer and cut it into strips. Using her teeth and her right hand, she knotted a few strips together and then wound the material around her left arm above the wound and tightened it as best she could creating a makeshift tourniquet.

She shrugged into her jacket and checked the pocket for Mace. Yes! Her fingers found the canister. She withdrew it to examine the mechanism to make sure which buttons to press. Her luck, she'd spray herself. Her eye caught the Warning on the back of the canister.

Oh no! "Keep out of reach of children. Use only in a well-ventilated area. Can cause severe incapacitation, temporary blindness, and difficulty breathing and choking."

She couldn't use the Mace within the narrow confines of the caboose because of the danger to little Petey and Isabella. So much for that weapon. She got up and placed the canister on the counter. What else could she use? She had a paring knife and a carving knife. Get real. In her condition, close combat with lethal weapons between a battered and unsteady opponent and a healthy young woman would be foolhardy. The best outcome she could hope for would be a bloody standoff

Move while you can. You have to try to get Petey and Isabella to safety. Forget fighting. Cooperate and get Loretta to release her little hostages. Put the money and the damn tapes into the safe. Time was on Loretta's side. Everything was. Loretta had told Agnes that Casey killed Kennedy. She could manufacture some story where Casey and Kennedy taped the activities at the A-frame for blackmail. They'd had a falling out that turned violent, and Casey killed Kennedy and had taken the money and tapes.

After storing the goodies in the safe, what did Loretta intend to do with Casey? If Loretta could get Casey to put the money and tapes inside the safe and lock her in the closet, Casey would look guilty as hell. Focus, girl. She had no evidence of anything to do with the White House except for the paperwork and the recordings she'd made of Fisher's demands.

Ha! The little hand-held recorder was on the counter next to the ruined phone. Get Loretta to talk. She picked up the recorder and studied it for a minute. Rudimentary. Record. Stop. Play. Rewind. There were also buttons for Fast Forward, Pause, Eject, and Volume. She had only taped two brief conversations, so the batteries were still fresh.

She toyed with the little machine to make sure she could operate it without looking at it. She put it in her jacket pocket and then, without looking down, shoved her hand into the pocket, felt for the control buttons, and pushed Record. She spoke in a low voice. "I thought we were friends, Loretta." She pressed the Stop button and removed the recorder from her pocket. She pressed Rewind and then Play. "I thought we were friends, Loretta." So strange to hear her own voice, but even at low volume, the recorder had picked up her voice clearly. She tested the blind operation of the recorder twice more to give herself confidence.

She turned on the outside light, flooding the parking area with light. Nothing moved. She launched herself forward. Show time.

Chapter Sixty-Five

Casey was weak but vertical, and her eyesight wasn't hazy anymore. Through sheer determination, she left the station and covered the distance from the station door to the steps of the caboose. She'd made it down the stone steps from the White House. Could she climb up the three metal steps to the platform? Hiking herself up the stairs would require both hands, making her totally vulnerable. Loretta wanted her inside and had even left the door ajar as an invitation. Casey gripped the side rails, leaned forward, and hauled herself up to the first step. Two more. She could do this. Step two. Now three. At the top, she peered inside the long, narrow railcar.

Casey fingered the buttons on the recorder in her pocket and pressed Record as she stepped inside. "Petey?" she called.

"Here! I'm here," his high voice responded. Isabella scratched maniacally on the inside of the door of the storage closet to let her presence be known.

"I'm coming, guys. Coming!" Casey lurched toward the rear of the car.

"Took you long enough." Loretta jumped down from the cupola at the far end of the caboose, waving the knife in her right hand.

Casey stopped abruptly, struggling to keep her balance.

Loretta reached overhead to the cupola with her free hand and hauled the tote full of tapes and then the backpack down after her. "You could have made this so much easier," she scolded. "I have no reason to hurt you. I like you. I thought we were friends. You helped me when I needed you. Now I just want to store these tapes in your safe."

Such a calm, well-modulated voice. Casey was silent for a moment. "Okay.

271

Let them out."

Loretta cocked her head as if in disbelief. "Come closer."

Casey shook her head. "Let them out."

Loretta lifted the latch, and boy and dog burst forth. "Not so fast, Peter!" Loretta grabbed Petey by his shirt and yanked him to her. Isabella dashed to Casey's side. She bent over to pet and reassure her. Petey howled in protest until Loretta smacked him with the back of her free hand. "Quiet or I'll carve up your friends. Sit." She shoved him to the side bench. He whimpered but obeyed, his eyes enormous, holding the side of his head.

"Agnes will have called the police by now," suggested Casey, hoping to slow things down.

"No, she won't," Loretta laughed.

"So why did she help me escape?"

"She didn't know what you'd done."

Damned if Loretta wasn't enjoying herself.

"When I told her that you and Kennedy had a prostitution and blackmail ring going, she didn't bat an eye. She despises you. Doesn't like me either, but that doesn't matter."

Loretta beckoned for Casey to come closer and enter the closet. "In you go. Open the safe."

"No way."

"I thought you'd come to your senses."

"I don't trust you. You'll lock me inside."

Loretta advanced a few steps and waved the knife. "This can be easy or painful. Your choice. I don't really want to hurt you, but I will if I have to," Loretta threatened.

"So put down the knife and we can have tea," Casey suggested with a smile.

Loretta kicked the tote full of tapes toward the closet. "Tapes first."

"You might be right about Agnes, although she hates you as much as she does me. She's just crazy enough to think you are...were...her competition. You do know that Kennedy was using her to go in with him to develop the property."

"So many schemes. Too bad."

God, she was cold! Casey took another tack. "Does Fisher know Kennedy is dead? What happens when he can't get Kennedy on the phone?"

"You needn't worry about Fisher." Lorretta took a deep breath and pressed her fingers hard against her larynx and lowered her voice an octave. "Call Mrs. Kennedy immediately. Do whatever she tells you to do." Fisher's irritating voice reverberated against the walls of the caboose.

Stunned, Casey stood, mouth agape, staring at Loretta/Fisher.

Loretta laughed.

"You're...?" Casey looked to the side, momentarily disoriented. She didn't see the lunge coming until it was too late. Loretta pinned Casey against the side wall with the knife against her throat.

"Time to open the safe."

"No."

"I'll open it!" Petey's high voice startled them both.

Chapter Sixty-Six

Loretta kept the knife against Casey's throat but turned her head toward the boy. "You remember the combination?"

Petey looked to Casey.

She shook her head to discourage him. He didn't know the new combination.

"Don't hurt her," he begged.

Would he really go back into that place where he'd been locked up for hours in the dark? He hadn't been able to open the safe when he and Davey were playing. He must know he couldn't open it now.

"Okay." Loretta tilted her head toward the closet. "Go on. Put the contents of the bags in the safe. I'll be watching you."

Petey eyed the knife, his eyes wide. Poor boy was terrified. "MOVE!" screamed Loretta. He scrambled to the closet and disappeared inside. Moments later he emerged. "I need the flashlight."

"Where is it?" demanded Loretta.

"Probably under the sink with the cleaning products." Casey gestured to the galley next to Loretta. Unbelievable. Loretta had been playing her all this time. She was Fisher. She had watched her every move.

"Turn around," Loretta ordered. Keeping the knife on Casey's back, she opened the door under the sink, reached inside, and came up with a long flashlight. She pushed Casey forward a few steps and handed the flashlight to Petey.

Loretta hadn't closed the door. Next to the dishwashing detergent was a spray can of Ant and Roach Killer. Would it work? Worth a try. Get the little ones out of range. How to keep her talking? "What happens if Vlad and Olga return? They might not appreciate being fingered for Kennedy's murder." She paused, momentarily confused. "Wait a minute. I've got it wrong. Didn't you tell Agnes that I killed Kennedy? Do you plan to frame me?"

"Yes, you'll have to do. Vlad and Olga aren't coming back."

"How can you be so sure?"

Loretta glanced inside the storage closet. "You didn't believe me about the bomb, but explosives were Vlad's specialty. Railroad bridges, busses, open markets. He was too successful and had to emigrate. He and Kennedy collaborated on many projects. Including arson."

Keep talking!

"As you guessed earlier, William had discovered my little indiscretion. Vlad told me that William made him get a bomb and place it in the trunk of my car. If he didn't, William would hand him over to the authorities."

"Hurry up!" Loretta shouted. Petey was taking too long.

"Why tell you?" Casey was trying to piece together the whole story.

"He begged me to help him. He needed money and time to get away before the police showed up. I told him to go to Fisher in Rhode Island for new IDs, passports, and airline tickets." Loretta laughed.

"But there was no Fisher. Why are you laughing?"

"When I helped them carry their belongings to the van, I tucked one special box under the driver's seat. Tidy time." She smiled. "The morning news reported an enormous explosion on Route 95 around eight o'clock. Poof!"

Oh. My. God. So cold-blooded.

Petey's head poked out of the closet. "I can't get it to work," he whispered, his huge eyes on Loretta.

"Tell him the correct combination."

Okay. Time to cooperate. "Spin the dial all the way around to the right twice and stop it at 34—"

Petey said each instruction after her, then repeated the sequence and ducked back into the closet.

Loretta continued talking. "It's cleaner this way. You, my dear, will take the rap for me."

She said, "For me." Her words confirmed what Casey now suspected. Loretta stabbed her own husband. The horror must have shown on Casey's face.

"Yup, you got it right."

Loretta was bragging! She wanted Casey to appreciate how clever she was.

Petey reappeared at the closet door. Loretta took the flashlight from him in her free hand and bent over to look inside. "You put everything inside the safe?"

"Yes."

"Come on out now. I won't hurt you."

Snuffling, Petey emerged, eyes great fearful orbs, his dirty face streaked from earlier tears.

"Go to the door and wait."

As Petey passed by her with his head hung low, Casey said, "It's okay, kiddo. Take Bella with you."

"Your turn. On your knees. Be a good girl."

Casey hesitated.

"Slowly now. Crawl inside and you won't get cut."

Dead quiet.

"Or I can slice you up and shove you inside. Your choice. Easy way, or the other way."

Casey inched forward, bracing herself for a blow.

"Atta girl."

Casey bent over, grabbed the spray can, uncapped it and dove to the floor beside Loretta. She rolled over, bobbled the can for a second, and then pressed the nozzle, spraying Loretta full in the face. Loretta shrieked and dropped the knife. Both hands flew to her eyes. Casey held her breath and rolled out of range of the fumes.

She stood and shoved a howling Loretta to the floor. She picked up the knife and poked Loretta in the backside a little harder than necessary to encourage her to move forward. Still blinded, Loretta lurched into the closet. Casey slammed the door and latched it.

When Casey looked around, Petey and Isabella were gone.

Coughing, she walked toward the front of the caboose, knife in hand.

Sirens approached.

She sank to the bench.

Chapter Sixty-Seven

Heavy footsteps pounded up the metal steps to the caboose. Officer O'Malley burst into the caboose.

Casey stood and took a few steps forward.

When O'Malley caught sight of Casey, he skidded to a halt, fumbling with the snap to his holster. "Drop it!" he shouted. "I said, drop it!" He drew his gun and pointed it at Casey.

For a second, Casey was confused. She followed his eyes to the bloody knife in her hand. She tossed it to the floor.

"Help me! Help!" Came a pitiful cry from within the closet.

"What the hell?" O'Malley yelled.

Fortune blasted in behind O'Malley. "Stand down," he ordered, shoving the gun toward the floor and pushing the officer aside. He took in the scene and shook his head. "My God, Casey, what have you done now?"

She wanted to explain, but all she could muster was a weak, "Mike..." She reached into her jacket pocket for the recorder. She held it out to him as her knees collapsed, and she fell forward.

Chapter Sixty-Eight

One week later, Sunday, 11/25

C asey awoke early, stretched, and put on a pot of coffee. She'd spent the better part of the past week sleeping and, when awake, in a haze. Although she could remember various visitors coming and going, she'd be hard pressed to recall specific days or conversations. Her face was still multicolored from the concussion, and her upper arm had stitches to repair the wound inflicted by Loretta, but she felt clear-headed for the first time.

The very best news was that Captain had tracked and found Petey, and that the boy was safe and sound and temporarily staying with Fortune. As she sipped her coffee, she catalogued the issues before her. What was her status with the law for shooting the gun toward Wilson, and for spraying Loretta and shutting her into the storage closet of the caboose at knife point? Casey claimed self-defense, but both Wilson and Loretta offered significantly different accounts of the events compared to hers.

Thank goodness Casey had taped the conversation in the caboose, or Loretta might have been able to twist the story and frame Casey. Legal status from the violence at the station with Wilson, as well as specific charges for the murder of Kennedy and his servants, was still unclear to her.

Second, finances. Soon she'd need to think about money. Where did she stand? Agnes needed to pay her for her last month. When was the next quarterly tax payment due? Easy to find out. But what could she do to make money? Now that the tenants were gone, one dead, two presumed dead in the bombing, and Loretta in jail, what did Agnes plan to do with the property? Rent it again? Sell it? Would she ask Casey to play any kind of role in whatever she decided? Agnes hadn't been down to visit her, nor had she called to ask how she was doing. Casey couldn't depend on Agnes as a source of revenue.

Time to take the last of the White House records up to Agnes and collect her last month's pay. She'd given $500 to Jim for his getaway, but the police had kept it as part of their investigation of the debacle with Wilson.

She found a cardboard box and began loading the files.

When she'd moved them down to the station, she'd emptied out a whole drawer of Mary's old file cabinet. Now she smiled as she recognized Mary's easy, rhythmic, vertical writing on a few of the file tabs in the back. One file had pictures from the family in Ireland. Another contained old notes and letters.

Curious. The last one was entitled POA. Inside she found legal documents including the note written by Mary that had convinced the court to give Agnes Power of Attorney over Mary's financial affairs. At the time, there had been no reason to question the note that Agnes, a devout woman of God who was selflessly caring for her seriously ill sister, had presented to the court.

Casey had searched for these documents in Agnes' files but had been unable to find them. Apparently, Agnes never bothered to transfer the POA file from Mary's file cabinet to hers after the assignment of control was a *fait accompli*. Casey withdrew the handwritten note signed Mary Waddington and smiled. It was a poor forgery.

Casey placed the POA note beside a sample of Mary's real handwriting and studied them for a while. Even a novice graphologist could tell that different hands had written the two documents. Handwriting was brain writing, and Mary's brain was very different from Agnes' brain. Even sick as she was, Mary's script would never look like the POA note. Before, all Casey had was conjecture that Agnes had gotten control of Mary's finances by illicit means. Finally, she had what she needed to prove it.

Before she confronted Agnes, she needed more information about the penalties for forgery in Massachusetts. She picked up her new phone which Fortune had had installed and called a lawyer who had taken her handwriting class in Cambridge who filled her in on the current laws.

She added the POA records and the real sample of Mary's writing to a separate file of documents she planned to use in her graphology class, and then carried the lot up to the carriage house.

When Agnes saw who was at the door, her pretty features distorted into a dyspeptic grimace. She stood like a stone with arms crossed staring at Casey in silence. No idle chitchat. No greeting. No "How have you been?" or "Are you feeling better?" Nothing. Casey put down the box, crossed her arms, turned down her mouth, and stared back. Neither were willing to ask or say more.

So be it. Casey hefted the box, pushed past Agnes, and lowered it onto a chair next to the kitchen table. She smiled and sat and gestured toward the box. "I'll trade you the old records for my final check."

Without a word, Agnes left to get her checkbook. Casey withdrew the file with the samples from the box and laid two handwriting samples on the table.

Agnes returned and wrote out a check and handed it to Casey. "What are you doing?" she asked, eyeing the papers.

Casey assumed a casual, friendly tone. "Looking at these pages. I'd think that different people wrote them. Would you agree?" Both writings were by members of her class. One was spare, minuscule print script; the other, a light and airy tangle of loops.

Agnes looked from one writing to the other. "I suppose. They look different."

Casey took out three more samples. "How about these?" The first writing slanted far to the left with letters crowded together. The second writing almost fell off the page with a far rightward slant, and the third was Lorretta's controlled, vertical script.

"Where are you going with this?"

"Bear with me for a minute. What do you think? Are they written by the same hand?"

Agnes shook her head. "Doesn't look like it."

"How about this writing. Do you recognize it?" She retrieved a page of Agnes' informal script with its crowded, spiky letters and tics of annoyance.

Agnes frowned. "It's mine and you know it."

"Different from, say, this one?" Casey produces a note she herself had written.

"Yes. That looks like your writing."

"Good eye. Yes, it's mine. Now, how about this one?" She added Kennedy's handwritten list with his heavy, angular strokes that were carved into the page.

Agnes was out of patience. "You know very well who wrote that."

Casey was relentless. "One more set." She laid the note from the POA file, allegedly written and signed by Mary, next to a sample actually written by Mary.

Agnes glowered at Casey. "Your point?" she demanded.

"You got a few strokes right when you wrote this," she pointed to the POA note. "But any document examiner or handwriting analyst worth her salt can easily demonstrate that it's a poor forgery. Even you can see, Mary didn't write it."

"If you're so sure, why didn't you challenge it then?" Agnes didn't even pretend to deny Casey's accusation.

"Giving you Power of Attorney as Mary's closest relative made sense at the time. There was no reason not to trust you. Then."

Casey studied the forged note for a moment. "Before she died, Mary showed me the will she'd written. I advised her to have it notarized and filed with a lawyer, but lucky for you, she ran out of time. When she died, there was no will to be found in the desk where she'd kept it. By then, you had Power of Attorney and the key to the desk. I can't prove you destroyed her will, but I know you did. You got everything as next of kin. You knew that wasn't what she wanted."

Agnes glanced from one document to the other. "The Power of Attorney assignment has nothing to do with the will. Why bring it up now?"

"Because I just recently found the actual note you forged in Mary's file. Now I have the document I need to prove that you committed a felony."

"You're bluffing. You don't know anything about forgery analysis."

"I'm studying with one of the best court-certified document examiners in Boston. I showed her the writings—yours and Mary's. She didn't hesitate. Believe me, you do not want to go to court." Casey kept a straight face as she dished out her threat. She didn't doubt for a second that the POA note was a forgery, but she had no idea if a lawyer or a document examiner would take the case.

"Too late now. You should have challenged it two years ago. Now, if you're finished with your little show, I have things to do." She snatched Mary's sample from the table and turned to leave.

Casey grabbed Agnes' wrist to stop her. Agnes gripped the sample in both hands and pulled.

No! She'll rip it! Casey gave Agnes a swift kick in the knee.

"Ow!" Agnes howled and released the paper. She sat in a chair and held her knee. "No need to be violent."

"Not anymore." Casey continued the earlier conversation as if the altercation hadn't taken place. "It isn't too late. The statute of limitations on forgery is six years. Do you have any idea what the penalty for forgery is in the state of Massachusetts?" Casey cocked her head as she asked the question. She couldn't resist a small smile.

When no response was forthcoming, Casey continued. "Forgery is a felony that results in a permanent criminal record. The penalty can be as low as one thousand dollars or two years in the house of correction. Or…" she hesitated for emphasis. "Really big bucks and up to ten years in state prison. I can tell you from personal experience, the latter is to be avoided at all costs."

Casey collected the handwritings and returned them to her file. "I want to thank you for the things you've done for me, giving me a good job, leading Loretta to the attic, and calling the police. You surprised me, and I owe you one. So, here's what I propose. If you agree, I won't take you to court for forgery.

"I don't want to be greedy. If I had my druthers, I'd split up Mary's properties three ways—you, me, and Mary's nephew Jackson. But Jackson has decided to join the Jesuits. As you well know, the priests swear an oath of poverty. He'd have to give his portion to the Church. Instead, Jackson will sign his third over to me." Casey hadn't spoken to Jackson in months, but Agnes couldn't know that.

"So that leaves you and me. Here's the deal. You keep the cute little carriage house you're already living in, and I'll take the White House properties. If you decide to rent and move out West, you can hire me or a maintenance company and receive hands-free income. Or you could sell for a tidy profit." Casey rose to leave.

"Outrageous! I deserve more!"

"Mary gave you a prime oceanfront estate in Chatham, which you sold for a small fortune. You've lived high on the hog for two years rent-free, traveled, and gotten a new car and a new face. I'd say you've done very well.

"My proposal sure beats a hefty fine and prison time any day. A court battle would be lengthy, expensive, and extremely unpleasant. I strongly advise against it. Even with your unpracticed eye, you can see that the POA note is a forgery. I suggest we make a clean break. Your call."

"You wouldn't."

Casey looked Agnes in the eye. "I don't want to, but I can, and I will. Think about it. It's a very reasonable offer."

Agnes picked up her checkbook and led Casey to the door. She hesitated and turned her head to the side as if weighing her options. Her eyes narrowed as she looked down her nose at Casey. "I get the carriage house... and the note."

"Not a chance. The note stays in my safe."

Agnes lowered her head in resignation. "Okay."

Chapter Sixty-Nine

Monday, 11/26

The next morning, voices and a repetitive pounding sound out in front of the station distracted her. She wrapped herself in a robe and peeked out the window. Fortune and two little boys dribbled around the parking area. Davey shot at the basket. Off to one side, Captain guarded the game, accompanied by Isabella, whose little snout came up to his shoulder. Their heads followed the action as the ball passed between players.

Casey climbed up to the loft and dressed in jeans and a sweatshirt. Nothing she could do about her face, but she ran a brush through her hair because she had her pride. Fortune had been clear what he thought of her. She was surprised he'd come with the boys. Probably because they wanted to play basketball. Maybe Petey even missed her a little.

Don't get your hopes up, girl. He's a badly traumatized little boy, and you played a central role in the trauma. He was brave to come back here, but what did she know—children could be more resilient than older folks. In Ohio, Casey had loved a little girl, Gabby, Gabriella, who had lost her mother in horrendous circumstances yet seemed to survive without too many noticeable psychological scars. How could you tell if they were damaged? She had precious little experience to guide her.

She returned to the window and peeked out again just as Fortune performed a successful jump shot. She sighed. Lord, he was a hunk in jeans and tee shirt. He retrieved the ball and tossed it to Petey who was guarded by Davey. Fortune glanced into the window, directly at Casey. He grinned before turning back to the game.

Casey backed away, blushing scarlet, before she caught herself. Wait a minute. I live here. I shouldn't be embarrassed. He's got nerve, showing up uninvited, making a racket outside my home. She threw back her shoulders and marched to the door, unlocked it, and descended the steps to the parking lot.

Fortune bounced the ball to Petey and walked toward her. "I hope we haven't disturbed you. We were on our way down Church Street to the dump when the boys asked if we could stop here."

To Casey's surprise, Petey dropped the ball and made a beeline for her, arms extended, catching her in a big hug that almost bowled her over. She wrapped her arms around him and closed her eyes in relief and delight. When they disentangled, Petey looked up at her colorful face with a frown. "You okay?" he asked.

"Better every day. How 'bout you?" But he'd already picked up the ball and was dribbling toward the basket, Davey close on his heels.

"How's your arm?" asked Fortune.

"Stitches come out soon. It was a shallow wound, just messy." She hesitated a moment. "Thanks for finding Petey."

"Captain sniffed him out." Captain, hearing his name, trotted to Fortune's side, followed closely by Isabella.

Casey vaguely remembered a visit a week earlier when Fortune came with Captain to let her know they'd found Petey. Captain had made the mistake of backing Little Mother into a corner. She spat and hissed at him in warning. When he crowded her, she'd let him have it with a lightning swipe to the nose. He'd shrunk away, whining and bleeding a little, a lesson he wouldn't soon forget.

"How's his nose?" Casey asked, snugging Captain's ears. Isabella crowded in, pushing the big fellow aside for her share of attention. Gutsy little dog.

"It's his pride got hurt. Your little cat's got sharp claws."

Casey smiled. "The station is really Little Mother's house."

"One needs to be careful around the females in this place," remarked Fortune. He shifted from one foot to another.

Nervous? Well, she wasn't exactly welcoming, blocking the doorway. "How's he doing?" she asked, nodding toward Petey.

"Pretty quiet, but Davey seems to understand and just hangs out with him. Mom enrolled him in school—same class as Davey—and he's been getting used to that as well. Big changes for a little guy. Big change for Davey, too. His mother just returned to France." Fortune stuffed his hands into his back pockets and turned to watch the boys.

"Coffee?" blurted Casey, surprising herself and Fortune.

"Sure?" he asked. "Sure," he answered himself, not waiting for her response.

She stepped aside, gestured for him to enter, and followed. He sat at the table while she fetched mugs, remembering to offer cream, no sugar.

"I have a few updates," said Fortune. "Social Services has granted us— Mom and me—temporary custody of Petey until his legal status can be determined. We learned from papers locked in a desk in the White House that the trust fund was for a Peter Bement."

"Will Loretta remain his legal guardian?"

"Not clear, but I doubt it. I think, but I'm not sure about these things, that the officers of the trust have the authority to make that determination. Until a decision is made, he's with us."

"Then what?"

"Unless other relatives step up, he'll become a ward of the state. We'll petition to keep him. He'd have a stepfather, a brother, a dog, a grandmother, and a home."

"Has he asked about Loretta?"

"No. The only thing he's said—he asked if he'd have to go back there, meaning the White House. I promised him he wouldn't have to, and he seemed greatly relieved. I was surprised this morning when he asked to come down here." Fortune paused and looked directly at Casey. "He asks about you every day."

His deep-set, dark eyes were too much. Casey looked down, afraid to show Fortune how much this meant to her. She was surprised to feel a lump in her throat. "How's Davey doing with an instant new brother?"

"Well, it's a big change for him. They're sharing a room while we fix up the spare room. Davey's had to let Petey play with some of his toys and read his books. There have been a few disagreements, one or two scuffles, but they seem to have become fast friends. I need to be careful with attention. Mom has been super. She's a natural with children. As are you."

Again, Casey diverted her glance, not knowing how to take the impossible compliment. What good did it do her to be good with children?

"Didn't mean to embarrass you."

Didn't mean to let it show. Casey could feel his eyes on her as he sipped his coffee.

"Okay, then. Legal issues." Fortune sat back and adopted a tone that was all business. "Loretta has been charged with first-degree murder and assault. We have nothing but the tape to go on to charge her for the deaths of Vlad and Olga. She refuses to cooperate. We don't even have their last names and may never know who they were.

"There's reason to believe that William Kennedy and Loretta aren't their real names. We're following a trail of criminal activity prior to coming here. Petey's name and the assumed fact that his mother was Loretta's sister are the only anchors to their past so far. Laura Bement, aka Loretta Ashley, and her sister, Coral Bement, Petey's mother, graduated from a high school in Queens. Laura studied theater at NYU and appeared in bit parts in commercials and theater productions. She supported herself as a call girl for an escort service, where she met and married William Kenny. Not clear when Laura became Loretta or when they changed their last name to Kennedy." Fortune stopped his recital. "That's as far as we've got."

"I'm amazed you've discovered so much in such a short period of time."

"Actually, they've been on our radar for a while. I started asking questions the minute I found out about the camera. We also learned about the parties at the A-frame from a speed trap. O'Malley pulled over two of the visitors on their way home. He let them off with a warning, and I suspect, an exchange of cash, after they told him they were from out of town, just in for an executive education program. O'Malley later recognized them on one of the tapes."

"Huh. Amazing."

"We confirmed their participation in an executive education program they were attending and tracked them down, both from New York. One had continued to see a call girl, Jenny, and coughed up her number. Jenny talked so that we wouldn't prosecute her. She admitted to knowing Loretta as Laura Kenny, née Ashley, from earlier days. There's also a Kenny who is wanted for mail fraud in Rhode Island, but we don't know yet if they're related."

Casey shook her head. "What a tangled web we weave. They appeared to be such a respectable, wealthy, if private couple. I'd hoped Loretta could become a friend or at least a friendly neighbor. Their handwriting was the only clue that they weren't exactly what they seemed, normal. Then again, normal is just someone you don't know very well." She paused to reflect for a moment, aware that Fortune was watching her. "Any news about Jim and Wilson?"

"Jim is responding well to treatment and has been able to give a full statement. The Army has begun an investigation into his claims regarding Wilson, but that will take time. The gun is registered to Wilson, supporting Jim and your versions of events. There's no charge against you for firing the gun.

"I...uh...owe you an apology. When I spoke with Jim, he told me on no uncertain terms that you and he were never involved. I jumped to conclusions and—"

Before Fortune could continue, two boys and two dogs blasted through the door. Little Mother streaked from her nest on the couch across the floor and up the ladder to the loft in one fluid motion. She glowered down at the intruders.

"Whoa, there!" Fortune caught hold of the boys to slow them down. "Game over?"

"Yup," said Davey.

Petey turned to the kitchen, his eyes seeking out the cookie jar.

Casey followed his eyes. "Sorry, champ. Didn't know you were coming. I'll have cookies next time."

Petey shrugged. The boys approached Fortune. "Can we go to the dump now?" asked Davey.

Fortune rose. "Thanks for the coffee. We'll be off." Boys and dogs dashed outside in a whirlwind of energy.

Casey followed Fortune to the door. He turned unexpectedly, and she found herself within inches of his chest.

"See you later?" he asked, his dark eyes intense.

Completely off guard, Casey was at a loss for words.

He placed a hand on her cheek. "I figure anyone who loves animals and children can't be all bad."

Casey looked up into his eyes and forced herself to respond. "I've had the same thoughts. But I've been wrong before."

"We've all been wrong before. Give it a chance."

Casey started and backed away.

Fortune dropped his hand, confused.

Casey shook her head. "Sorry, just my reaction to... Chance." She hesitated a second and dared a smile. "I much prefer Fortune."

"Dad? Dad, are you coming?" an impatient voice called from outside.

"Good choice. Take care." Fortune's smile returned as he turned and walked out the door.

So quiet. Casey preferred the noise. She peeked out the window. The boys wrestled in the back seat of the station wagon. Captain rode shotgun next to Fortune. He raised his hand and waved as the car pulled out.

How does he know I'm watching? Take care, indeed. I've been horribly wrong before. Isabella popped through the cat door and joined her at the window. But I'd rather like to take a chance on Fortune.

Acknowledgments

Special thanks to Dave Pierce, President of the Chester Foundation, who gave me a very thorough tour of the Chester Railway Station and their antique, renovated caboose. He also provided the photograph of the inside of the little railcar which appears on the cover. I've tried to include a few of his details in the story and hope I got them right.

Once again, gratitude to members of my writers group: Mark Ammons, Cheryl Marceau, Frances McNamara and Leslie Wheeler, for valuable critiques and edits, without which there would be no story. Thanks also to beta readers Ron Kelly and Ellen Richstone who offered useful comments and critiques along the way. Special appreciation for Connie Hambly, Susan Oleksiw, and Barbara Ross who read and provided blurbs for the back cover.

Thanks to Level Best Books, especially Verena Rose, Shawn Reilly Simmons, and Deb Well as well as fellow Level Besties who constitute a vigorous, and vibrant community of authors. I'm also grateful to the members of Sisters in Crime/New England (too numerous to name!) who have been so very supportive over the years and members of Mystery Writers of America/New England.

In memoriam, I would like to thank my dear mentor and good friend Barbara Harding for teaching me everything I needed to know to become a professional graphologist. It was rewarding to work with Barbara and loads of fun to incorporate handwriting clues in my stories.

Thanks to Detective Forti of the Weston Police department for answering my random questions about treatment and ownership of found property.

Once again, dear readers, you make it all worthwhile.

Most of all, bless you dear husband Jeffrey for your continued encouragement and love throughout the writing process. You're the best.

About the Author

Katherine Fast is an award-winning author of over 25 short and flash fiction stories. She was a former contributing editor and compositor for six anthologies of *Best New England Crime Stories*. *The Drinking Gourd* was her debut novel, followed by *Church Street Under*, and now, *Caboose,* the third novel in the Casey Cavendish series.

In her prior corporate career, she worked with M.I.T. spin-off consulting companies, with an international training firm, and as a professional handwriting analyst.

She and her husband live in Massachusetts with their German Shepherd and three cats.

AUTHOR WEBSITE:

Katfast.com

SOCIAL MEDIA HANDLES:

https://www.facebook.com/people/Katherine-Fast/100074399272274

https://www.linkedin.com/in/Katherine-Fast-3127294

Also by Katherine Fast

The Drinking Gourd

Church Street Under

Over 25 short stories

www.ingramcontent.com/pod-product-compliance
Lightning Source LLC
Chambersburg PA
CBHW021505110726
47899CB00001BA/304